Down in Flames

Also by Cheryl Hollon

Published by Kensington Publishing Corp.

Down in Flames

Cheryl Hollon

KENSINGTON BOOKS
www.kensingtonbooks.com

KENSINGTON BOOKS are published by

Kensington Publishing Corp.
119 West 40th Street
New York, NY 10018

All Kensington titles, imprints, and distributed lines are available at special quantity discounts for bulk purchases for sales promotion, premiums, fund-raising, educational, or institutional use.

Special book excerpts or customized printings can also be created to fit specific needs. For details, write or phone the office of the Kensington Sales Manager: Attn.: Sales Department. Kensington Publishing Corp., 119 West 40th Street, New York, NY 10018. Phone: 1-800-221-2647.

Kensington and the K logo Reg. U.S. Pat. & TM Off.

First Printing: July 2019
ISBN-13: 978-1-4967-1179-3
ISBN-10: 1-4967-1179-3

ISBN-13: 978-1-4967-1180-9 (ebook)
ISBN-10: 1-4967-1180-7 (ebook)

10 9 8 7 6 5 4 3 2 1

Printed in the United States of America

To my terrific siblings:
Gary Hollon and Eileen Hoffman
Sheila Hollon Collins and Larry Collins
Mark Hollon and Deanna Wormack Hollon

Acknowledgments

I can't believe that this is my sixth published book. How did that happen? It happened because there are people who make sure the thousands of details happen.

The Bookends Literary Agency was my dream agency from the first time I heard Jessica Faust speak at the SleuthFest conference in 2007. She is a force of nature propelled by caffeine and curiosity. When she suggested that my cozy proposal might be a perfect fit for her newest agent, Beth Campbell—she was right. Beth is the perfect agent for me. She is both sympathetic and relentless in giving me an unflinching assessment of each book. From our first meeting, Beth and I could finish each other's sentences. It is such a joy to hone and perfect each manuscript with Beth's guidance.

Now that Beth has left the agency to pursue another chapter in her publishing life, I'm in the skilled hands of brand-new agent James McGowan. He has the personal trait I most admire—persistence. He, like Beth, started with Bookends as an intern and simply stayed, and stayed, and stayed. I'm looking forward to his guidance on future projects.

Kensington Publishing is a delight to work with. Selena James, Rebecca Raskin, and Lulu Martinez work very hard to bring the best possible book to print. Speaking of print, thanks for the magnificent production talents of Rebecca Cremonese. There are so many more Kensington folk who are dedicated, patient, and passionate about books. I enjoy the opportunity I get to meet with Team Hollon at the Kensington offices during the ThrillerFest conference each year.

Thanks to Claire Hill for her creative publicity campaign in promoting this series. I would never have made those glass demonstration videos without your encouragement. Sometimes a push is exactly what is needed. Thanks.

This book features a new glass art for me—beadmaking. To get enough hands-on experience to give this book credibility, I signed up with Zen Glass Studio and took a three-day class in flameworking. My instructors—Josh, David, and Mike—were incredibly patient with my fumbling, stumbling, and terrified attempts to make the pieces that I planned to have Savannah teach. Check out their workshops and classes at www.zenglass.com.

My parents continue to inspire me with their enthusiasm and obvious pride in having a daughter who is a "real" author. The arts have always had first place in our family. We all sing, play instruments, write, quilt, knit, and enjoy woodworking. Some of us paint, dance, and play sports. But all of those were practiced only after all homework was finished. Thanks, Mom and Dad.

I found my tribe within the Sisters in Crime organization. I'm the Past President of the Florida

Gulf Coast Sisters in Crime Chapter and enjoy the incredible support of so many wonderful writers, readers, booksellers, and librarians.

I have an incredible face-to-face critique group. We meet in my sunroom one Sunday a month to torment, terrorize, encourage, and drive each other into writing stronger, tighter, and clearer stories. We've been meeting since 2008 and I have learned to look forward to these word-centric tussles. Thank you, Sam Falco and Christa Rickard.

Without inspiration, nothing good comes from my writing. I depend on my muse, Lujoye Barnes, to supply copious amounts of encouragement. She's my compass. When I get stuck, my first question is, "What would surprise Joye at this point?" Works like magic.

Thank you, Ramona DeFelice Long, for taking my early glimmers and showing me the way to make a better story. I laugh almost as much as I weep when I read through your comments. Your dedicated service is vital to my writing process. I'm so glad I found you.

The world's greatest writer champion continues to be my trophy husband, George. He's my first reader, trusted adviser, taskmaster, and long-suffering spouse of an obsessed writer. When I'm deep in my story world, with no sense of time, you draw me back into our wonderful life. "A bushel and a peck."

Chapter 1

Monday afternoon,
Webb's Glass Shop

"Fire!" screamed Rachel Rosenberg. She pointed at her twin sister. "Faith started a fire."

Savannah Webb sniffed the distinctive odor of burning hair. She ran over to Faith's student bench, grabbing the fire extinguisher on the way. She quickly scanned each twin's short white hair, which appeared untouched. Faith was near tears but pointed to a pink cashmere sweater that lay in a smoldering heap on the floor behind the metal work stool.

Faith snuffled like a toddler. "I tossed it over there."

As normal, the twins had been the first students to arrive. Also, as usual, they dressed alike and wore head-to-toe vibrant pink. From pink ballet flats and slacks embroidered with flamingoes, to cotton sweater-sets with flamingos screen-printed on the front. All topped by large flamingo earrings and pink polished nails.

Using two rapid spurts from the extinguisher, Savannah sprayed the burning sweater. Then she stomped on the remains for good measure. She turned to her perennial students, her throat still pulsing from the surge of adrenalin. "Are you all right? Did you get burned?"

"No." Faith sat very still with her eyes wide, staring at the sodden lump of pink char. "I forgot about the rule banning loose clothing. I got a chill and drew the sweater over my shoulders. My sleeve must have dangled across the flame." Faith's eyes began to fill with tears. "I'm sorry."

The twins were typically aloof, tightly controlled, but friendly. Emotion at this level felt awkward.

Savannah heard the pitch of her voice rise. "What possessed you to turn on the torch? We haven't started class."

Faith's eyes grew even wider. "I just don't know. It seemed to call to me to turn it on. I couldn't resist. I've never had that happen before."

Savannah covered her mouth with a hand and pressed her lips together. *I'm so relieved they're okay!*

Rachel huffed a great breath and put both hands on her hips. "You've always been clumsy. You should have waited for Savannah to tell us exactly how to light the torch. Perhaps this class isn't such a good idea."

Savannah put an arm around each twin and drew them into a warm side hug. "Ladies, you know that at Webb's Glass Shop, a class wouldn't be complete without you two. You've attended every class of-fered for the last—how many years?"

The twins looked at each other and Rachel shrugged. "It's been at least five years, don't you think?"

"Yes," said Faith. "We were walking by and no-ticed the poster in the window offering beginning stained-glass classes and we went right in. You know, of course, that your dad was a wonderful in-structor."

Savannah smiled. "Yes, he was." She paused for just a second. His loss was still a raw spot. "Now that he's gone, you've been my security blanket and my dear friends. I need you. Don't decide about the class right now."

Faith wrung her hands. "But I could have burned the shop down. You might have lost the whole build-ing." She put her hands over her eyes and began to cry.

"Stop that. I'm well prepared for any little acci-dent. My friend over at Zen Glass Studio says that if there's not at least one fire a day, he's not mak-ing money. He runs a lot of students through his shop. Close calls are part of the deal."

Savannah felt her heart pounding and she huffed out a breath. Near accidents caused an aftereffect, but they were far better than a real accident. She felt her confidence drop as she thought of her six be-ginner students wielding molten glass inches in front of their faces.

Rachel gently pushed Savannah back and folded Faith into her arms. "Don't fret, sister. It wasn't a problem. You saw how quickly Savannah put out the fire."

Faith lowered her hands and gulped a shuddering breath. "I'm so sorry."

Savannah put a hand on each twin's shoulder. "You both enjoyed the sand-etching class, didn't you?"

The twins stepped apart, looked at each other and then glanced away.

"Remember that and give flameworking a chance. I won't hear a word about quitting until you've gotten to the end of today's class."

"But—" chirped Faith.

Savannah pointed like a teacher. "Back to your workstations."

Rachel and Faith returned to their work stools. They folded their hands and raised their chins. They looked ready to pay attention to the first lesson in making a glass bead.

Savannah sighed deeply. Her relief that no one had been injured was both personal and calculating. An accident could tarnish the reputation of the family-owned glass shop that she had inherited from her father. Even though her small business was doing well, it would all collapse in the wake of burning the whole building down.

She turned to the other three new students. "This might have been the best unplanned lesson ever. This is not a risk-free art form." They were wide-eyed and solemn with nodding heads. "I'll expect your full attention during the safety briefing."

She scooped up the sodden lump of burned sweater with a dust pan and dumped it into the trash bin. It stood next to the fifty-gallon drum that contained their unusable glass. It was nearly full and would need dumping into the bright blue city recyclables bin in the next day or so.

Today was her first afternoon teaching a workshop in glass-bead creation. The method called flameworking, or sometimes lamp-working, utilized acetylene torches fastened to the front of each table, facing away from the students. The beads were formed by manipulating colored glass rods through the flame.

Safety for the students was always Savannah's primary worry when working with an open flame, so she had been testing the torches one by one when Faith let the sleeve of her sweater catch fire.

To accommodate her growing student clientele, Savannah had installed all the student workstations in the newly acquired expansion space of Webb's Glass Shop. She owned the entire building, so when one of her long-term tenants retired and closed their art-supply retail business, she took the opportunity to expand. Luckily, the expanded classroom was adjacent to her current location. Savannah hired contractors to remove the adjoining wall and created a larger student space.

That left two more businesses in her building that still held on to their leases. One was a nail salon and the other a consignment shop. She rarely raised her rent more than two percent a year because loyalty meant so much more to her than risking an empty rental.

Because the flameworking torches needed powerful exhaust fans to remove noxious fumes and expel clouds of glass dust, she had placed the workstations on the back wall facing the alley and had a contractor knock small holes into the outside wall for the fans. The construction work on the six-station teaching space was finished mere minutes before the class began at one o'clock this afternoon.

There was a little space for her personal station, but students brought money in the door, so that work would be finished later. All but one student had shown up early to learn bead-making. They had also gotten an unplanned show and prime example of the dangers of working with an open flame.

The bell over the entry door jangled. "Am I too late?" asked a thirty-something tall woman dressed in muscle-hugging black athletic wear. "Have I missed something important?" Her pale face flushed and a sheen of sweat formed on her brow.

Savannah walked into the display room and led her into the new classroom. "A little, but you're in good time." Savannah shook her head. "We've had a bit of delay getting started. Anyway, you're the last one to arrive, so our class is complete. If you could take a seat at the end workstation, we can all make our introductions. After that I'll make some important safety and housekeeping announcements, and then we'll begin."

Savannah pointed to the late-arriving student. "Welcome. We'll start introductions with you. Give us your name, where you live, and what you want to get out of this class."

The pale lady looked extremely uncomfortable at the notion of speaking. She cleared her throat not once, but three times. "I'm Myla Katherine Nedra, but everyone calls me Myla Kay. I'm a seasonal resident from Ann Arbor, Michigan. I'm recently widowed, and I couldn't stomach the idea of a cold winter in our big house all alone, so I rented one of the tiny bungalow cottages in a courtyard within a few blocks of here. This class should be a great distraction and will hopefully be a way to get to know the neighborhood."

Savannah raised her eyebrows. *That's an unusual way to introduce yourself—recently widowed.* Most women would be reluctant to admit that so quickly. She's confident.

"Thank you, Myla Kay. You must be in that street of tiny houses near my house. I live right down the block from you. I find the tiny-house zone in the Kenwood Historic Neighborhood fascinating, although I could never live in one. Which one did you rent?"

"I chose the converted Blue Bird school bus."

Savannah bobbed her head. "I walked through that one while I was at the Tiny Home Festival last year. The bus has a very colorful history. Remind me to tell you about it."

She's awfully young to be a widow.

Savannah looked toward the next student. He adjusted the collar of his green Columbia fishing shirt and stood in front of his work stool. He said in a booming voice, "My name is Lonnie Mc-Carthy. I'm from Pittsburgh. My wife and I are staying downtown with friends for a few weeks and I have some basic experience with making stained glass. I want to present my wife with some hand-made beads for her fancy Pandora bracelet." He gave everyone a politician's wide-toothed smile and sat.

The third student, with brown hair framing soft brown-eyes, looked as gawky as her sixteen years of age. She popped up before Savannah could signal her turn. "Hi, I'm Patricia Karn." Her voice was high and thin, exactly like her teenage figure. "I'm here from Indian Rocks Beach. I'm a native Floridian but my parents are from Akron, Ohio. I want to make beads as Christmas gifts to send up to my six cousins up North. I'm home schooled and this class will fulfill my art elective credits for the year."

"Thanks, Patricia. Did you bring your signed release?"

"Yes, ma'am." Patricia pulled a folded slip of paper from her back pocket and handed it over.

The next student sat until Savannah nodded toward him. He was white-haired with a close-clipped beard and mustache. He gripped the back of the chair and stood, favoring one knee. Even at his full height, he was a little stooped. "I'm Herbert Klug." He gave a sheepish shrug of his shoulders. "I'm here because my wife wants me out of the house."

Everyone laughed. His timing and stage presence reminded Savannah of a stand-up comedian.

He smiled at the reaction. "No, I'm kidding. That's not exactly true. I'm a retired research professor. My lab was downtown at the Bayboro Campus of the University of South Florida." His well-modulated voice had everyone's attention. "Although I haven't created anything in glass as an artist, I have certainly made plenty of glass pipettes for my lab. This is my chance to explore flameworking as an artist." He maneuvered cautiously back onto his work stool.

He must have been an excellent instructor. Edward had been prodding Savannah to hire more staff. Edward was still coming to grips with his new role as her fiancé. He was cautious about giving her advice about her business, but felt compelled to solve her tendency to overcommit, quickly followed by overworking. *However, just because he's a research professor doesn't mean he'll have an affinity for teaching civilians. I'll see how he survives the chaos of the class.*

Next were Faith and Rachel. Savannah knew they were more than eighty years old, but their looks and actions declared middle-sixties. The twins deftly avoided all discussions about their age. They stood up together. "Hello, everyone. I'm Rachel Rosenberg and, obviously, this is my twin sister, Faith."

"We've been coming to all of the Webb's Glass Shop classes for years," said Faith.

Savannah stepped between them and put an arm around each twin. "Webb's Glass Shop, like any artistic enterprise, needs patrons. These two ladies have been attending classes for years and knew my father, who started this business from nothing. Without this level of support, the arts have no chance to survive." She turned her head to each twin. "I appreciate your patronage more than I can say."

"Yes." Rachel looked at Savannah. "We find the challenge of learning new skills keeps us young."

They sat down with their backs to the workstations and Savannah felt all eyes upon her.

She had taken the opportunity to brush up on her flameworking skills at the nearby Zen Glass Studio. She wasn't like her dad, in that she was open to using any resource available to make her classes the best they could be. He had been more of an "if it isn't available here, it isn't worth having" management style.

The Zen studio was less than a mile away and, like hers, was a small shop that catered to beginning glass students and offered work space and time for advanced students. The owner, Josh Poll, cheerfully advised Savannah about how to set up the student work space along with a demonstration workbench.

Josh had been turning away students and felt another teaching venue would be good for both Webb's Glass Shop and Zen Glass Studio. There were enough snowbirds and retirees seeking adult education or lifestyle classes to keep the arts-based businesses solvent. It was another example of how the business owners supported each other. They were still competitors, but all boats rise on an incoming tide.

"Thanks, everyone. First things first. I need to cover the safety issues. It is important to wear formfitting clothing, pinned-back hair and closed-toe shoes. Glass does occasionally drop onto the floor—but mostly it will stay on your work surface. If it does drop on the rubber mats, it will flame up. Let me handle it. I'll pick up the glass with pliers and stamp on the flames. It cools surprisingly quickly, but don't touch it." She lowered her head a touch and winked at Faith. "No loose sweaters on the shoulders or jackets tied around the waist. Understood?"

The students nodded their agreement.

"Okay, then. Everyone, follow me."

Savannah walked over to the back door, went outside and held the door for everyone to follow.

She pointed to the newly installed tanks that sat in a fenced-in enclosure. She pulled out a key and unlocked the gate.

"This is the butane tank—just like the ones you might use for your barbecue grill." She pointed to the controls. "Here's the knob to turn off the gas. I will probably never ask you to do this, but if I ask—turn the knob to the right. Remember this phrase: Righty tighty, lefty loosey. It's a memory trick for: Turn right for OFF and turn left for ON. That's universal. Okay, back inside."

She led everyone to a stainless-steel container not far from the end of the long workbench. There was a workstation space on the far-left side of the back wall that Savannah planned to use as her own, so it had a higher quality torch and more advanced tools.

"This is the control for the oxygen tank. The same thing applies—Righty tighty, lefty loosey."

"Question," said Herbert. "I thought we would be using those portable torches that you can get at the hardware store."

"Those don't get hot enough long enough for us to work the glass. We need our temperatures to be at least 4500 degrees. Mixing the butane with oxygen gets us there. Good question. What did you use in your lab?"

He shrugged his shoulders. "Since I was only modifying thin lab glass, I just used the Bunsen burners that were already in the lab."

"We need more heat since we're going to combine solid glass rods," said Savannah. "Now for the first aid salve you're most likely to use more than anything else. Let me introduce you to Bernie the aloe plant." On a plant stand against the right-hand wall was a moldy clay pot that contained a strange plant with ugly spikes sticking out in every direction. "If you get a slight burn, pluck off a stem, split it open, and slather the juice all over the burn. It will seal it so you can keep on working. Obviously, if you get a bad burn, we'll take further action, but for minor ones, Bernie is your friend."

Patricia stiffened. "I know this sounds silly, but I've never worked with fire before. I'm actually very nervous."

Herbert learned over and said in a low voice, "Don't let that stop you. You need practice in order to get comfortable." He quickly glanced over to Savannah and then straightened. "Oh, I'm sorry. It's not my place to answer questions. Force of habit, I'm afraid."

"But you're completely right." Savannah noted his deft handling of Patricia's fears. "It's perfectly normal to be cautious, but not to the point where you don't learn. I spent my first weeks near Seattle at Pilchuck Glass School making paperweights. I made so many I could do them in my sleep."

Patricia raised her hand. "Did you meet the famous Chihuly? I love his work! I practically haunt his museum downtown."

Savannah raised her eyebrows. "We're very lucky he decided to put a museum here. Anyway, the demand for his time was incredible, so he couldn't come near the beginning studio, but I met him later when I was one of the senior apprentices. He radiated amazing charisma—you couldn't help hanging on his every word." She paused, remembering her apprentice days.

"Gosh," said Patricia. "I've never met anyone who worked with him."

"It was the experience of a lifetime." Savannah felt a dreamy smile softening her jaw. She shook her head a bit. "Anyway, back to our class. Let's begin by becoming familiar with the tools lying on your workstation."

Each student's work area was set up with the tools they would need for the class. Savannah then described the names of the tools laid out neatly on each side of the torch. She explained how to use the tweezers, a graphite marver, a mosaic cutter, a bottle of bead release, a tungsten bead reamer, a rod rest for the glass rods, and a mandrel for holding the bead as it was formed.

She held a pair of bright blue glasses up for everyone to see. "Here's your most important safety equipment. These are didymium glasses that not only protect your eyes, but they filter out the orange sodium flare, so you can see how to manipulate the molten glass."

She walked over to her teaching workstation. "This is your primary tool for flameworking. It's called a hothead torch, which provides as big a flame as you can get with this style torch. The bigger the flame, the more BTUs and the faster you can work the glass.

"Your torch has two nozzles. Each nozzle has a dial for butane and a dial for oxygen. The small nozzle on top is for light work with the smaller rods of glass that don't require maximum temperature. The second nozzle right underneath the small one is for larger rods of glass as well as for your finishing steps—we'll talk about those later.

"To light your torch, you can use either a striker"—she held it up and made sparks by compressing the handles—"or a match." She held up a small box of wooden matches. "Most students find it easier to simply use a match or cigarette lighter." Savannah shot a glance at the Rosenberg sisters and made sure she had their full attention. She selected a match and lit one using the grit panel on the side of the box. "Turn the knob slightly to the left to start the flow of gas—remember lefty loosey—then hold the match right against the torch." The torch whooshed a bright orange flame.

Savannah blew out the match. "Now you turn on the oxygen. You want to adjust the two so that the flame is steady." Savannah turned the flame down until it was a steady pure blue. "Now go ahead and try it at your station."

Everyone except Herbert used matches. He expertly clicked the striker so that it sputtered huge sparks, lit his torch, and adjusted the oxygen and butane knobs to achieve a perfectly steady blue flame.

Not his first rodeo.

Savannah adjusted the gas-flow knobs on each student's torch so everyone had an efficient setting. Both Rachel and Faith overreacted to the sweater fire to the point that their flames were barely lit at all.

"Ladies, you couldn't toast a marshmallow on those flames." She adjusted their torches. "Can you hear the difference between a bad mix of air and butane and a good one? This is a good one." Then she increased the oxygen and the torch responded with a loud rushing sound. "This is a bad mix." She readjusted the torch so that if fell nearly silent. "Good. I want everyone to practice adjusting your torch."

After a few minutes, even the twins seemed more confident with the adjustment knobs on their torches. "Okay, now we're ready to start. The process we need to practice first is to punty up a clear glass rod with a colored rod. We will be repeating this process many times, so the more practice the better. It is not fun to be working on a piece and have the colored glass fall off the punty."

Savannah held up a rod of clear class about twelve inches long and a short three-inch rod of lime-green glass. "Punty is the name for any piece of material that is used to hold and manipulate glass. It's also used as a verb, such as 'punty this piece of glass.'" She demonstrated the steps required to join a single-color rod to a clear rod. "The trick here is to heat both glass rods to the same temperature, so they will form a good join."

Savannah explained each step in the basic process of making a glass medallion with an attached glass loop. After she showed the finished medallion to each student, she slipped the whole business into an upright kiln to keep it warm. The students caught up by selecting their medallion colors. Then they puntied each color onto clear rods.

"How hot does the glass get while in the flame?" asked Patricia.

"Good question," said Savannah. "Glass begins to melt at six- to eight-hundred degrees. It varies with thickness, of course. As you get more experienced with manipulating the hot glass, you'll be able to tell its temperature just by looking at it."

The class progressed, with Savannah working with each student on their first attempt at a medallion. Except for Herbert. He crafted a perfectly symmetrical oval with four swirls of colored glass in a pattern. "Wow. That's gorgeous. Your science-lab experience is serving you well."

He ducked his head a bit. "I have to confess. I've tried my hand at the creative side of glasswork before, but I became fascinated with all the demonstrations you can find on the internet. However, I'm delighted by how much more I retain with in-person instruction."

Myla Kay formed her first medallion using a Salvador Dali–like selection of vivid high-contrast colors—yellow, azure, lime, and royal purple.

"Well done, Myla Kay," said Savannah. "That was risky. Sometimes a high contrast selection of colors will result in a horrible muddy mixture, but yours is terrific. Beautiful!"

Myla Kay smiled broadly. "I have some experience with color. I like to paint. Actually, I like to paint a lot."

"Well, that explains your sense of color. Good job."

There were no accidents, and at the end of the class each student left behind a newly formed glass medallion annealing in the kiln. As the Rosenberg twins—always first to arrive, and last to leave—wished her a good day and walked out the door, Savannah programmed the kiln to start the cool-down cycle in four hours from now. The kiln would do its work after hours. When she first took over the glass shop, she'd felt uneasy leaving the kilns powered on. Not anymore. The kiln was absolutely safe, and it rested on fire-proof bricks, which were even safer.

Amanda Blake, office manager and instructor for Beginning Stained Glass, walked into the flameworking classroom. "So, how was the first day of bead-making class?" Amanda's voice sounded flat and toneless.

Savannah glanced up at her, concerned. "Exhausting, but exciting. I can't believe that two hours have flown by! Are you on your way to see your mother?" Savannah noted the somber outfit. A zaftig woman of size, Amanda's appearance typically displayed her bohemian side. Today she wore muted shades of beige. Her normally neon spiked hair was brushed down into a soft, wavy, fawn-like color.

"I did the Monday inventory of supplies and got everything ready for day two of the stained-glass class. The new students are great. They're attentive and calm—perfect. I'll help you clean up here and then push off for an evening of reading to Mom."

Without another word, Savannah walked over and folded Amanda into a huge hug. Amanda reacted by stiffening, then relaxed into the comforting gesture. In a flash, she was sobbing like a toddler. *Poor dear.* Savannah gave her a light squeeze and rubbed her back in small, soothing circles.

After several long moments, following a whole-body shudder, Amanda stepped back and snuffled. "Thanks for the attack hug. I'm going through an emotional roller coaster. I'm either stiff and stoic or a crying waterspout. I don't know how I would cope with the hospice visits without you, Edward, the Rosenberg twins, and even young Jacob giving me the support I need."

Savannah nodded. Jacob was her late father's final trainee in a long line of apprentices who benefited from learning to make glass art. His parents had purchased his adorable service beagle, Suzy, to let others know by a special bark if Jacob began to have an anxiety attack. She also soothed him with her calm presence. If left alone, he could escalate into a full-blown asthmatic crisis. The inhaler was stowed in the pocket of Suzy's blue service pack. "We're all here for you." Savannah continued to rub Amanda's back. "We've weathered through a few crises together."

"As your investigative posse—we have certainly made a difference."

"What are you reading to her?"

"You're not going to believe this. She *looks* like she would be the perfect candidate for listening to a cozy mystery with a magical cat who solves the murders. But, nope. She is having me read a Tim Dorsey thriller."

"Which one?"

"*The Pope of Palm Beach*, the newest installment of the Serge Storm series. When she still had good mobility, she never missed his signings down at Haslam's Book Store. I think his books keep her wondering what horrible thing he will make happen next."

Savannah shook her head and grinned. "You can't fault her logic. I didn't sleep properly for a week after I read that one. I'll stop by tomorrow night and read to her for a while."

Amanda beamed. "She would love that. Oh, I

nearly forgot. You can bring Rooney. The nurses love fur baby visits. His big, cuddly dog energy would liven up the evening for everyone."

Savannah imagined the disruption her yearling Weimaraner would bring to the peaceful facility for hospice patients who didn't have a home setup for receiving palliative care. On the other hand, the staff were experts in end-of-life experiences. They would know right away if his behavior was appropriate. "I'll think about it. If he's in a calm mood—absolutely."

"Anyway, if there's nothing else, I'm off." Amanda hiked her patchwork hobo handbag onto her shoulder and left by the back door.

The over-the-door bell sounded a single ting. Eighteen-year-old Jacob Underwood entered the front door and let his service dog, Suzy, lead the way into the shop. Jacob had a strange knack for keeping the bell practically silent when arriving. Savannah thought it was a personal challenge he was playing against himself.

He walked into the flameworking studio and handed Savannah a black journal. He didn't look her in the eye as he said, "Webb's Studio needs more supplies." Jacob's condition used to be called Asperger's syndrome, but after the recently revised medical definition, he was medically classified as a high-functioning autistic.

"Thanks, Jacob. I appreciate that you ask each artist what supplies they want for their works in progress. This is very good practice in communicating with clients."

Savannah had recently promoted Jacob to the position of journeyman in charge of Webb's Studio. It was a new venture housed in a converted warehouse with by-the-month rental work spaces for intermediate and advanced students.

"I'll just gather the requested supplies tonight and drop them off at the studio for you to pass out tomorrow." Savannah looked at Jacob to be sure that he understood.

He nodded again and picked up Suzy, then managed to get out the front door without the bell making a single sound.

She chuckled. *Looks like he won the game today. Jacob 1, doorbell 42 million.*

As Savannah entered the final key to shut down the cash register, she heard a sharp yelp directly in front of Webb's Glass Shop, followed by a sickening thud. Next, she heard squealing tires and then a roaring engine. Out the front window, she glimpsed a white car flying down the street.

Jacob! Please don't let it be Jacob. Savannah bolted out, nearly tearing the bell off the door.

Jacob stood outside on the sidewalk as stiff as the tinman from *Wizard of Oz.* He let out a keening scream, which was overlaid by a howl from Suzy.

Jacob abruptly stopped screaming. Suzy went silent as well.

As Savannah moved to stand in front of him, a yard away, a tsunami of relief rushed over her. She quietly said his name. She was careful not to touch him. A critical precaution to reduce the chances of Jacob having a panic attack.

Savannah noticed that Suzy appeared calm, so Jacob didn't need his inhaler. He stared down the street without acknowledging her presence. She made no attempt to get his attention.

Savannah followed his gaze out on the street. Crumpled faceup near the curb lay a woman dressed in khaki trousers and a white Queen's Head Pub logo shirt.

"Nicole!" Savannah shrieked. Nicole was completely unresponsive. Not even an eyelash fluttered.

Terrified, Savannah became hypersensitive to every sound around her. The murmur of onlookers, the slowing of traffic in the street, the mockingbird singing nearby.

Nicole was a good friend. She worked in the pub right next door, owned by Savannah's fiancé, Edward.

Shaking herself into action, Savannah placed two fingers on Nicole's throat. She detected an irregular heartbeat. It was barely noticeable, and her infrequent breaths were shallow.

She pulled back Nicole's thick blond hair to reveal heavy-lidded eyes. There were streaks of road filth down her face and her legs didn't line up properly. From the back of her head, a terrible wound leaked a small stream of blood, which made its way to the curb.

This is bad.

"Call 911," she yelled to the gathering crowd of bystanders, pointing at a balding man with his cell phone already in hand. "Hurry! She's still alive."

The man dialed.

A sour taste hit the back of Savannah's throat. She knew better than to try to move a victim of trauma. Instead, she gathered Nicole's limp and clammy hand in both of hers. "Nicole, can you hear me? Stay with me, girl. Help is coming."

Chapter 2

Monday afternoon,
Webb's Glass Shop

The St. Petersburg Fire Department truck arrived first, followed by Sunstar Paramedics EMTs, who specialized in Advanced Life Support first-responder procedures.

After the SPFD paramedics stabilized Nicole, they consulted with the Sunstar paramedics to ensure that everything possible had been done for the best care of Nicole.

The tallest SPFD paramedic spied a very pale Jacob and raised an eyebrow. He stepped over. "Son, are you feeling okay?"

Jacob held Suzy in his arms, staring at the spot in the street where Nicole had lain. He didn't respond.

The paramedic continued, "Did you see the accident?"

Jacob dipped his head the tiniest bit and opened his mouth for a long moment, then closed it again. Suzy licked his chin. Jacob turned to stare at Savannah.

"Do you know this boy?" the paramedic said to Savannah.

She turned. "He's my apprentice. His name is Jacob, he's autistic, and he's holding his service beagle, Suzy. He witnessed the accident. I've just left a message for his mother. She's a judge. They're interrupting the trial to inform her of this incident. Is he okay?"

"He's pale, but not sweating. His breathing is good." He reached out to touch Jacob's forehead, but Jacob backed up a step and Suzy's ears perked up.

Savannah turned to the man. "He never wants anyone to touch him. Suzy will give out a warning yip if he needs his inhaler for an anxiety attack."

The paramedic shrugged. "I'll get him a shock blanket anyway. It won't hurt." He pulled one out of his black bag, unfolded it, then draped it around Jacob's shoulders without touching him.

Jacob exhaled a deep breath and Suzy's ears relaxed.

Savannah phoned Edward. *He should be here. Didn't he hear Suzy?* The call went straight to voice mail. "Edward, come out front right away. Nicole's been hit by a car. I need you." Her stomach churned, her breathing quickened, and she felt her chest tighten.

This could be fatal.

A Channel 9 news vehicle pulled over and a reporter lunged out the passenger door before the white van had come to a complete stop. "What's happened here? How bad is she hurt? Did anyone see it?"

Savannah responded with an are-you-kidding-me? scowl and turned her back.

Undaunted, the reporter waved to the driver, who turned off the ignition and walked around, opening the back of the van to grab a microphone, which he tethered to a large camera. He handed the microphone to the reporter, who stood in front of their van so that the logo was in the shot.

Savannah ignored the news van and watched the paramedics as they wrapped a brace around Nicole's neck and strapped her onto a board.

Nicole's purse had been thrown to the curb by the impact. The contents were strewn in an area over six feet long, except that her phone was still in an inside zippered pocket. Savannah scooped the contents back into the bag and put the cross-body strap over her head.

"I'll take that along, miss," said the paramedic, a sturdy young woman with short black hair. "She's going to be needing that for insurance and identification." Savannah took off the handbag and offered it over.

"How does it look? Will she be all right?" Savannah felt the catch in her voice.

The paramedic headed toward the driver's seat and looked at her teammate. "We can't tell yet, but it is very serious. We'll be taking her to Bayside Medical Center. You should get her family there as soon as you can."

The paramedic stuffed Nicole's handbag into the front seat of the ambulance and returned to her partner as he inserted an IV into Nicole's left hand. They lifted her onto the gurney, then rolled her up into the ambulance. The woman paramedic climbed into the back with Nicole and they drove off with lights flashing and siren blaring.

Jacob hadn't moved a muscle, his shock blanket was still draped around his shoulders, but he had tucked a corner over Suzy. Savannah put out her hand and pulled back just before she touched his shoulder. His gaze snapped to her face and he stepped back a pace. "Your mom will be here soon to take you home." He nodded but faced back to the street.

Jacob watched the ambulance leave. He stood silent and held Suzy.

Savannah hadn't heard from Jacob's mother. Frances was the sitting judge for the Pinellas County Sixth Judicial Circuit and specialized in juvenile and family cases. Court was normally only in session until about 4 P.M., but Judge Underwood sometimes forgot to turn her cell phone back on. She answered after the fourth ring. "Hi, Savannah, what's wrong? You never call me at work."

"Sorry, Frances. You need to pick up Jacob from Webb's Glass Shop. Nicole Borawski from Edward's pub has been severely injured in a hit-and-run."

"Oh my God. That's terrible. How bad is she hurt?" Her speech was harried and staccato.

"It looks very serious. Jacob saw it and seems to be stunned mute. He won't talk to me."

"That's not a good reaction from Jacob. Is he cold or shaking?"

"No, he doesn't appear to be in shock. One of the paramedics tried to examine him, but Jacob would only accept a shock blanket. The paramedic stopped trying and let him alone. Jacob is very quiet and won't answer any questions."

After describing to Frances Underwood what she thought Jacob had seen, she called Edward. This time he answered.

"Hi, luv. I'm sorry. I saw your call. I was elbow deep in a huge order of hand-formed crab cakes. When I start making them, it's a can't-stop job. What's up?"

Savannah told him.

He was stunned into silence. but after a moment, he told her he would arrange for someone to take care of Queen's Head Pub and that she should follow Nicole to Bayside Medical Center. After he rearranged staffing, he would meet her there.

The next call Savannah made was to Nicole's wife, Elizabeth. The couple had only been married a little more than a year—they'd recently celebrated their anniversary at Queen's Head Pub. Her office was just across the Howard Frankland Bridge in Tampa.

Panic made her voice tremble. "I'll be at the emergency room as soon as I can get there."

"Do you have someone who can drive you?" Savannah asked. "You're upset, and you shouldn't be behind the wheel."

"No, that would take too long to arrange, and I can't wait. I'll be right there."

Savannah spied Judge Underwood's car making its way down Central Avenue. She waved her whole arm and watched Frances pull over, slam on the brakes, throw the car in park and leap out onto the sidewalk. Frances flew to Jacob's side. "Darling, are you okay?"

Jacob turned and shook his head slowly from side to side.

"Okay, I'm going to take you home for root beer. Is that okay?"

Jacob tipped his head. She turned to Savannah. "I've got him. Get going to the hospital. Nicole will need her friends." She gripped Savannah's upper arm. "I hope she recovers."

Savannah hopped in her gray Mini Cooper and set out for the hospital.

Chapter 3

Monday evening,
emergency room

Savannah stood inside the emergency room entrance and noticed that her keys were jangling. Her hand was shaking and she could feel her heart race.

She took a deep, calming breath. She held her elbows tightly to her sides, knowing that she dreaded hearing news of Nicole's condition.

Those tangled legs, fluttering pulse, and bleeding skull—she didn't think Nicole would be leaving the emergency room alive.

The waiting room was decorated in the exact opposite mood of bright and cheery. It was dismal, depressing, and painted a dull flat gray. Savannah wondered if this was the plan, or perhaps lifeless décor was the only kind that could withstand the high traffic. The man behind the reception desk was thin, pale, and had shaved his head as a solution to his natural baldness. His mucky brown eyes stared at her through thin round frames.

"What's the condition of Nicole Borawski?" Savannah asked.

"Can you spell that?" The reception man opened a red binder with about a dozen sheets of paper, one for each patient.

Savannah frowned. "B-O-R-A-W-S-K-I. Her first name is Nicole. N-I-C-O-L-E."

He flipped a few of the pages and stopped. "Yes, she's here. Are you a relative?"

"No—"

"Okay, then the only thing I can tell you is that she arrived and that she is in critical condition."

Savannah lifted her head to look at the ceiling. *At least Nicole made it here.* "Thanks. Her wife will be arriving shortly."

"Wife?" The receptionist pursed his lips, then pressed them into a thin line. "She'd better have the proper identification if she expects to be let in to see a patient."

Savannah raised one eyebrow and turned back into the waiting room.

The coffee was bitter and stale. Even when she followed the handwritten instructions taped on the wall on how to make a fresh pot, the only difference was that it was now hot, bitter, stale coffee.

She repeatedly clenched her hands into fists and released them, trying to ease the tension that plagued them while she worried about Nicole. Savannah sat on the green chair with her head in her hands. She tried to recall if she had locked the doors at Webb's Glass Shop before leaving.

The automatic doors swooshed open and Elizabeth Hartford frantically looked around the room. She was slightly taller than Savannah's six feet, with short, scruffy locks of sun-bleached hair and the kind of weathered tan that comes with years of sailing on racing yachts. Her eyes were red-rimmed and her gaze landed on the information desk. With the unconscious grace of an athlete, Elizabeth ran over to it, but the receptionist had stepped away.

Elizabeth pounded a rat-a-tat with her fist on the desk. Then she looked at everyone, desperately searching for someone in charge. She said to the room in general, "My wife is supposed to be here. I was told she was in an accident. Her name is Nicole Borawski. Can someone help me?"

Savannah walked over and gently touched Elizabeth on the arm. "Elizabeth, I don't know if you remember me. I'm Savannah Webb. I own Webb's Glass Shop next door to Queen's Head Pub. Nicole is here. The receptionist will be back in a moment. I'm sure."

Elizabeth's tanned skin was tinged with a yellow paleness. She blinked her deep brown eyes repeatedly. "What happened? What do the doctors say?"

"I'm not her next of kin. They'll only tell me she's in critical condition." She gently turned Elizabeth back to the receptionist, who was sitting down in his chair. "This is Nicole Borawski's wife,

Elizabeth Hartford. She needs to know what's happening."

The receptionist looked up. "Ms. Hartford, may I have your identification and insurance cards, please? I'll also need proof of your"—he pressed his lips together—"marriage to the patient to indicate that you are her next of kin."

"I don't understand. Where's Nicole? I need to see Nicole," she said frantically.

Savannah firmly held Elizabeth and spoke quietly but clearly into her ear. "I know it's hard, but you must calm down. They need to make sure it's you, first. They will give you all the information you want as soon as they confirm your identity. It's the privacy act, I think, but it doesn't matter. He doesn't know anything. You need to get in there and see the doctor. Do you have your ID handy?"

Elizabeth blinked rapidly, unzipped her windbreaker and removed a worn Spider-Man billfold from the back pocket of her shorts. She placed her driver's license and medical insurance card on the counter.

The receptionist took them. "Do you have proof of your marital status?"

Elizabeth frowned. "I don't carry our marriage license around with me, if that's what you mean." The pitch of her voice boomed in the large waiting area. Elizabeth was used to yelling over the sound of crashing waves and grinding winches while racing through the ocean.

"Calm down." Savannah's whisper contrasted sharply with Elizabeth's volume. "This will go easier if you take the high road."

Elizabeth woodenly turned to Savannah with absolute terror shining in her eyes. "I don't have proof."

"Wait a second, wouldn't your insurance company have that information? Isn't that on your card?"

"I don't know, I've never been questioned about our relationship before."

"You haven't had an emergency since you married?"

Elizabeth shook her head.

Savannah picked up the insurance card from the window shelf. "Look. There's a number to call. Hang on." She dialed the number and explained the situation to the insurance agent. In less than a minute, Savannah handed her cell phone to the receptionist. "Maybe this will be proof enough." She accompanied her comment with a ferocious look.

The receptionist took the phone. "Hello, this the Bayside Hospital emergency room." He listened for a few seconds. "No, of course we don't discriminate, we treat everyone who comes in. Personal information is different." He listened again. "Okay, but—" He pursed his lips but continued to listen. "Okay, fine." The receptionist handed the phone back to Savannah.

"Is everything clear, now?" Savannah said between clenched teeth.

"Yes, ma'am. We treat all your kind." He took Elizabeth's ID and insurance card from the counter. "I'm going to copy these. Meanwhile, please fill out these forms. All of them." He handed Elizabeth a thick set of forms that were attached to a clipboard.

He also gave Elizabeth a pen with the hospital's logo printed on it. "Have a seat. As soon as you complete the forms, we'll get you logged in as the next of kin and the doctor will be able to tell you what's happening."

Elizabeth glared at the receptionist, then spoke each word slowly, calmly, fiercely. "Can you please tell me if she's alive?"

Chapter 4

The silence in the waiting room smothered the tense group like a wet woolen blanket.

The receptionist shifted back in his chair, the shock of the request plastered on his face. He stuttered, "The . . . the . . . last I heard, she was . . . was alive. I'm not a doctor, you know." He pointed to the clipboard in Elizabeth's hands and regained his composure. "The quicker you manage to fill those out those forms, the quicker you can see the patient—your wife."

Savannah took Elizabeth's arm and led her over to one of the horrible plastic chairs. "Sit right here and get those forms filled out. In the end, this will save time. The receptionist doesn't know and won't tell you anything. You must be brave, but hurry."

With a trembling hand, Elizabeth poised the pen over the first blank, but that's as far as she got. Savannah took the clipboard and pen from her and quickly filled out the information she knew. She asked Elizabeth a few questions about the remaining blanks. Then Savannah pointed to the signature line and held the clipboard steady while Elizabeth scrawled a wavering signature.

Savannah pulled Elizabeth up. She led her by the elbow over to the receptionist's desk, then handed in the clipboard. "That's all the forms done. When can Elizabeth see the doctor?"

The receptionist pursed his lips and reached for the telephone. He spoke to someone in a syrupy voice and replaced the handset. "Doctor Smith will be right out." He stood, leaned over the counter, and pointed to a plain door along the same wall as his cubicle. "He'll be coming out that door. You can wait right over there in those seats." He pointed to the chairs nearest the door.

They sat. Elizabeth turned even more pale and rubbed her tummy.

"Are you going to be sick?" asked Savannah.

"Oh, I hope not."

After what seemed like an hour but was probably only two minutes, the door opened. A very young man no taller than five feet two looked from Savannah to Elizabeth and back to Savannah. "One of you is Elizabeth?"

"That's me," Elizabeth said as she stood. Savannah stood as well.

"Your wife is critical and unstable. Are there any other family members here?"

"Not yet. One of her brothers is on his way, but

he hasn't arrived. I left him a message and he texted that he'll be here as soon as he can. I don't have a number for the other brother."

"I'll tell the receptionist to send him right in. There isn't very much time. I'll take you back to be with your wife. We're minutes from taking her to surgery. It looks like there's internal bleeding."

Elizabeth covered her mouth with one trembling hand, covered her tummy with the other. She looked at Savannah, her eyes pleading. "Come with me, please. I can't do this alone."

Savannah looked back at the receptionist and then to the doctor. "Will it be all right?"

The doctor heaved a great sigh. "Trouble getting your status verified?"

They both nodded.

The doctor raised his voice. "Jared, I'm taking them both back. I'll be putting in another written complaint."

The receptionist shrugged his shoulders. "That's your prerogative. I know what's right and what's wrong."

Elizabeth straightened her shoulders and narrowed her eyes into a blazing glare.

"Obviously you don't," the doctor said, "or you wouldn't be adding pain to an already unbearable situation. I'll be suggesting a course in diversity training when I report this to your supervisor. I'll be checking back until I'm sure you've changed."

Savannah's brows arched upwards. *That should strike fear into his stone-cold heart.* She shook the doctor's hand. "Thanks."

Dr. Smith led them through the plain door down a short hallway. "That idiot is an eyelash away from getting fired. My written complaint should provide that last bit of overwhelming evidence." He paused for a second outside of a large room and looked at Elizabeth. "On behalf of the entire hospital, I apologize for his behavior." He gently touched her shoulder. Elizabeth flinched, her eyes tearing up, but didn't pull away. "This is hard enough." Without another word, he led them into the room.

Four beds were spaced along the walls, each bed surrounded by gray curtains on sliding rings. Three empty beds had smooth white sheets with two pillows, a cotton blanket, and a thick thermal throw. He stopped in front of the bed with the curtains closed.

"I must warn you that she sustained grievous injuries to her head and body. Her prognosis is grave." He opened the curtain to let them inside.

Elizabeth cried, "Oh, Nicole!" and rushed over to the side of the bed.

Nicole lay completely still with her eyes closed. Her complexion was slate gray. The same shade of the hospital gown she wore. A respirator covered most of her face. A large brace was fastened around her neck and multiple fluid bags were attached to a pole feeding an IV in her left hand. Nicole's bright red fingernail polish provided the only color.

"Nicole, can you hear me?" Elizabeth grabbed Nicole's right hand and kissed it. She tucked it against her chest. "Can she hear me?"

Dr. Smith lowered his voice to a whisper. "You should assume that she can. We don't know for sure, but it appears to help."

Elizabeth leaned over to gaze at Nicole's closed eyes. "Darling, this is going to be fine. You're going to get better, believe me." She lifted Nicole's hand to the side of her face. "I love you so much, you can't leave. Not now. Do you hear me? You can't leave me alone."

An orderly parted the curtain and poked his head in. "Dr. Smith. They're ready for her in surgery."

"Quick," Dr. Smith said. "Say your goodbyes, we have very little time to save her." He pulled the ringed curtain around a bit to give Elizabeth at least the notion of privacy.

Elizabeth's cheeks flushed up an ugly mauve as huge tears steaked down her cheeks. She bent down to whisper. "Nicole, I know you can hear me. You've been my life. I know things have been difficult lately. Please don't leave me." She dropped her head onto Nicole's shoulder and sobbed uncontrollably.

Savannah placed her hands on Elizabeth's shoulders and pulled gently. "You must let them work on her. We all want to see her recovered and healthy."

Elizabeth shrugged off Savannah's hands. "No. I can't let you go. I need you."

"Ma'am!" the orderly broke in sharply. "Step back, please. I'm sorry. We have to take her now."

This time when Savannah took hold of Elizabeth, she complied and stumbled backward without taking her eyes from Nicole.

The muscular orderly zipped the curtain open as wide as the tracks allowed. He lifted the portable oxygen tank he pulled behind him and placed it between Nicole's feet. Another orderly made sure the IV stand would roll smoothly and nodded to his buddy. The first orderly transferred Nicole's oxygen source from the wall to the portable tank. He unlocked all four wheels, then moved Nicole down the hallway to a set of double doors, twisting around to speak to Elizabeth. "You need to go to the surgery waiting room on the fourth floor." He flashed a winning smile. "The nurses will keep you apprised of her status. They're a great bunch up there. Very sympathetic to all kinds of patients." He cast a disapproving look toward the reception-ist's desk, then gave Elizabeth a sympathetic smile. "Everyone is treated with respect up there." He trotted through the double doors.

Chapter 5

After the frantic hustle in the emergency waiting room, the surgery waiting room reminded Savannah of a visit to a library. It had only taken them about five minutes to locate the room. On the door was a sign. NO CELL PHONE USE PERMITTED INSIDE THE SURGERY WAITING ROOM.

The room felt cool and looked heartless. Not a single comfortable chair. The temperature was set ridiculously low—even by Florida standards. Savannah cursed the designer who'd had no idea why people would be using the chairs. Idiot.

Monday night was apparently a slow time for surgeries. An elderly couple sat next to each other adjacent to the Mr. Coffee station. They were asleep. The man had his head resting on the pale green wall behind his chair. The woman's head rested on his shoulder.

"Now what happens?" Elizabeth's shrill voice pierced through the quiet room like fingernails on a chalkboard. The elderly woman startled awake and looked confused.

"Shush." Savannah gently led Elizabeth by the elbow to a seat near a telephone hanging on the wall. "You'll wake those poor folks over there."

The sign next to the phone read DIAL 326 FOR AN UPDATE TO SURGERY STATUS. "I'm sure we'll be hearing something very soon. Try to relax. I know it's hard, but you must try."

Elizabeth shrugged off Savannah's arm, picked up the phone, then punched in a 326. "Hello, this is Elizabeth Hartford. Nicole Borawski has just arrived for surgery. I wanted to let you know that I'm her wife and that I'm ready for any information you can give me. I'm right here in the waiting room."

There was a long pause.

Elizabeth said, "Yes, I can hold." She covered the mouthpiece. "She's going to check to see if Nicole has made it to the operating room."

Another long pause was followed by, "Yes, I'm her wife." Another pause. "Okay, we're sitting right here by the phone."

A door next to the coffee stand opened and a chunky woman dressed in balloon-printed medical togs walked over to Elizabeth and Savannah. She was carrying a folder with a notepad inside.

"Elizabeth Hartford?"

Elizabeth nodded.

"I have—"

Before the nurse could continue, Edward burst through the doors and hustled across the room. He spoke to Savannah as soon as he saw her. "Where's Nicole? What's happening?" He stood between Savannah and Elizabeth, putting an arm around each. "I'm Nicole's boss. What's going on? Is she in surgery?"

Savannah took Edward's hand and squeezed it hard. He was extremely upset, but she didn't hug him. He had been brought up not to embrace anyone in public.

"Let the nurse finish, Edward. She's just now giving us an update."

"Thanks. We've finished prepping Nicole and they're taking her into surgery now. Her vital signs are indicating that she has significant internal injuries. I want to prepare you for the possibility that she may not survive."

"Oh no!" Elizabeth broke away from the little group and covered her face with both hands. "This can't be happening. We've only just begun our lives together."

Savannah looked at the nurse and could see the sympathetic concern in her world-weary eyes. "I'll let you know immediately if her condition changes." She returned through the door.

Edward turned to Elizabeth. "How are you holding up, pet? Would you like a cup of coffee?"

Elizabeth bit her lip and exhaled a long breath. "Yes, this may be a very long night and I need to stay alert."

In the far corner of the waiting room, Edward found a Mr. Coffee on a small counter next to a beverage vending machine. The counter had a small sink and a built-in storage cabinet for supplies. He picked up the carafe, sniffed the brew, and wrinkled up his nose. "Stale." He dumped the contents, grabbed a paper towel and scrubbed out the carafe. He dumped the previous filter and wiped down the basket along with every reachable surface in the coffee area.

Next, he bought two bottles of water and used them to start brewing a fresh pot of coffee. As soon as it was finished, he smelled the coffee in the carafe. He smiled, then poured coffee into two paper cups and took them to Savannah and Elizabeth. He went back and poured one for himself.

Savannah's phone pinged a message from Jacob's mother.

JACOB HASN'T SAID A WORD YET. HE'S EATING HIS COMFORT FOOD.

Savannah texted back a frowny-face emoji and then added an alarmed-faced one as well. She realized how much Jacob contributed to the smooth running of her business. She worried about how he would recover. He was dealing with enough challenges. He had grown from a gangly teen into a responsible young man on her watch. She thought that her late father would be proud.

Savannah glanced over at Edward, who watched the wall clock tick second by second while clenching his fists, releasing them, then clenching again. She considered at this point that he had known Nicole longer than anyone else since he moved here from the UK. She went over to stand by his side and held on to his arm with both her hands. He stopped clenching his fists.

"Has anyone notified Amanda?" Edward asked.

Savannah puffed out a held breath. "Honestly, I didn't even give her a thought." There had been too much going on for Savannah to consider contacting anyone but Elizabeth and Edward.

"She knew Nicole before she came to work for me. Amanda recommended her, and after I interviewed Nicole, I hired her on the spot. I haven't regretted that for a second."

Savannah squeezed his arm again. "I didn't know that."

"How do you think she's doing?" Edward tilted his head toward Elizabeth. "I've just realized that I don't know her very well at all. Nicole wasn't the type to share her feelings at the drop of a hat, but I should have tried to reach out more often."

The coffee was delicious and gave them something warm to hold.

They had barely finished Edward's coffee when the door opened to a young man with short sandy hair and pale blue eyes. He looked quickly at the old couple and then walked toward Elizabeth. "I'm sorry to be late. I got here as quickly as I could. How's Nicole?"

"Phillip!" Elizabeth stood and threw herself into the young man's arms. "Oh, Phillip. It's terrible. She's in grave condition."

Phillip frowned and patted Elizabeth awkwardly. "It's okay. I'm sure she's going to be fine. This is my big sister you're talking about. She's tough as nails." He pushed Elizabeth gently away and led her back to her seat. She was still snuffling.

Phillip reached into his back pocket and gave Elizabeth a new packet of tissues. She pinched the package with her trembling fingers but couldn't open it. Phillip took it back from her, opened the package, then pulled out a tissue and placed it in her hand. She blew her nose and wiped her eyes. "Thanks for being here. It makes this nightmare manageable, but not really." She wiped her eyes again.

"Can we ask for news?" Phillip asked her in an urgent tone.

Elizabeth took another tissue out of the packet, sat down, and continued to wipe her eyes.

An awkward pause grew within the small group. Savannah broke the silence.

"Hi, I'm Savannah Webb and this is Nicole's boss, Edward Morris. I don't think you've met. Sit down," said Savannah to Phillip. She led him to the seat on the other side of the still weeping Elizabeth. Savannah and Edward stood in front of them, looking helpless.

Elizabeth wiped her eyes and shifted toward Phillip. "You must be tired. It's a long drive from Zephyrhills. Even worse when you're rushing toward an emergency."

"Where is Nicole?" asked Phillip. "Can I see her?"

"She's in surgery now." Elizabeth glanced at the telephone hanging on the wall. "They'll call as soon as there is news."

"I can't believe this." He put an arm around Elizabeth and side hugged her. "What happened?"

When Elizabeth's mouth fell open but nothing came out, Savannah answered for her. "It was a hit-

and-run right in front of my shop." She turned to Edward. "My apprentice, Jacob, saw the whole thing from the sidewalk. Seeing the impact was brutal for him. The paramedics asked him some questions, but he just stood there. He was in shock, and I had his mother come to take him home."

Savannah stopped talking. She realized that Phillip didn't know her, Edward, or Jacob.

Edward filled the silence. "The traffic down Central is usually pretty calm. We're all pretty careful about crossing," he turned toward Savannah. "She wasn't texting, was she?"

Savannah spoke. "No, it wasn't that. Her phone was zippered into her handbag."

Phillip spoke up. "It's weird. Nicole has seemed distracted, and honestly, we haven't been that close lately. I thought I had done something to make her mad. Did she say anything to you?"

"No," said Elizabeth, "but she has been a little preoccupied and distracted. I thought she might be steeling herself to confront her parents about accepting me again. She would try to talk to them about me every few months."

"No luck with that, I'll bet," said Phillip.

Elizabeth frowned and pulled another tissue out of the packet. "None."

"Let's sit, Edward. I feel like we're hovering." Savannah took the seat on the other side of Elizabeth and Edward sat next to Savannah.

He leaned in to whisper, "How's Jacob? He must be in a right state."

"I haven't spoken to his mom yet. But I'm afraid this could really cause some serious damage to his confidence. There was something disturbing about how fast the driver was going and how quickly he left the scene."

After several long minutes of silence, the entry door squeaked, and Officer Joy Williams entered the room and looked over at the solemn group of four.

Savannah was struck by the thought that her friend appeared strangely official and remote. Her uniform was tailored to her curvy shape and her cornrows were drawn back and tied to the nape of her neck

They all looked up toward her as one.

Officer Williams stood in front of Savannah. "Hi, Savannah, Edward. I'm sorry about Nicole, but I've been assigned to investigate the hit-and-run. I need to ask you some questions now, before any details disappear." Nodding to Elizabeth and Phillip, she said, "I'll need to talk to you next." She asked Savannah, "Is there somewhere we can find a little privacy?"

Savannah stood. "Let's go down to the coffee shop."

Savannah took Elizabeth's hand and squeezed it tight. "I'll be right back." She mouthed a kiss to Edward and they left for the café on the first floor. After going through the serving line for a coffee for Officer Williams and a sparkling water for Savannah, they found a secluded table.

"What is the first thing you recall?" asked Officer Williams. She took out her notepad and scribbled the date, time, and Savannah's name at the top of the page.

"It was the sound of Nicole getting hit." Savannah realized her voice had suddenly gotten scratchy. "It was a thump. It didn't register with me what it was until I heard a squealing of tires and an accelerating engine roar." She stopped to swallow hard. She inhaled a huge breath and tried to relax the tight knot positioned at the back of her neck. "The next thing I heard was Jacob screaming and Suzy howling. They were right on the sidewalk. They saw the whole thing."

"What did you do then?"

"I ran outside and saw the back end of a white car turn right at the very next street."

Officer Williams looked up from her notepad. "I don't suppose you got a glimpse of the license number?"

"No, it was too far away, and my focus was on Jacob and Suzy."

"Next?"

"As soon as I got Jacob to look at me rather than in the street at Nicole, he stopped screaming and Suzy stopped howling. Then I went into the street, knelt beside Nicole, and checked to see if she was alive. She had a faint heartbeat, but she was unconscious." Savannah fell silent, the image of Nicole completely limp seared into her memory.

"And then?" Officer Williams prompted.

"I yelled for someone to call 911 and then I brushed Nicole's hair out of her face and talked to her. She didn't respond. The EMTs got there in just a few minutes."

"What about Jacob?" Officer Williams scanned the café. "Where is he?"

"I called his mother to get him. He was a wreck. I left him there on the sidewalk as soon as his mother arrived. She texted me a bit ago to say that he was at least eating his favorite McDonald's order at home."

"Okay, I'll have to speak to him at some point. He is our only primary witness. Is that all?"

Savannah cleared her suddenly scratchy throat. "Here, let me give you his home number." She reached out for the notepad and Officer Williams hesitated for a moment, then handed it over along with the pen. Savannah wrote down the number and returned them.

I am certainly not myself. I didn't even peek at her notes when I got the chance.

"I'll need a list of your students. If they were still in the area, they may have noticed something."

"Absolutely. I'll e-mail their contact details to you the first chance I get." Savannah glanced over at the clock on the wall. "There are only six students."

Officer Williams smiled her thanks. "Was that her wife in the waiting room?"

"Yes, her name is Elizabeth Hartford. She's waiting up there with Nicole's brother, Phillip."

"I need to talk to both of them. Let's get back. Thanks for bringing me up to speed."

As soon as they returned, Officer Williams indicated to Savannah and Edward that they should go to the other side of the waiting room. Then she stopped in front of Elizabeth. "Ma'am, are you Elizabeth Hartford?"

Elizabeth sniffed noisily and lifted her eyes. "Yes, I'm Nicole's wife."

Phillip piped up. "I'm Nicole's brother, Phillip Borawski. Have you caught the hit-and-run driver?"

Officer Williams continued to stand in front of

Elizabeth. "Not just yet, but if you don't mind, I would like to ask some questions about Nicole."

They both nodded.

"Have you noticed anything unusual in Nicole's behavior with you or any of her friends?"

Elizabeth inhaled a trembling breath, looked over to her brother-in-law, then turned back to Officer Williams. "Nicole was truly kind to people in need. She didn't just complain about social issues. She actually did something about them where it counts—at home, going about her daily life."

"That's absolutely correct," Edward confirmed, nodding his head. "She frequently helped members of staff with small loans and she kept an eye out for the homeless vets who frequented the dumpster in the alley behind the pub. She donated our leftovers to a food locker. Nicole also made sure they knew about the free kitchens, the free health clinic, and all the support services."

Elizabeth added. "She was especially interested in helping young people who were addicted to opioids. She frequently used her own money to check them into detox programs. Now that I think about it, Nicole was—"

The plain door beside the wall telephone opened and Dr. Smith walked over to the group. Savannah searched his face and found turned-down lips, a wrinkled brow, and his shoulders were slightly slumped. The lump in her stomach grew to the size of a boulder.

Elizabeth stood first and everyone followed.

"Elizabeth, I'm so sorry. I regret to tell you that your wife didn't make it through surgery. Nicole is dead."

Savannah gasped and felt her muscles stiffen and a sudden chill race through her body. *Nicole! Nicole is dead?* She turned to Edward. He ducked his head into his chest and reached out to her. They held each other in shock.

An agonized groan started deep in Elizabeth's throat and rose into a keening cry. She turned and buried her face in Phillip's shoulder. "Oh, Nicole. I knew you were courting trouble. This is what it cost—a terrible cost."

Chapter 6

*Late Monday evening,
Savannah's home*

Savannah pulled into the drive just as Edward arrived on his vintage Indian motorcycle. She had stayed a little longer at the hospital while Edward had returned to close the pub.

Rooney met them at the door, sitting tall and regal like the royal prince he thought he was. He sensed something serious. He didn't writhe with anticipation of their greeting hugs and scratches. He didn't clamor to be taken for his evening run. Rooney seemed to understand that Savannah and Edward were upset.

Instead, when she collapsed on the couch, he curled up into Savannah's lap as if he were still a tiny puppy. He was large for a Weimaraner, and he took up most of the three-seater sofa so that Savannah was left crunched up at the far end. She shrugged her shoulders at Edward, who had settled into the adjacent leather club chair.

She was conscious of the comfort she felt at having him live here. Instead of feeling dependent, she felt empowered by his unstinting support. It hadn't been an easy decision. It was still less than a year after her father's untimely death—the event that had led to so many changes. Owning Webb's, consulting for the police, meeting Edward. It had been an upheaval, but one that was settling into something wonderful. She squeezed Rooney. Thinking of Nicole, Savannah knew that everything she had gained in the past year could be stripped away in a matter of seconds.

Keeping himself busy, Edward got up and rustled up some pan-fried salmon with balsamic-glazed broccolini over a pile of fragrant basmati rice. As the smells of dinner started wafting through the house, Savannah roused herself and fed the pets, set the table, and pre-loaded the dishwasher. It was a comforting domestic routine, but far too quiet. Nicole's death hovered over the couple, stifling their usual chatter.

The unnatural silence stretched long into the meal. Savannah became acutely aware that the only sounds were the clicks of knives and forks on plates. *I've never seen him this upset. How will he handle Nicole's death?*

She cleared her throat and took a large gulp of wine. "Have you told the staff about Nicole?"

Edward swallowed and inhaled a deep breath. "Yes, that was hard. I went back to the pub to tell everyone we were closing for rest of the evening. I never know what to do when people start to cry."

He put his knife and fork down to clench his fists then rest them flat on the table. "Everyone is stunned. She was genuinely loved." He picked up his knife and fork again. "It's going to be bloody difficult to replace her. In fact, I'll have to hire at least two new staffers."

"Interviewing is going to be tricky with the Best Burger in the Burg contest going on."

"I know this is petty, but the timing couldn't be worse. This is my biggest promotion campaign of the entire year. I won last year with an Angus black-and-blue burger. This year is a little more traditional."

"But you closed the pub tonight because, well, it was the right thing to do. Is it possible that you're already out of the competition?"

"No, most of the voting will happen this weekend. I feel awful complaining."

"You should feel bad. It may be tough for you, but Nicole's family is going through pure agony."

"Right. I'll stop."

Savannah nodded and felt guilty for enjoying the pleasure of Edward's perfectly prepared salmon. "I'll help wherever I can."

"The main thing is to just carry on." He looked down into his plate and paused for a long time. "Oh, Mum called today," he said in a strained tone.

Savannah sighed heavily, put her fork down, and placed her folded hands in her lap. "Are we going to discuss this again? Now?"

Edward again put his knife and fork down on each side of his plate. "You've got to understand that long-distance flights are expensive during the holiday season. She needs to know where the wedding will be and the exact date. Mum and Da are not rich."

"I know that, but it seems a bad time to be discussing this. How can you even think about it right now?"

Edward stood and came around the table. He kissed the back of Savannah's neck. "Luv, right now seems like the best time in the world to me. We've had a shocking reminder that tomorrow is not guaranteed. Every day is a gift."

"Mmm, delicious." Savannah tipped her head back to look into his sad, intense eyes. "I've been looking at this wrong. You have a way of grounding me."

Edward returned to his seat and continued to eat in silence.

Savannah picked up her fork and it hovered over the delicious fish. "Okay, I promise to think about the details. There are a lot of decisions to make. Where to have the wedding, when to have the wedding, who do we invite. I need a dress. It's overwhelming right now."

"There will never be a convenient time for either of us. Can you at least let me give her a broad idea of when?"

Savannah took another bite of her fish. She looked over at Edward.

Why on earth is this so difficult? I love him to pieces. He's a wonderful person—supports me as a business-woman—accepts and even helps me with my obsession about crime.

"I'll think about it. Let's get our staffing issues resolved first."

Edward gave her an exasperated look.

"It's not a delaying tactic. We both must get that resolved very quickly. I've got a new class I'm in the middle of teaching. I can't cancel that without financial repercussions. I've got one student who I think could be a promising instructor."

Edward continued to look exasperated.

"Well, you've got a bigger staffing problem. Nicole will be next to impossible to replace. Training a new manager could take a while."

Edward's face softened into a gentle smile.

"Let's see where we are by the end of the week. I'll look ahead at my teaching schedule and give you a date. I promise." Savannah sealed that promise with a kiss.

After the kitchen cleanup, they retreated to the living room with red wine. As soon as Edward plopped down in his oversized chair and pulled the handle to recline, Snowy jumped onto his chest, used her fluffy paws to knead dough, then curled into a white ball. Rooney claimed his spot on the couch with his head in Savannah's lap. After a few minutes, Snowy, Edward, and Rooney fell into a sound asleep.

Something bothers me about Nicole's hit-and-run. Elizabeth's reaction at the hospital is really causing me heartburn. Ugh! I shouldn't be thinking about this now.

Still trapped by Rooney's huge head, Savannah whispered, "Edward." No response. She whispered harder, "Edward."

His eyes fluttered and opened wide. He took a deep breath. "Um, what?"

"How are you feeling? Do you want to talk?"

"It might be the old stiff-upper-lip part of me to

try to protect you at my expense." He automatically began giving Snowy tummy scratches. "But I'm stunned. It's not real in my head that it all happened. I didn't see it happen, but I was there when the doctor told us she died. I just can't wrap my head around it yet."

"She was part of our everyday lives. A huge part of your pub family."

Edward slumped into a solemn gaze. Snowy's big kitten paws grabbing his hand startled him out of a trance. A tiny smile crooked his face. He turned to Savannah, "Bang on. I didn't appreciate that." He had stopped stroking Snowy. She stretched her paws out and wrapped them around Edward's wrist.

Savannah tilted her head back and looked up at the ceiling. "I feel drained but outraged."

Edward squinted his confusion.

"I felt somewhat like a circus ringmaster from the moment I heard Jacob scream until we got the awful news. I was juggling my focus between keeping Elizabeth calm, listening to her brother's concerned questions, and worrying about Jacob. Now I feel like the plug has been pulled and all my feelings have drained away."

"That's just how I feel as well. Hours of anxious waiting culminating in horrible news."

They both stared at the floor in companionable silence.

"Have you talked to Jacob's mum, yet?" asked Edward, gently stroking a steadily purring Snowy.

"No, but I should before it gets too late." She reached into her back pocket for her phone, without disturbing Rooney. She dialed, and Frances picked up after a few rings.

"Hi, Frances. I thought you should know that Nicole died on the operating table."

Silence.

"Frances, are you there?"

"Oh, no. I mean, yes, I'm here. It's only that she was so young."

"I'm concerned about Jacob's reaction."

"This will be an additional stressor for his condition. He really liked Nicole. She had a knack for looking out for Jacob and Suzy when they went to Queen's Head Pub. She watched over him without smothering. I didn't have to worry about them when they were there."

"How is Jacob?" Savannah asked. "Is he all right?"

"His reaction is a bit unusual, but maybe I should have expected this. He won't speak to me at all. In fact, he won't speak to anyone. It's like he has regressed back to his toddler days. He was very late to talk—almost six years old. But then when he started talking, it was at the comprehension level of a ten-year-old. Big words—complete sentences—adult level language. It was quite a leap. I'm sorry. I know I'm rambling, but I'm deeply worried and I automatically try to formulate a closing argument."

"I can't even imagine. We're all so concerned."

"I also have heard from Officer Williams. She feels that since Jacob is her only known eyewitness that somehow she's going to have to find a way to get him to give a statement."

Savannah heard her voice rise. "But that could make this worse."

"You know I won't let anything jeopardize his

recovery. Right now, he needs to know everything is safe."

"No problem. Tell him that there's no need for him to come in to work. None of his currents projects are urgent. He needs to know that. He takes his work seriously, of course, but all of his projects can be shelved right now."

"Thanks for that. I know it's a lie and it's sweet of you to try to spare him. He feels a powerful responsibility for his work. Anyway, I'm taking him back to his therapist for an emergency appointment in the morning. I want a thorough assessment. We'll see what she makes of this."

"Let me know what she thinks if you can. I hope this is just a temporary reaction to the shock of witnessing a violent accident."

Savannah asked Frances to keep in touch before they hung up, then recounted the news to Edward.

He shrugged his shoulders. "Only the experts can tell."

Savannah scanned the room for the TV remote. "Let's see if this made the news." It was the usual search behind cushions, in crevasses, and under blankets until Edward picked it up from the floor beside his chair.

The local news, Channel 9, was covering their Weather on the Nines segment. The anchorwoman, Holly Gregory, returned, and the background was a view of the street in front of Webb's Glass Shop. Savannah and Edward watched the TV news broadcast in silence.

> *"There was a hit-and-run accident in the twenty-five hundred block of Central Avenue at*

around five o'clock. The victim has been identified as Nicole Borawski, bartender and manager of Queen's Head Pub. She died in the operating room at Bayside Hospital earlier this evening. The police are asking for the public to provide information regarding a white vehicle seen speeding from the scene.

To submit an anonymous tip via text message to the St. Petersburg Police Department, text SPPD and your tip to 847411 (tip411) or call the tip line at 727-411-TIPS to report anything about the accident.

To submit an anonymous tip using the tip-411 web form, click the button on the SPPD website."

"Have you heard anything back from Officer Williams?" asked Edward as the segment ended.

Savannah scanned her phone. "Nothing. Oh, wait. I missed her call. I must still have my phone on silent."

"From while we were in the surgery waiting room, I think."

"She left me a voice mail." The time stamp indicated that it had been recorded after they received the terrible news.

"Hi, Savannah. Look, I'm sorry about your friend Nicole. I know your first reaction is going to be to investigate the hit-and-run, but I want to warn you that sometimes things are just what they seem. This looks like a tragic but perfectly ordinary hit-and-run where the driver has panicked. Don't get yourself tied up in knots trying to imagine more than the reality of a bad decision on the part of the driver. Most of these cases involve a driver with DUIs, and they usually turn themselves in after all

the effects have worn off. That said, it's vehicular homicide. She audibly shuddered, as if a bug had crawled down her back. *"I hate these cases. They're all tragedy and never end well."* She sighed heavily. *"Call me tomorrow for lunch. Bye."*

Savannah felt a shuddering chill race up her body and she wrapped her arms around herself. She looked into Edward's sad green eyes.

"Strange."

Edward frowned. "What do you mean?"

"Joy seems to think I'll go roaring off to investigate Nicole's death."

"Why would she think that? Did you say something to her at the hospital?"

"Not really, but now I've had time to think. Elizabeth and Phillip seemed to have a different view about this."

Edward tilted his head. "It was an accident and the driver could have outstanding warrants or drugs in the car or was drunk or high or maybe the car was stolen." He looked down at the peacefully purring Snowy and then looked back at Savannah. "Right?" Silence filled the room like an incoming thunderstorm.

"I need a hug," said Savannah.

Edward lowered his head a bit. He gingerly slipped out of his chair, carrying Snowy without waking her, then tucked her between Rooney's head and shoulder. Snowy's emerald green eyes opened for a sleepy blink and she fell back into a deep kitten sleep. He slowly scooched down into one end of the couch behind Savannah. Edward pulled her into his lap without waking either pet. He wrapped his arms around Savannah and nuzzled into her neck. "Better?"

"Perfect." Savannah sighed and snuggled into the family pile. She was just beginning to drift off when her eyes flew open. "If this was an accidental hit-and-run, why didn't I hear screeching brakes? All I heard was the impact, Jacob screaming, and then Suzy howling."

Edward mumbled, "Uh-huh."

"I still don't understand why the driver didn't brake . . ."

Chapter 7

Tuesday morning,
Webb's Studio

Savannah unlocked Webb's Studio, her newly opened second business location. She felt a powerful sense of accomplishment. A few months ago, she had risked her hard-won financial security in favor of opening an artists' studio warehouse for intermediate and advanced students. The refurbished space had been more expensive than she had originally planned, but now it was filled and had a short waiting list.

Two locations were occasionally a scheduling challenge, especially since she would be spending more time at the original shop with the flameworking class starting up. She relished challenges but loved the security of routine as well.

"Good morning, Arthur. How are you feeling

today?" she asked when she noticed one of her usual students.

Arthur Young peeked out the open doorway of his work cubicle. His brown hair was beginning to thin and he dressed in his typical khaki cargo shorts with a snug-fitting blue golf shirt. He wore boat shoes without socks. Arthur played second-chair cello in his previous career with the Florida Orchestra. His medical issues had derailed his dream of achieving coveted first-chair status.

"I'm having a great morning. No tummy troubles and I'm just about finished with the stained-glass panel I'm making for my lovely bride."

"How is Nancy?"

Arthur's brown eyes drooped, and he turned both hands palms-up. "She's still fussing about how long my recovery is taking. She wants me back in the orchestra, clawing my way up to first cellist. I'm not sure I want to get back into the gossip, drama, and fierce competition of claiming first-chair honors. Irritable bowel syndrome doesn't always take a straight line to perfect recovery. It was a miracle I managed to hang on to second-chair last season."

"When do you think you can go back?"

He hung his head. "Nancy doesn't want to hear this, but I don't think I'll ever perform again. That's why I'm working so hard on this beautiful panel. I'm going to enter it in a contest." He beamed a mischievous smile. "I think she'll enjoy being the bride of an accomplished stained-glass artist."

Savannah beamed. "You have a good heart, Arthur." She suspected that Nancy reveled in the status of being a musician's wife. "That may work. You're a clever fellow—Nancy is a lucky woman."

"Thanks, but in our many years together, I know the real truth of that. I'm the lucky one."

Savannah folded her arms. "Arthur, I have a ginormous favor to ask."

"Anything, ask away."

"You may have heard about the hit-and-run accident yesterday." Arthur nodded. "Well, Jacob witnessed it and is experiencing a dreadful reaction. He won't be around to manage the studio for at least a few days. Could you take over for him?"

"Of course. Sure, I'd be happy to." His quick glance at the studio's bathroom betrayed Arthur's confident response.

Savannah raised both hands into a stop position. "You don't have to worry about the phone. I'm going to forward all calls to my cell. Jacob has more than enough supplies in stock here for the next week, so all you'll really have to do is just be the point of contact for the other artists."

"I can handle that." He swallowed hard. "I'm sure of it. Excuse me."

He dashed over to the restroom and quickly pulled the door closed.

Savannah palmed her forehead. *That may have been a mistake. He's fine except when he's not. He'll just have to tell me he can't do it. I have no other choice—the other artists are too ditsy. It's a challenge just to get them to pay their studio rent.*

She raised her voice. "I'm going back to Webb's Glass Shop, Arthur. Call if anything comes up." She stood in front of the bathroom door. "Are you going to be all right?"

"Sure, sure."

Shaking her head, Savannah headed over to Webb's Glass Shop.

He's right. If he can't handle this, how on earth will he ever perform with the Florida Orchestra again? She thought for a moment about Arthur's society-obsessed wife. *Nancy is not going to be happy. I wouldn't want to be around an unhappy Nancy.*

At Webb's Glass Shop, Savannah parked and went through all the little procedures needed to get the shop ready for customers and students. As soon as she unlocked the front door, her cell phone rang. It was Jacob's mother. "Hi, Frances. How's Jacob?"

"This is not good, Savannah. He's not speaking at all."

"Oh, no. That's horrible."

"His therapist has diagnosed selective mutism with a short-term memory loss. He wrote his answers on a pad of paper. He doesn't remember the accident at all."

Savannah matched her calm tone. "Is it permanent?"

Savannah knew that Frances spent a lot of time in court handing down sentences to juveniles convicted of major crimes. As a result, she had extensive experience delivering bad news to terrified parents. Savannah felt that Frances was treating her the same way.

"Jacob's therapist doesn't think so, in his case. His brain is fundamentally wired in a different way and it's very likely that his speech will return. She doesn't hold out much hope for his memory. Anyway, he needs quiet and rest for a few days and we'll go on from there."

"Thanks for letting me know so quickly. I appreciate it."

"I'm not sure if he's capable of resting at this point. He is anxious about not following his daily routines. This is going to be a challenge. I'm staying home today, but I have an important hearing tomorrow that I can't postpone."

"Tell Jacob not to worry about losing his job. He will *always* have a job at Webb's. Everything is going along just fine. His current restoration project has a hard deadline, but I'm going to call the customer and see if there is some wiggle room. I can finish it, of course, but Jacob prefers to work an entire piece all by himself."

Frances chuckled. "Yes, I can see where he would be possessive. He freaks out when I attempt to help him with his laundry. He takes the clothes I've stowed, out of his drawers, refolds them, and then stacks them the only way he thinks is right."

"I can see that." Savannah smiled.

"I'll give you a call tomorrow and we'll assess the situation. I would say for now that he won't be in for the next few days. I'm taking him back to the therapist every day until he can come back to work in the studio."

"Thanks, Frances."

"It's for him, Savannah. He needs to return to Webb's Studio. He needs his daily routines."

Chapter 8

Officer Joy Williams knocked on the doorjamb of Detective Parker's office. His office looked like all his filing cabinets had committed mutiny. There were piles of papers stacked on every available flat surface. Though he was bent over with his back to the door, he greeted her by name. "Officer Williams, come in. There's nowhere to sit, but I've got to get these files sent to the records department within the next two hours or they will be shredded without being scanned."

"How did you know it was me?"

"You always lightly tap twice. I'm a detective, remember?"

"I've never seen your office like this." She had expected to see his normally clear desk with maybe one open folder on its frequently Windex-sprayed surface. "Is this because of the move?"

Parker stood and placed another stack of folders on his desk. Each stack was equidistant from its neighbor. "Yes, we're to have smaller offices in the new building. That means we will have no personal filing cabinets." He looked longingly at the row of four black metal five-drawer filing cabinets. "I'm going to miss having my notes near me."

"Smaller offices?"

"Yes, unfortunately for the future of my personal filing cabinets. I bought these myself. I know how I work best. I received a drawing of the office layouts—smaller for everyone. Very energy efficient. I hate working with electronic documents. But never mind that. What's your question?"

"It's more a feeling, sir. No one has come forward to confess to the Nicole Borawski hit-and-run accident. Isn't it normal for that to happen within a few hours of the accident?"

Detective Parker turned down a corner of his mouth. "No one has come forward?"

"No."

He turned back to the file drawer and placed another stack of files on his desk. "Upgrade the priority of the case. Since a death occurred, when a driver willfully leaves the scene of an accident that involves a death, the offense is punishable as a felony of the first degree."

"Not many citizens know that."

"True. It could mean a thirty-year sentence."

"Yes, sir."

"Because of this nightmare"—he waved a hand at the disgorged filing cabinets—"I'm going to give you the lead in this case."

Officer Williams felt her eyes get large. "Sir, I appreciate that—"

"Don't get overconfident," he said with a good-humored smile. "I'm not at the top of my game right now, so I'm going to shamelessly take advantage of your eagerness to advance in rank."

She smiled in return. "Yes, sir. I appreciate this opportunity."

"There are some nonnegotiable conditions. You'll need to check with me twice a day at a minimum—even more if something significant happens. Don't make any major decisions without my expressed approval."

Officer Williams frowned.

"Don't give me that look. That's the way everything works here. You must keep your supervisor apprised of your plans and actions."

"Okay, why?"

"There's less to mop up after something goes haywire. Now, go back to the scene and find out more from the witnesses. If you've got a feeling something isn't right, then something is probably not right."

Another tap on the doorway caused them both to turn. "Ready for the move?" Coroner Charlotte Gray's eyes twinkled as brightly as her teasing tone. When she caught sight of Detective Parker's exasperated frown, she said, "Oops, sorry. Touchy subject?"

Detective Parker sighed. "It will be good in the long run, but for now it's a huge pain." He turned and picked up the final stack of folders and plopped them on his desk with a loud thump. "That's it. Records are coming along with their archive boxes and then I'm ready to move to the new building. You?" He looked at Officer Williams.

She smiled wide. "I don't keep anything here except a few snack bars and my coffee cup."

"You?" He nodded at Coroner Gray.

"I've been ready for weeks. Two small boxes that I can carry over myself."

Detective Parker put his hands on his hips. "I find the minimalist trend irritating. Officer Williams, don't you have an accident scene to investigate? Check with Traffic to see what they have before you take a look." He turned to Coroner Gray. "I'll see you at lunch." He shooed them out of his office.

Officer Williams was lucky to find a parking spot near Webb's Glass Shop. She drove a patrol car, but didn't like to flaunt the privileges of her position. There were some officers who routinely blocked the street just because they could. Not her.

She had printed the accident report before leaving the station and she studied the notes the responding officer had written. It was a well-written account of what he determined was an accidental event. The sketch was clearly drawn and neatly labeled.

Getting out of the car, she walked over to the spot where Jacob must have stood when the speeding car hit Nicole. She held up the sketch to her view of the street. Everything was there. It all matched. Everything except—there were no skid marks approaching the site of the impact. There were signs that the driver accelerated as he left the scene That means that the driver hadn't braked either before or after hitting Nicole. Not typical at all. The responding officer had noted that in the report.

The speed limit in this section of Central Avenue was twenty-five miles an hour. It was low because of the many shops and high activity of pedestrians along the fifteen-block designation for the Grand Central District. For quicker traveling, drivers used the one-way streets of either First Avenue North going west toward the beaches, or First Avenue South going into downtown.

The time of the accident was around five P.M. Officer Williams thought that seemed a little early for drunk driving, but not that unusual. However, to not even try to stop? This didn't add up. She knew that the most common reasons were fear of consequences, bad driving record, drunk driving, lack of character, and stark panic.

She walked down to the end of the block and looked at the corner intersection where the report said that the white car turned. From there the white car would have turned left on to First Avenue North and would have been miles away before anyone realized that an accident had occurred.

An ordinary white car, even if speeding, wouldn't be particularly noticeable.

On the off chance than the speeding car was noticed by neighbors along First Avenue North, Officer Williams canvassed the houses nearest the intersection. She found two neighbors at home, but neither of them noticed anything yesterday afternoon. At the rest of the houses, she left her business cards with her question written on the

back. You never know, and she felt it was important to cover everything.

She returned to Central Avenue and pulled on
the front door of Queen's Head Pub. It was
locked. She went around to the rear of the restaurant and pulled on the back door. It opened into
the kitchen, where a short, thin, dark-haired man
with even darker eyes was chopping red onions.
He turned to Officer Williams, dropped the knife
on the counter, raised his hands, and splayed his
fingers.

"I'm legal," he squeaked and began to back away.
"I have papers." He started to reach for his back
pocket but halted and raised his hands again.

"Relax, relax, I'm not here to check papers. I
have a few questions about the hit-and-run that occurred yesterday. Were you here?"

"No, ma'am, Officer, ma'am. My shift is over at
two o'clock. I make the salads." His hands reached
higher.

"Relax. Put your hands down. I just want to talk.
What's your name?"

"Samuel Joven, sir. I mean Officer, ma'am." He
slowly lowered his arms to his sides. He held them
stiff, like a toy soldier. "You will want to talk to the
owner. He will be here soon. Chef will be here
soon as well."

"Yes, I'll want to talk to all of them. First"—Officer Williams drew out her small notepad and a
pen from her back trouser pocket—"did you know
Nicole Borawski?"

"She's the boss when the boss isn't here."

"So, yes, you knew her?"

"Yes, but not very well."

He's making me pull everything from him bit by bit. Maybe he is illegal. "What are your hours, Samuel?"

He tightened his hands into fists, then straightened them. "As many as Nicole schedules. She's good about it. I mean she was." He made fists again.

"Fine, but what was normal for you?"

Samuel stopped making fists and folded his hands tightly in front of him. "I arrive at about ten in the morning to make the salads and then, like I said, I leave around two. I'm part-time. I also work at the Old Key West Bar and Grill only one block from here, and also at Punky's Bar and Grill about five blocks from here."

"When was the last time you saw Nicole?"

"Let me think a second." He tilted his head. "It was last week. She came in early to do something and she said hello and we chatted for a bit."

"What day last week?"

His knuckles where turning white from lack of blood. "I think it was on Tuesday or Wednesday. I'm not sure. I work every day, so I get mixed up sometimes."

"Was Nicole having any problems with anyone here in the restaurant?"

"Not that I know about, Officer, ma'am. I don't talk to anyone. I need this job."

Officer Williams had just returned her notebook and pen to her back pocket when Edward walked in from the dining room. He stopped abruptly when he saw her.

"What's wrong?"

Chapter 9

Officer Williams knew Edward well. Not because he was Savannah's fiancé, but because he was one of Savannah's principle assistants in the past investigations they had solved with the help of Amanda and Jacob. He usually met with Savannah and the posse right here in his pub. Of late, their meetings were social, as Savannah was not currently acting as a consultant with the police.

"Good morning, Edward." Joy smiled. "Nothing's really wrong. It's all part of the routine associated with a sudden death."

"Sorry for that. Good morning, Joy." Edward craned his head around to look back at the door of his large commercial refrigerator. "We're not open yet."

"I know. I'm here officially, so I'm Officer Williams. I'm sorry, I know you must feel that I'm intruding. But, Edward. I need to ask you some pointed questions about Nicole."

He stood completely still for a long second, then took out a gallon carton of half-and-half. "Why would you need more information about Nicole? It was an accident. Have you caught the driver?" He spoke over his shoulder.

Officer Williams drew out her notepad and pen. "There are some curious aspects to this incident. It seems it might not have been an accident."

Edward motioned for Officer Williams to follow him. "I need some coffee. What will you have? Oh, I remember. It's a cappuccino."

They both entered the main dining space and bar. Behind the bar was a white porcelain bust of Queen Elizabeth. Next to that was Edward's pride and joy: A refurbished espresso machine stood gleaming and ready for action. He dumped some locally roasted Kahwa beans out of an airtight canister, flung them into the grinder, and threw the switch. The noise was deafening. He worked swiftly and smoothly to make her cappuccino and his double espresso.

He pointed to the table in the corner. "Let's sit over there. We can talk without the whole kitchen hearing us." He placed the white mugs on a tray, grabbed a plate and piled it up with almond biscotti. "Hey, Samuel. I'll finish with setting up chairs. Start your prep work. I'll be back in the kitchen in a few minutes."

Officer Williams swallowed some coffee, then placed the notepad on the table. She scribbled a few notes. "Edward, I'm so sorry for your loss. Nicole was a friend and I know this is difficult, but you know I need to ask these questions. When was the last time you saw Nicole before the accident?"

"It was immediately before she was hit. She was leaving for the day and I walked into the built-in commercial cooler. It's loud, so I didn't hear anything." He blew on his coffee, then took a small sip followed by a long drink. "By the time I got out to the street, she was unconscious. Then I ran back in here to let the rest of the staff know. I reassigned responsibility for closing up the pub, so by the time I got to the hospital, she was already in surgery." He reached for a biscotti, opened his mouth as if to take a bite, but put in on his saucer untouched instead. "I didn't see her again before she died. My last words to her were 'See you in the morning.'"

Samuel poked his head out from around the kitchen door. "Sorry. Mr. Morris, do you want me to stay around to start prepping for dinner?"

"Yes. That would be great." Edward turned back to Officer Williams. "I'm going to have a difficult time replacing Nicole. She was completely qualified and capable of opening her own restaurant. For some reason, she didn't want that. She liked overseeing someone else's. I think it was all the paperwork. Although she did a fair bit of it for me. Maybe it was the responsibility. Anyway, I'm going to miss her."

"We are all going to miss Nicole."

"Do you know who might have witnessed the accident?" asked Officer Williams.

"As far as I could tell, only Jacob. I was trying to

come up with the next day's special. I usually try to use whatever is coming close to its sell-by date or whatever I have too much of . . ." He paused and reflected. "I didn't even hear the ambulances. When Savannah called me the first time, I was still in the walk-in cooler—no reception in there. Her second call went through and I dashed out front. By the time I reached the sidewalk in front of Webb's Glass Shop, Savannah was in the street with Nicole and Jacob was standing on the sidewalk holding Suzy."

"Anyone else? What about the shops across the street?"

"That's certainly possible. I didn't notice."

"I'll have to check with the owners. Who did you notice?"

"I think Amanda was there, but I'm not really sure. Then someone, I think it was just a passerby, called 911." He looked down into his nearly empty cup.

"That's right. Then what happened?"

"The ambulances had taken her away within a few minutes after that. A large crowd had gathered by that time, but I didn't notice who was there. I wasn't thinking properly from the start."

"What a shame you didn't see the vehicle or driver."

"I wish I could help. All of that was well and done by the time I got out there."

Officer Williams drained the last of her cappuccino, then scribbled in her notebook for a couple of minutes. She raised her head. "Just one more thing. Did you hear anyone talking about the tires screeching before Nicole was hit?"

Edward tilted his head and looked up at the ceiling. "I don't think so. It was a circus."

"What about any sounds of a vehicle peeling away?"

He reached for another biscotti but stopped when he noticed the one untouched on his saucer. "I don't remember any sounds at all out on the street before Savannah phoned me."

"Interesting." Officer Williams frowned, then stood and gave Edward a quick pat on the shoulder. "Tell Savannah I said hi."

Edward smiled. "I will, thanks."

She continued canvassing the small businesses in the immediate area. She interviewed the owners of the art supply store, a yoga studio, and a nail salon. No one heard anything before Jacob's scream and no one saw the car.

The next building offered a possible source of witnesses. The Mustard Seed Inn provided transitional housing to homeless adults who have begun their recovery from alcohol, drug abuse, and/or mental illness. Some of the windows of the three-story former hotel looked out over the street where Nicole was hit.

Officer Williams entered the aged and worn lobby. It was deserted. She walked over to the reception counter and tapped the bell. It echoed loudly in the quiet building.

A minute passed. Officer Williams tapped the bell several times, stronger and louder. Immediately, a small, sandy-haired woman in a tan dress with a flowered work apron came huffing down the hallway. "Hello, Officer. Sorry . . . I was in the back . . . I'm the only one here . . . at this time of day." She slipped behind the reception counter, still panting. "Sorry . . . my COPD is giving me fits today." She pulled out an inhaler and administered three shots of its mediation.

"Take your time, ma'am. I'm here to ask a few questions about the hit-and-run that occurred on Monday night in the street in front of this place."

"Oh, I had already gone for the day." Her voice was thin and squeaky. "I have the early morning shift here. It's the quietest shift—other than the third shift, of course." She glanced at her inhaler. "I don't like crowds."

"Who was on duty?"

"Our normal receptionist has the flu, so corporate sent over a substitute."

Officer Williams raised her eyebrows. "Did you get their name?"

"No, I was on my way out the door. She just said that she was the replacement and I scooted home."

"Will she be here tonight?"

"No, our regular will be back. He's been out for over a week, but I heard that he'll be back today." She inhaled shakily. "I'm sorry to be so little help."

"What about the residents? Were any of them looking out their windows and maybe saw something?"

"There was some chatter at breakfast the next morning, but nothing that I would feel comfortable repeating."

"Fine. Let me have the phone number of your managing organization. A card if you have it."

"Certainly." She opened a drawer and gave Officer Williams a pamphlet with a business card stapled to the front. "I keep these for folks who walk in wanting to use our facility."

Officer Williams handed over one of her cards. "Please call me if anything occurs to you or if one of the residents mentions something." She left the lobby and shook her head. This was probably a case where Savannah would be more effective than a uniformed police officer. She made a mental note to ask if Savannah could stop by and interview the second shift receptionist and any observant residents. With one more shop to go, Officer Williams was tempted to skip it and report that no one had witnessed the hit-and-run. But her strong desire for justice kicked in and she walked into Buster's Antiques. If this one interview cracked the case, she would crucify herself for skipping it.

She found the owner in the back of the store behind a huge wooden desk covered in stacks of papers, knickknacks, a full cup of black coffee, and the smaller half of a chocolate croissant. A beautiful black-and-white French bulldog balanced on two scrawny human knees in perfect comfort.

"Good morning. Are you looking for something in particular?" he said without looking up from the tiny laptop teetering on a stack of school exam notebooks.

"Good morning, sir. I'm Officer Williams and I'm investigating the hit-and-run accident that occurred in front of your store yesterday afternoon."

"So?"

Officer Williams inhaled deeply and stood as tall as she could. He was very tall, or had a very tall chair, as she felt like she was asking a school teacher for a hall pass to use the bathroom.

"So, did you witness the accident?"

"Ah, well now. I was wondering if anyone would ask about that."

Officer Williams frowned, then drew out her notebook and pen. "Well, I'm here to do that right now. Your name, address, and phone number, please?"

"Keith Gilbert. My store is named after this little French bulldog, Buster." He scratched the dog's ears and received a lick on his hand in return. "I'm the owner and I live in the apartment upstairs. So that's 2536 Central Avenue, St. Petersburg, Florida, 33712. My phone number and address are on this card." He plucked out a business card from the disorganized mess and handed it to her.

"What did you see?"

"Well, Officer, it's like this. I was out on the sidewalk sweeping up the trash that the lazy good-for-nothing folks around here can't be bothered to put in a trash can that's only five feet away."

Officer Williams frowned and cleared her throat. "Sir, get to the point."

"Anyway, I was leaning on my broom, taking a little rest, when I saw a white car speeding down Central Avenue. Folks don't speed so much down here after the city police set up that speed trap earlier this month. That trap really slowed everyone down—yes, it did. Maybe they should do that again."

"The accident?" prompted Officer Williams.

"Oh, yeah. The white car plowed right into that lady who runs the Queen's Head Pub. I heard it—it was an awful sound."

"Then what?"

"Well, then the idiot just kept on going and I saw the car turn to the right at the end of the block. That's all I saw."

"Was there anything noticeable about the white car? A make or model? Maybe a bit of the license plate?"

"Oh, no, nothing like that. It was an ordinary small white car, not big like a van or SUV. By that time, young Jacob had started to scream and then his dog added her howling. I didn't notice anything after that. I went over to see if there was anything I could do to help, but Savannah Webb from the glass shop had it handled."

Officer Williams made some notes and then looked into Samuel's eyes. "One more thing. When did you hear the brakes screech?"

"Brakes? I didn't hear brakes. I heard tires."

Chapter 10

Savannah felt wooden from the shock of Nicole's death and the aftereffects of Jacob's diagnosis. A heavy sensation in her stomach seemed to have moved in as a permanent resident. Jacob mute? He didn't speak much, but she would miss his teenage cracking voice. She hoped he would recover quickly.

But even if Jacob returned to normal, Nicole would always be dead. Grief had become Savannah's unwanted companion with the death of her father. Now it felt wrong to try to ignore loss.

In the meantime, life lurched on and she would be scrambling to staff both locations properly. Arthur could be counted on to interact with the studio clients and Amanda was now a pro at the beginning stained-glass class. The main issue remained a gap in restoration work. The most profitable segment of her business.

Amanda's morning stained-glass class had gone well, and she had not yet returned from visiting with her mother. Savannah had told her to spend a little extra time with her today. Suncoast Hospice was less than ten blocks away on First Avenue South, so if Savannah needed her she could be back in minutes.

The hospice center's bungalow-style design reflected the many homes that surround it, creating a comfortable setting. Amanda would be able to spend a lot of time with her mother in a supportive environment. Her mother wasn't eating well, but having Amanda there encouraging her appeared to make a significant difference in her food intake.

Savannah spent a few minutes checking the individual workstations, making sure each of them had the right tools for today's lesson. She had taken out yesterday's cured medallions and placed them in the center of each student's work space. The warming oven wasn't quite up to temperature but was rising quickly and would be fine by the time it was needed.

Just as she closed the oven cover and replaced the protective glove back on its hook, the doorbell jangled, and the Rosenberg twins arrived in a blaze of autumn colors. They had mixed things up by wearing opposite parts of identical yellow and orange pantsuits. Their multicolored scarves tied the look together, with dangling orange leaves for earrings.

Savannah looked at their feet and was relieved

to see closed-toe yellow flats. "Good footwear, ladies. You certainly look festive."

"We take your safety instructions seriously, dear," said Rachel as she hung her orange Prada handbag on the back of her work stool.

"We love to shop, and your requirements give us the opportunity to spend without guilt," said Faith as she hung a matching yellow Prada on the back of her work stool.

"I wouldn't exactly say that we shop," said Rachel.

"No, we're too busy," said Faith.

Savannah smiled. "But you two must have a huge wardrobe. I've never seen you wear anything twice."

"We have rules," said Rachel.

"After we have worn an outfit three times . . ." Faith pulled back her stool a little and scooted onto it.

". . . we donate them to CASA," finished Rachel. "It's a charity."

"I gathered that." Savannah hid a big grin with her hand.

"It stands for Community Action Stops Abuse," said Faith.

"Their vision is a community without domestic violence so that home is a safe place." Rachel sat in her work stool.

"They've been around for over forty years now," said Faith.

The bell dinged as Herbert walked in. "I donate to CASA as well." He set his ice-water-filled container on his work space. "No clothes, of course. I donate the toiletries that I've picked up from hotel rooms. Oh, and those sample packets my dentist hands me. Women who have fled with only the clothes they're standing in need a toothbrush, toothpaste, shampoo, and soap."

After the remaining students arrived, Savannah lit her torch. "Today we're going to make a larger medallion using four colors. In addition, we're going to attach a glass loop. So this will be multiple steps, but some of them you already know. First, watch again as I punty my four colors."

The bell over the entry door jingled, and Savannah saw Officer Williams walk into the shop and wave to her. "Miss Webb, I need a few minutes of your time."

"Of course." She turned to the class. "Just a moment, everyone. I'm sorry for the delay." Savannah turned off her torch, placed her glass rods on a metal rest and walked over to meet Officer Williams in front of the check-out counter. Savannah whispered, "What's up with the Miss Webb?" Normally she and Joy were on a first-name basis.

Joy whispered in return. "I'm here in an official capacity. Detective Parker has given me the lead in the hit-and-run investigation. He's monitoring closely, but still it's a firm step toward promotion."

Savannah nodded. "How can I help you, Officer Williams?"

"I'm here to gather information from your students. They may have seen something that could help."

"Sure thing," said Savannah. "Would you like to use the office?"

"No, this is just a preliminary interview to see if

there is any need to investigate further. I'll just speak to them in the classroom. Does this wreck your schedule?"

Savannah smiled. "We'll run over a bit. Don't worry, I've put plenty of slack time into this class." She led Officer Williams into the flameworking classroom.

"Good afternoon. My name is Officer Joy Williams. I'm here to gather any information you might have on the accident that occurred on Monday at around five o'clock just in front of this business. First, does anyone have any objections to answering questions in this open setting? If you do, I can interview you separately."

Everyone shook their head in the negative.

Officer Williams smiled as Savannah pushed over a tall bar stool. "Thanks, my feet do get a workout in the door-to-door questioning process." She perched on the stool and brought out her pad and pen. "Now all I need at this point is your name, and where you were at the time of the accident. To save classroom time, I'll get your addresses from Miss Webb's records, if that's all right with everyone. Is it?"

Everyone agreed.

"Excellent, let's start with you on the end." Officer Williams pointed to the far-left position.

"Hi, I'm Myla Katherine Nedra." She hopped up from the stool, but lost her balance for a moment and grabbed at the workbench. "Whoops, I got up too quick. I'm on a new pain medication and I haven't fully adjusted to it. It gives me vertigo for a few days."

Officer Williams raised her eyebrows as she was writing that down.

"Where was I? Oh my, everyone calls me Myla Kay." Myla Kay's smile was almost as broad as her Southern accent.

"I thought you were from Michigan?" Savannah wrinkled her brow.

"I am, my late husband was a Michigander, but all my folks are from Alabama." Myla Kay sighed. "My accent comes back when I'm loopy"—she paused for a second—"or upset."

"Okay." Savannah shrugged.

"Anyway, I was walking back to my house. It's just a few blocks to the north of here." She looked at Savannah. "Right near our instructor here. I didn't know anything about the hit-and-run until I saw it on the evening news."

Officer Williams wrote in her pad then looked at the next student.

He cleared his throat. "I'm Lonnie McCarthy. I was driving toward the condo my wife and I are renting downtown. We don't watch the news when we're on vacation, so I didn't know anything until I got to class."

"And next?"

"My name is Patricia Karn." Her voice sounded scratchy and very near to tears. "I met my parents over at the cupcake store and then we returned to our hotel on the beach."

Before Officer Williams could signal her readiness for the next student, she heard, "My name is Herbert Klug. I left immediately after class. I was lucky enough to be parked right outside the shop. I was long gone before the accident."

Officer Williams turned to the twins and her eyes widened. "Ladies, can you tell me what happened after class?"

Rachel batted her eyes. "You can't treat us special, Joy—I mean Officer Williams."

Faith glared at her sister. "Don't make this out to be a big mystery. She's a busy woman." She turned to Officer Williams. "We don't drive anymore, so we ordered an Uber ride on our credit card. So, if you need our alibies, we have evidence."

"If an alibi is needed for you two, I'll ask for that receipt." Officer Williams grinned as she scribbled in the notepad. "And last, what about you, Miss Webb?"

"I gave my statement to the traffic officer." She noticed Joy's disapproving frown and backpedaled. "But I'm happy to go through it again. I heard Nicole get hit and then Jacob began to scream, followed by Suzy howling. I was out in the street in seconds, but I only caught a glimpse of the car."

"Anything distinctive about it?"

"Nothing at all. A small white car speeding around the corner of the block. It barely registered with me."

"Before the accident, was anyone in the shop with you?"

A look of concentration flitted across Savannah's face, then vanished. "Yes, my office manager, Amanda Blake, stopped in for a few minutes."

Officer Williams nodded then recorded her findings on the notepad. She stowed the pencil and the notebook. "Thanks, everyone. I appreciate your patience." She looked over at Savannah. "I need a quick word."

They walked over to the front door. Officer Williams pointed over to the Mustard Seed Inn. "I talked to the receptionist over there but got absolutely nowhere. Do you think you could go over at the same time of day that Nicole was hit and ask if anyone saw something?"

"Of course. I'd be happy to help."

"I would appreciate it. I can't recommend that the department hire you yet. There's no connection to the art community at all, so this is just as a personal favor. Most of the residents are reluctant to share any information with the police. I can't say I blame them, but you might be able to get cooperation where all I'm getting is resistance."

Savannah smiled. "I'd be happy to try."

"Thanks, I'll get out of your way now. Have a great class."

"Sure." Savannah watched her friend go out the front door, then she turned back to the students. "Well, that was surprising. Let's get back to work."

Savannah demonstrated several different techniques for joining short rods of color to clear rods. "Here is your chance to experiment and find out which technique works for you. Everyone works with glass differently—some right-handed folks use their left hand to do the heavy lifting while using their right hand for more precise moves. Switch things around. Find what works for you." She took off her protective glasses and perched them on top of her head. "Now it's your turn. Choose your four colors from the scrap box. Punty up."

Herbert was blindingly fast and had his colors ready in five minutes flat. The twins were still choosing colors, while Lonnie needed a reminder on how to light his torch. Patricia was trying out alternative hand positions.

After helping the twins catch up to the rest of the class, Savannah again showed the steps for making a medallion. "Now for the loop. You use a clear rod that you attach to the medallion and then heat the next inch of the rod and form a loop with a twist, letting gravity assist you." She formed the loop and separated the clear rod from the piece.

"Again, this is only one way. Let me show you some other methods I've seen other artists use over at Zen's Glass Studio."

By the end of the class, everyone had fashioned a looped medallion with Herbert needing no assistance and the twins needing major support. As everyone was getting ready to leave, she asked Herbert to stay behind for a few minutes.

"You are excelling in this class. I mean, in everything. Your flameworking skills are extraordinary. Your color combinations are gorgeous. So imaginative. How are you enjoying it?"

"I've only occasionally practiced doing anything remotely artistic, but I'm shocked by how much I appreciate the satisfaction I get in creating my own pieces. I'm having a ball."

"Good. I thought your continuous grin could be an indication, but I wanted to make sure before I hit you with a proposal."

His brow crinkled. "Proposal?" She saw him fiddle with his wedding ring.

Savannah laughed. "Really, Herbert. Not that kind." She lifted her left hand. "Although this is not a diamond, it is my fiancé's grandmother's ring. I'm engaged to the pub owner next door."

He grinned back. "I'm sorry. No, I mean congratulations. I've put my foot in it, haven't I? Anyway . . ."

"I would like for you to consider working here at Webb's Glass Shop as an assistant instructor. It would only be part-time, but it would help me out. With you as a student assistant, I could handle larger classes."

"But I've only taken a couple of classes. That's abrupt."

"I've learned that life doesn't really wait. The right moment is almost always right now. I wouldn't assign you to new students at first. There would be an extended apprenticeship where you would assist me with the class until you're ready."

Herbert nodded. "I understand. Let me see how I do with the rest of this workshop. I'm pretty sure that I'll say yes, but I want to observe with a prospective teaching role in mind."

"Sure," said Savannah.

"It will give you a chance to look into my background."

Savannah let her head dip to nearly touch her chest. "Of course, but I would like for you to fill out an application form before that. I can give you one to take home."

"Thanks, I'll take one just in case, but I still want to observe how you teach."

"Fair enough. I hope you will consider teaching. I think you will love it, and even better I think the students will benefit."

After checking the kiln and tidying up the work-stations, Savannah heard the doorbell clang. "Hey, could you use a little pick-me-up?" She turned to see Edward advancing toward her with a tray. "I've got a new pumpkin latte and I need your opinion."

"A new recipe? But I thought you were going to be shorthanded until you can get a new manager. What gives?"

Edward set the tray on one of the workstations and pulled a work stool over and patted the seat. "Sit. There's a new pumpkin muffin, too. I'm having trouble concentrating, so I'm creating instead. Nicole's death has knocked me for a loop. Something is wrong with how it happened. The way I cope is to cook my way out of it."

Savannah just stared at the muffins and cups of steaming lattes. "I agree that there is something wrong—specifically, the lack of braking. That puts this smack dab into murder, as far as I am concerned."

"I agree."

"We're going to have to investigate this. It will be hard. Amanda is with her mother and Jacob can't speak, but we can't leave this alone. Not only that, but Officer Williams has asked me to go across the street and talk to the residents of Mustard Seed Inn. There are windows that overlook the street. It's possible someone could help."

Edward sighed deeply. "I've been thinking about how little I know about Nicole's personal life. It's embarrassing."

"Why would you say that?" Savannah frowned. "You've been a wonderful boss to not just Nicole, but everyone who works for you." She tapped him on the shoulder. "Stop that—it's not helping. You probably know more than you think. Start thinking."

Edward stared down into his coffee cup.

"Out loud," said Savannah. She reached for one of the pumpkin muffins and took a large bite. "Oh, my. These are good. Come on. Talk."

"Right. Well, Nicole worked on most weekend nights, so she didn't go to concerts. She and Elizabeth went to movies on Monday nights."

"What about family? We know about her brother. Who else?"

Edward took a sip of his coffee and frowned. "I've let this get cold."

Savannah tapped his arm again. "Come on, family?"

"Her parents haven't spoken to Nicole since she told them about her plans to marry Elizabeth. Her brother took her side and has been ostracized as well. Nicole mentioned an uncle who stepped in to help, but I don't know his name."

"Okay, so if this uncle is her father's brother, we should be able to find him."

"But Amanda usually does all the internet business."

"Yes, but we'll have to give it a try. I can google!"

"What's in her personnel file?"

Edward slapped his forehead. "What a Wally. I'll get it." He stood up. "Wait, I've got to get back to the pub." He checked his watch. "We're open until eleven P.M. and I don't have anyone working here today who can close. I'm going to start training one of the bartenders today. Anyway, I'll be home with her personnel file." He stood and bent over to give her a kiss.

"I'm going over to the Mustard Seed Inn first. After that I'll see Amanda's mother and after that I'll have a run with Rooney and feed everyone, including myself. See you tonight. Bring us a bread pudding for our late-night snack." She gave Edward a warm hug followed by a hot kiss. "Wake me if I've fallen asleep."

Savannah closed the shop later and walked across the street into the Mustard Seed Inn. Officer Williams had told her that the place was deserted, but she found the opposite. The lobby was crowded with residents enjoying coffee and tea from a well-used setup in one corner.

The plump, balding fellow behind the reception desk looked up with a friendly smile. "Are you here for the AA meeting? We're just about to start. Have some coffee or tea and—"

"No, thanks. I'm Savannah Webb. I own the glass shop across the street. I'm trying to find out if anyone in this building saw the hit-and-run accident yesterday at about this time."

"Hi, I'm Tim." He stretched out his hand. "I've seen you around the neighborhood. That was an awful accident. How is she?"

Savannah shook his hand. "I'm sorry to say she died in the hospital."

Tim sighed deeply and looked down for a long moment. "I'm so sorry. Nicole was good people. She was responsible for signing up some of our residents in our rehabilitation program."

"Thanks. I'm working with the police as a consultant and would like to know if anyone saw the accident." *That's a bit of a stretch, but it will be true soon. I hope.*

"I didn't see it, but I went outside to see why the ambulances and police cars were in the street. Hang on. Gregg said something when we were standing in front of our building." He looked over to a thin fellow with a salt-and-pepper scruffy beard. "Hey, Gregg, come over here for a second."

Gregg walked over, and Savannah noticed the sallow skin and neat clothing that hung on his bones. "Whatcha need, Tim?"

"Gregg, this is Savannah Webb from across the street. She's helping the police to investigate Nicole's death."

"Oh, man. She died?"

Tim nodded. "Yes. Didn't you say you saw something strange?"

"Yeah, I called in to that tip line that I saw the car that hit Nicole. I haven't heard from them at all. Is that what you mean?"

Savannah tilted her chin down and sighed. "I didn't know that you had called in. But the police department is in turmoil right now with their move. It's causing all sorts of problems with their records. Anyway, is there somewhere we can go for some privacy? I would like for you to tell me what you reported."

Tim interrupted. "You guys can use the community room until the AA meeting starts. I can hold everyone out here until you're finished. No one is that anxious to start, anyway. Will that work?"

"That's great," said Gregg. "Follow me. It's right down this hall."

They went into a plain room set up with folding chairs positioned in a rough circle. Gregg sat in what Savannah expected was his regular chair. She left one seat vacant between them, sat, then took out a pen and notepad from her black backpack. "Now, what did you say on the tips line?"

"I gave them just my first name, Gregg." He looked at Savannah as she wrote. "That's all I'm prepared to give. I have family that don't know where I am, but I've told them I'm safe. I don't want to see them until I'm clean."

"That's fine. I'm putting down just Gregg."

"And then I said that I live in the Mustard Seed Inn in a third-story room that overlooks the street."

Savannah halted writing. "You were looking down into the street?"

"Yeah, that's what I told the recording. I saw the whole thing."

"Go on." Savannah resumed writing.

"I had just gotten off work. The time was just about the same as now. I always wash up before the AA meeting. I work in a car repair shop and I need a shower to get the smell of grease and oil off me. Then I pulled on jeans and a T-shirt."

He paused.

Savannah looked up. He was picking at his grease-embedded hands. "Go on."

In a strained voice he said, "I was ready to go downstairs, but for some reason I looked out the front window. I never do that." He glanced over at Savannah. "I wish I hadn't."

Savannah waited in silence.

Gregg swallowed hard, then cleared his throat. "Did you know that Nicole was the one that got me in this program?"

"No."

"Yeah, last month she caught me behind the Queen's Head Pub getting scraps from the dumpster." He folded his hands and clenched them. "That was rock bottom for me. I was so far gone that food wasn't where I spent my panhandling money. That went for liquor. I only ate free food, and that meant scrounging scraps out of dumpsters behind restaurants."

Savannah listened without judgment and just waited.

He sniffed and rubbed the heels of his hands in his eyes. "Anyway, what I said on the recording is that I saw a white car deliberately swerve for Nicole right in front of Webb's Glass Shop." Gregg stopped and shook his head like a puppy.

"And then?"

"The car hit her, then sped away without even slowing down." He looked at Savannah. "She had no chance at all. It was deliberate."

Chapter 11

Tuesday evening,
Jacob's room.

Officer Williams parked her black, white, and blue patrol car on Fourth Avenue South in front of the south garage entrance to the Beacon 430 apartment building. She punched into the keypad the three-number code Frances Underwood had given her and heard the door unlock. As instructed, she took the elevator to the third floor, made three left turns, and stood on the WIPE YOUR PAWS doormat.

She tapped on the door and Frances opened it to a sleek and modern corner apartment. An open-plan granite-countered kitchen was to the left, with an island that held the sink and had room for three tall stools for dining.

"Thanks for interviewing Jacob here at home," said Frances. She stepped back and waved Officer Williams inside, gesturing in the direction of a sleek

gray sofa sectional with a chaise lounge. There were
no pillows. A small dog bed was positioned at the
corner where the sofa and the chaise met. The
dog bed was obviously special ordered in a matching fabric to the sofa. The large-screen television
was mounted to the opposite wall. "I hope you
don't expect much. He still isn't speaking."

"But he's still texting?"

"Yes, thankfully. Here's his number." She handed
Officer Williams a sticky note. "I'll just tell him
you're here."

Frances tapped on a white door on the right-
hand wall. "Jacob, Officer Williams is here to talk
to you. Don't forget your phone."

"You have to remind him?"

"Yes, unlike most teenagers who are glued to
their phones, he hates it. On the other hand, like
most normal teenagers, he exhibits the most irritating behaviors."

A long minute passed. Frances stood in front of
the door and turned to Officer Williams. "It takes
him a while to leave his room. He has a routine
that he follows. It usually only takes a minute or so,
but it may take longer since you're here." She listened closely at the door. "Good, he's washing his
hands now."

Frances motioned for Officer Williams to sit in
the center of the sofa. "Jacob prefers the chaise so
that Suzy is close."

The door opened, and Jacob walked into the living room and placed Suzy in her bed. He pulled a
smartphone from his back pocket. Then he slipped
off his shoes and stretched out on the chaise. It
was the perfect position to watch the television.

Frances sat next to Jacob. She looked at Officer Williams. "Whenever you're ready."

"Thanks." Officer Williams looked at Jacob, who was staring down at his phone. "We'll start with a quick message to make sure we're communicating, so that I have a complete record for our files." She pulled out her phone and began to text.

HI JACOB. YOU KNOW ME DON'T YOU?
YES, WE HAVE MET MANY TIMES.
DO YOU UNDERSTAND THAT I'M THE OFFICER IN CHARGE OF INVESTIGATING THE HIT-AND-RUN ACCIDENT THAT YOU WITNESSED ON MONDAY?
YES
WHAT DO YOU REMEMBER ABOUT THE ACCIDENT?
NOTHING

Officer Williams looked quickly at Jacob's mother to gauge her reaction to the interview. This was an unusual approach. Frances was calm and intently watching Jacob's flying fingers.

LET'S GO BACK TO EARLIER IN THE DAY ON MONDAY. DO YOU REMEMBER ARRIVING AT WEBB'S GLASS STUDIO?
YES
DO YOU REMEMBER LEAVING AND STANDING ON THE SIDEWALK?
YES
THAT'S VERY GOOD. WHAT HAPPENS AFTER THAT?

Jacob reached down to scratch Suzy behind the ears. Her soulful eyes were stuck to his face like glue. She gave a little whimper. He lifted her and folded her into his arms automatically. She fit perfectly.

I REMEMBER A BRIGHT RED FLASH AND THEN SUZY STARTED TO HOWL.

VERY GOOD, JACOB. YOU'RE DOING FINE. IS THERE ANYTHING ELSE?

Jacob sat still, then turned his head to look out the sliding glass doors to the balcony. The silence lasted for several quiet minutes. He patted Suzy, then turned back to his phone and resumed texting.

NO, NOTHING.

Frances stood. "I think that's all for now. He finds this upsetting, and I have yet to agree to a treatment plan with his therapist."

"Why?"

"The main treatment for selective mutism is behavior therapy. Sometimes medication plays a role in successful treatment. Behavioral therapy should be the first choice, and would be my first choice, but Jacob's therapist wants to start with medication." Frances glanced at Jacob. "He knows I'm uncomfortable resorting to drugs without fully exploring other treatments. This is not our first rodeo."

Officer Williams raised her eyebrows. "What if the therapist insists?"

"I'll be looking for a new therapist."

Officer Williams thought Judge Underwood would win that argument.

Chapter 12

Savannah found Amanda sitting in a sturdy lounge chair at her mother's bedside. Mrs. Blake looked too tiny and frail to be in such an oversized bed. The head of the hospital bed was raised, and Mrs. Blake was curled up on her side like a child, listening to Amanda read. Her eyes were bright and focused on Amanda's expressive face.

The bright blue book, *Clownfish Blues*, was open and Amanda was reading from it in multiple voices and gesturing with her free hand. She looked up. "Hi, Savannah. Mom, it's my boss, Savannah. You remember her, don't you?" Savannah thought Amanda sounded a little nervous asking that last question.

"Of course I remember her." Mrs. Blake turned toward Savannah. "Give us a kiss, dear. It's lovely to see you." She reached out a pale arm. Savannah walked around the huge bed, gently held the bony fingers, and kissed her papery cheek.

"How are you feeling, Mrs. Blake?" Savannah bent over to look into two piercing eyes.

"Please call me Viola, dear. I'm doing as well as I can. Thank you for letting Amanda take some time off work to read to me. I love the way she animates a book. I think she's better than those books on tape she used to buy for me."

"Mom!"

Mrs. Blake looked over to Amanda. "Don't 'mom' me, young lady. You're very good. You should read to the little kiddies at the library."

Savannah laughed. "Do you mind if I take Amanda away for a minute? I need to ask her some questions."

"You mean about that young woman who was killed by the hit-and-run driver?"

"Mom! How did you find out?" said Amanda.

"I'm not dead yet. I can push the buttons on the remote and watch the news." She sounded indignant, but Savannah saw a twinkle in her eye.

Amanda looked up to the ceiling and spread out her hands. "What can I do?"

Mrs. Blake shooed them away with her hands. "Get out and chat. I need to rest my eyes for a little while."

Amanda adjusted the pillows behind her mother's head and tucked the soft blankets around her tiny form. "I'll be right back."

They found a bench in the hallway not too far away. "What's up? What questions?"

"I suspect that Nicole's hit-and-run was deliberate. I won't be able to let this lie. To set my mind at ease, Edward and I are going to investigate. Well, he doesn't know it yet, but as soon as I tell him that it was no accident, I know he'll help me."

"But I'm not able—" Amanda began to bluster.

"I know, I know." Savannah gave Amanda a side hug. "You cannot leave your mother's side and I don't want you to. I just need for you to tell me everything you know about Nicole's life. Her interests, her relations, her hobbies, anything."

Amanda fiddled with the pages of *Clownfish Blues*. "I didn't know her all that well, but she did come next door sometimes to take a break." Amanda raised a hand. "Not when I was holding class, of course."

"Of course. Anything will help. You know her brother and her wife. You're the one who recommended her to Edward in the first place."

"Yeah. She was a server at that New Orleans restaurant down the street. What was the name? Oh, Ricky P's. They're out of business now. That's a shame; they had genuine beignets and a creole shrimp étouffée to die for. Sorry, I can't seem to stay on track with things. Nicole seemed way too smart to be working as a waitress, so I suggested that she apply for the manager job at Queen's Head Pub. Edward was running himself ragged."

"Did you know she was estranged from her parents?"

"I did." Amanda lowered her voice. "She made a comment last Mother's Day that I was lucky to have the relationship I have with my mom. Nicole was down that day. I don't think she was jealous in a mean way, just knowing what she was missing made her sad."

"It can be a difficult day for me sometimes, too. I was only nine when my mom died. I didn't have that much time with her. Every year after that, Dad always made a reservation in a nice restaurant. We would get all dressed up, go out and be thankful that we had her in our lives. He would remind me of the things that she did to show how much she loved us."

"Your dad was one of a kind."

"He was." Savannah pressed her lips together for a moment. "In the last month or so, did Nicole mention anything that was bothering her—like politics? Discrimination? Her family? Anything?"

"Nothing like that at all, but she did have a passion for the mural artists."

"I didn't know that."

"Yeah, there's one in particular with a funny name that she was wild about. He was a graffiti artist who had just been awarded his first work in the SHINE Mural Festival last year. Nicole and Elizabeth went to see him several times while he was painting his assigned wall."

"What's his name?"

"I don't know his real name. He signs his work as SNARK."

"SNARK?"

"He's a real character. No one admits to knowing who he is and he paints his murals mostly at night, covered head to toe in a ninja outfit. Only his eyes were uncovered."

"Right. I read about that in the *Tampa Bay Times*.

Wasn't he the winner last year and didn't show up to receive his award?"

"That's him. Instead, he left a note in an envelope taped to his winning mural. The note instructed the committee to leave his prize in cash taped to an obscure mural. The prize wasn't huge, but it did add an element of mystique to his reputation. He encouraged the festival organization to offer bigger prizes the following year."

"That's unusual."

"Nicole said he was here from Los Angeles and has a huge following there. Any building that has a SNARK graffiti automatically increases its value assessment by at least a hundred thousand dollars."

"Wow! Any idea why he keeps his identity secret? Did she know?" asked Savannah.

"She thought it was something to do with art forgery. Apparently, he can expertly mimic any artist of any period and usually includes a famous image in his murals."

Savannah raised an eyebrow. "That's amazing. I need to look at his works a little closer."

"I think Nicole was obsessed with his identity. She mentioned that discovering his identity was something she wanted to do. At one point, she tried to talk Edward into using one of the pub's walls for one of the festival murals."

"Well, that wouldn't work. Edward is very clear about his branding at the pub."

"Right. He didn't want the hassle at the time." Amanda stood. "Look, I need to get back to Mom. If I'm out of the room too long, she falls asleep. She's been sleeping a lot the last few days. When I think about it, it's been more like the past few weeks."

Savannah stood as well. "Of course. Just one more thing. Do you think Nicole had unmasked SNARK?"

"Elizabeth thinks she did, and I agree with her. I think there was some tension between them about that. Elizabeth was concerned that Nicole's obsession about SNARK might be dangerous."

"Dangerous? In what way?" asked Savannah.

"I wouldn't go that far. Certainly not healthy though," said Amanda over her shoulder as she went back into her mother's room.

Savannah went out to her Mini and before she started it up, she pulled out her phone and called Officer Williams to report her findings from the Mustard Seed Inn. She held back telling her about her conversation with Amanda regarding SNARK because she wanted to run it by Edward first.

After that she searched the internet for the mural artist SNARK. The results revealed that the artist was quite a character. Obsessive about not revealing his identity to the point that his Wikipedia page read like the biography of an international spy. That could be a branding technique, or he could be hiding something sinister. Savannah closed the app.

Maybe Elizabeth was right to be concerned.

Chapter 13

Savannah's heart lifted when she pulled into the carport of her Craftsman bungalow. Edward's vintage Indian motorcycle was tucked into the carport with just enough room left over for her Mini—he was home early.

It must mean something that I feel happy knowing he's home. I wish I were more comfortable with the idea of marriage.

She unlocked the door, walked into the living room, and plopped her keys into the ceramic bowl on the table by the door.

Rooney scrambled up from the rug in front of the fireplace and wriggled to a sitting position in front of her. "Good boy, Rooney. You're such a good boy." Savannah rewarded him for his calm greeting with a big cuddle. Rooney immediately canceled out his good behavior by bowling Savannah over with big puppy licks. She ended up on the floor with Rooney on her chest. "Rooney! Sit." He fell all over himself trying to lick her and sit at the same time.

Edward came in from the kitchen holding a TV tray stacked with a dessert, tea, napkins, and spoons. "Well, that went well." He smiled. "Are you done wrestling?"

Savannah scrambled up from the floor and gave Edward a long kiss. "Hi. What's this?" She eyed the tray.

"This is ginger tea and a hot gingerbread pudding with a side of vanilla ice cream. It's a new recipe. Sit. We'll try it out here."

Savannah sat on the couch and Edward sat beside her. She tilted her head. "Isn't this the second new recipe today?"

Edward twisted his lips to the side. "Guilty as charged. I'm cooking my way through my feelings. How is it?"

Savannah spooned a large bite of the bread pudding with a smidge of ice cream. She let the flavors roll around in her mouth, then rolled her eyes back into her head and hummed her pleasure. She followed that with a sip of the tea. When she could finally speak, she said, "Edward, this is the best you've ever done. This has to go on the menu." She turned back to the dessert and they were both silent until there was nothing left.

"I talked to Amanda at hospice."

"How's her mother?"

Savannah sighed deeply and could feel her eyes

fill with tears. "Oh, Edward. It's not going to be very long before she passes. This is going to overwhelm Amanda."

"But her mother has been frail for a long time. Surely Amanda must understand that her mom is slipping away?"

"Intellectually, I think she understands that these are her mother's last days—but emotionally, she's not really prepared. No one ever is."

They both sat silent for a few minutes. "Losses are hard," said Edward.

Savannah stood and grabbed the dessert tray. "Help me clear up in the kitchen. I think I've found a reason for Joy to give me a chance to participate in the investigation of Nicole's accident."

Edward followed her into the kitchen. "How? There's no connection to the art community at all. That's the only way for you to get hired as a subject matter expert—your expertise is in art."

"Au contraire." Savannah began rinsing the dishes and putting them in the dishwasher. "Amanda said that Nicole was a fan of one of the mural artists who paints on our buildings. He has a secret identity. I looked him up when I was in the hospice parking lot. He not only creates murals for our annual festival, but also sprays political images on sidewalks, train cars, trash cans, walls—any urban surface where he can plant his stenciled images. I could talk to the organizers of the SHINE Mural Festival and see what I can find out about contacting some of the local underground graffiti artists. I think Nicole was determined to unmask his real identity and that's why she was killed."

"That's a bit of a stretch. Do you think Joy will

be able to take you on as a subject matter expert on that alone?"

"I would like to think so. Though you and I are both critically short-handed . . . You've lost an experienced manager. I've lost an apprentice for who knows how long, and Amanda is dealing with her dying mother. I probably should just keep out of this one."

Edward snorted. "That's never stopped you before. I'm convinced that if you hadn't fallen in love with glass, you could have had a lucrative career as a private detective."

"Right, but I overcommit all the time." Savannah finished the last dish, wiped out the sink, and cleaned the counters. Drying her hands on a towel, she said, "It usually turns out all right, but it adds stress to our already hectic lives." She paused. "You finish here. I'll call Joy again. I think she'll agree with me about SNARK."

Joy answered on the first ring. "Hey, Savannah. It's late. What's wrong?"

"Oh, sorry. I didn't realize. Nothing's wrong. Well, a bit suspicious would be more accurate. I want to run something by you and maybe get myself back on the clock as a consultant."

"I don't really see a connection for you to join the investigation. Nicole was a bartender, she doesn't have a connection to your area of expertise. She was not an artist."

"Yes, but according to Amanda, Nicole was obsessed with unmasking the identity of a graffiti artist known as SNARK. He's affiliated with the local SHINE Festival and seems to be a social media phenomenon."

The phone was silent.

"Joy? Are you there?"

"Yep, just thinking." She was silent for a few more seconds. "Okay, that is a connection to the art community—a very tentative one, but it could qualify you as a subject matter expert. I'll run it by Detective Parker in the morning. I'll let you know, but don't act without my authorization. He might not agree. This is a very sketchy connection."

"No problem," said Savannah. "Thanks."

Edward leaned against the counter with his arms folded. He grimaced. "I still don't see how it plays a part in Nicole's death."

Savannah turned from the sink. "All graffiti is evidence of either social or political dissent, but stencils have an extraordinary place in history. They've been used to start revolutions and to stop wars for centuries. Maybe she discovered an underlying message in his work. Maybe. I don't think this was an accidental hit-and-run. I suspect we are investigating a murder."

Chapter 14

Officer Joy Williams knocked on the doorjamb of Detective Parker's nearly empty office. The change since her last visit was huge. The only items remaining were the empty filing cabinets and his small round conference table with its four side chairs. A single sheet of paper lay on the conference table, and Detective Parker stood staring at it with his hands on his hips.

"What!" Detective Parker barked without lifting his eyes from the sheet of paper.

"Sir, I need just a moment of your time." Officer Williams stepped into the hollow sounding office.

"You can have all my moments, Officer Williams." Detective Parker folded his arms across his chest. "The powers that be have decided that my new office is not ready for occupancy, but they didn't tell me that until the movers had whisked away the contents of my office. Everything. Everything. My pencils, my pens, my stapler, my PC, my phone. Even my cell phone charger." He heard his cell phone beep. He pulled it out of his inner jacket pocket and looked at the battery life remaining. "I'm down to fifteen percent!" He stood there a minute, looking at his draining cell phone, then looked at Officer Williams.

"What's that smell?" asked Officer Williams.

"Smell?" Detective Parker sniffed the air. "There's nothing left in here except—" He looked down at the dull gray carpet. "A million instances of spilt coffee, Cokes, greasy lunches eaten at the PC, and birthday cakes. Some parts of this building date back to the nineteen fifties. What you smell, Officer Williams, is over sixty-five years of memories."

Then his eyes began to sparkle, and his lip twitched. He lifted his head back and laughed like a child. "Why am I getting into such a state? We used to investigate crimes with nothing at our fingertips but wits, a pen, and a notepad. We can do that again. What did you need?"

Officer Williams hesitated. She wasn't sure now if he was angry or amused. She hoped he wasn't angry. "Sir, I—" She didn't know if she should continue. He had never seemed so distant.

"Go on. Make your report. I'm over it." He pulled out one of the conference table chairs for Officer Williams and sat in another one. "What's the latest?"

She sat, pulled out her notebook and cleared her throat. "Sir, I've been reviewing the evidence on the Nicole Borawski hit-and-run incident. I couldn't find the filed report from Traffic. I have the hard copy I printed out. I don't normally do that but it's a good thing I did. The electronic one has vanished from the server."

Detective Parker frowned.

Officer Williams hastily plowed on. "So, I contacted the officer who investigated the scene and asked him if he had updated his findings. The lead investigator insists that he filed all the paperwork later that day, but he couldn't find it either. He's going to enter the report again from my hard copy."

Detective Parker folded his hands tightly and placed them on the surface of the conference table. "It's got to be because of the move. Malfunctioning servers strike fear into my very core. This won't be the only report lost."

"Yes, sir. Anyway, he says that his report indicated that there had been no skid marks to indicate braking prior to hitting Nicole. In fact, he thinks the car was traveling at high speed, since it looks like Nicole was thrown quite a distance from the front of the pub where she worked."

"And your conclusion, Officer Williams?"

"I also interviewed the students who attended Savannah Webb's class, but none of them saw anything. I'll confirm what they told me with other witnesses, of course. But when I was interviewing the nearby businesses, I had a gut feeling that a resident from the Mustard Seed Inn looking out onto the street would have had a bird's-eye view of the incident."

"And?"

"Well, the desk clerk was the only one there and she indicated that her residents were not likely to be very forthcoming to a police officer, even if they had important information."

"And?"

Officer Williams let a crack of a smile break her poise. "And so I asked Savannah if she would make a few inquiries as a favor. I figured she would have a better chance, since it's just right across the street and she would be known to the residents as a local."

This time Detective Parker cracked a smile. "And?"

"Well, here's the fly in the ointment. One of the residents called in to our TIPS line and reported that the white car had deliberately aimed for Nicole and then sped away."

"Did you look for the tip?"

"Yes, sir. It's not in the system."

Detective Parker narrowed his eyes.

"Sir, I think it's obviously more than a hit-and-run and we should revise the report."

"There is no report." Detective Parker slapped his open hand on the conference table. "Darn!" The smack made Officer Williams jump straight out of her seat.

She stood for a second, then sat again and took a calming breath. "I wonder how many other vital reports are being lost because of the move.

"This is a serious problem. I'll report it to the captain. We'll have to be extra diligent and double check everything that happens for the next few weeks. Thanks for bringing this to my attention. Have you interviewed the victim's family?"

"Some of them, yes. I talked to Elizabeth Hartford on Monday night when I went to the hospital.

That's Nicole's wife, sir. She was obviously distraught, so I need to interview her again."

"How was their relationship?"

"They've only been married a little over a year, but I'll ask Nicole's coworkers about them."

"Good."

"I've also left a message for her brother, Phillip. He was also at the hospital, but he hadn't been at the scene of the hit-and-run, so I didn't finish interviewing him then, but I'll follow up with him. He should be a good source for the marriage as well."

"Any other family?"

"Yes." Officer Williams flipped back a few pages in her notepad. "Nicole's parents are here in St. Petersburg along with an uncle. I've made appointments with them for later this afternoon. She has a younger brother who lives nearby, and the eldest brother lives in Switzerland with his wife and two children."

"Lucky guy." Detective Parker scowled. "Everything runs smoothly there."

"There's more, sir. Savannah Webb called me late last night. After talking to the Mustard Seed Inn witness, she has the same suspicions that I have about Nicole's death."

"Not surprising. It was right in front of her shop. She would notice that there were no skid marks even before she found a witness."

"I think she's also concerned about Jacob."

"Why?"

"He was front and center for the whole incident and has stopped speaking since it occurred. I interviewed him at his home with his mother present. He only remembers a flash of red and his service dog howling. Luckily, he's fast at texting."

"He's not talking?"

"No, he's been diagnosed with mutism along with a short-term memory loss. So, although he doesn't remember anything right now, he could recall every detail, Jacob-style."

"Any prognosis for a quick recovery?"

"Not yet. His mother is on top of it, of course. I expect Judge Underwood will let us know the minute that Jacob has recovered his speech."

"She will." Detective Parker was silent for a moment. "So, our driver might or might not know that he has been seen. Correct?"

"Yes. Also interesting is that Savannah's store manager, Amanda Blake, reported that Nicole was obsessed with a graffiti artist named SNARK, who keeps his identity a secret. Nicole was determined to expose him. Given that connection to the art community, Savannah is proposing that we reinstate her consultant status."

Detective Parker steepled his hands and pressed them against his lips. He dropped his hands flat onto the surface of the conference table and heaved a huge sigh. "Given the holy mess our records are in now, let's do that. I don't want to leave any investigative thread dangling for lack of accurate information from our data servers. Tell her that she's authorized for a total of ten hours of work and to report to you every day."

"Anything else?"

"As I said, I interviewed the students in Savannah's flameworking class that ended right before the accident. Of the six students, only two are not able to verify their movements. The Rosenberg twins used an Uber to get home, so they're in the clear."

"Not that they were ever suspected." Detective Parker's grin signaled the return of his usual good humor.

"No." Officer Williams returned the grin. "A student named Myla Katherine Nedra was walking to a nearby rental home. No one saw her, so that's a problem." She got out her notepad and flipped the pages. "A tourist student, Lonnie McCarthy, was driving toward the condo he and his wife are renting downtown. Patricia Karn met her parents at the Cupcake Spot and the clerk there remembers them. Finally, Herbert Klug left immediately after class. His red SUV was parked right outside the shop and was gone for a only few minutes before the accident."

"So, you have eliminated Patricia Karn and the Rosenberg twins with verifiable alibis," said Detective Parker. "Check with Savannah, she may have already eliminated the rest of them for you."

Officer Williams rose and stood in the doorway. "You knew she was going to investigate anyway."

Detective Parker rolled he eyes. "Oh yes, but at least this way we can officially keep tabs on what she discovers. Although I appreciate that she's energetic and cooperative, sometimes she lets her enthusiasm overcome good sense."

As Officer Williams left Detective Parker's office, two men, each rolling a furniture-moving skid, entered. She heard the irritation in Detective Parker's voice as he barked, "What now?"

Officer Williams hustled down the hall. *I wouldn't want to be either of them right now.*

Chapter 15

Savannah left Webb's Glass Shop by the back door and walked the few yards down the alley to the back door of Queen's Head Pub. Edward was using a wooden paddle to mix a giant kettle of ground meat at a stainless-steel worktable.

"Hi, honey. Something new?" She smelled an aroma of sweet honey mixed with a spice she couldn't quite identify. "Ground ginger?"

"Good guess. I'll make a cook out of you yet."

"Not likely. What are you experimenting with now?"

Edward tilted his head at her with fake-glowering eyes.

"Oh, of course," she said. This is the last week-end of the Best Burger in the Burg competition. I'm so sorry, but I completely forgot. With everything else going on, it slipped my mind. What can I do to help?"

Edward pointed to a box of latex gloves. "Put on a pair and you can help me measure out today's supply. I'm running late, but if you help I can get each burger the same weight, then I'll form them and put them all in the chiller."

Savannah pulled the hamburger mixture from the kettle and placed the meat on a small scale. "How much for each?"

"Six ounces."

In a few minutes, she and Edward had an assembly line going where she weighed the meat, and he formed them into patties and placed them on a large aluminum tray. When a tray filled up, Edward used a self-sealing wrap to keep them individually fresh.

"Do you think you're going to win again this year?"

"No, not a chance. I would love that, but Nicole's death changes everything. She handled so much of the everyday details, I won't be able to concentrate on each hamburger like we did last year."

"But the secret is in the meat, isn't it?"

"Not really, the secret is in everything. The freshness and quality of the meat. The seasoning and cooking skills of the grill chef. The perfect pairing of the condiments. A toasted bun, perfect fries, and, of course, perfect service. I had all of those going for me last year. This year?" He turned his hands out, palms up. "I'll be lucky to place in the top ten."

They worked quietly but quickly until every burger was formed and stored.

"Thanks for that. You saved about half the normal time it takes me." He frowned. You usually don't come over here during the day. What's up? Who's minding the shop?"

"I closed it up for a bit. Wednesday is a slow day, anyway. But I wondered if there could be any information about Nicole's private life in her employee locker. She has one, right?"

"Of course." Edward whipped off his gloves and signaled for Savannah to do the same. They washed their hands and Edward removed the long apron tied around his waist. "I didn't even think about that. The lockers are in the utility room. I normally do that as soon as someone gives notice."

"That makes sense," said Savannah.

"I need to ask Elizabeth if she wants Nicole's things. There's usually not much personal stuff in a work locker, but you never know."

"Yep, I'll text her now." Savannah tapped in a text message and got an instant reply. "She says yes, absolutely she would like Nicole's locker stuff. She'll be right over." Savannah returned her phone to her back pocket. "She must be at home. I forgot that she would get compassionate leave from work."

Edward opened a gray steel door at the back of the pub and led Savannah into the small space crammed with electrical panels on one wall and a row of six lockers on the other. "There are twelve lockers, and almost everyone uses them. Most of the waitstaff at other places lock up their valuables in their cars. We're so short of parking slots, my employees have to park at least a block away."

"So, did she use a locker?"

"Yes. This one." Edward pointed to the top compartment of the locker farthest from the door. It had a shiny new Yale lock fastened to the hasp.

Savannah pulled on the lock. "Yep, that's locked. Do you have bolt cutters, by any chance?"

Edward pulled his keys out of his pocket and selected a tiny key. He unlocked the first locker nearest the door. The only thing inside the locker tucked into a dark corner was a bolt cutter. "Say hello to Liberator."

"You've named it?"

Edward chuckled and quickly snipped Nicole's lock. It clattered to the floor, and he replaced the bolt cutter and relocked the compartment. "I hadn't owned Queen's Head for more than a week when two employees quit and left their stuff locked up. That's when I bought my buddy, Liberator. The guy from Ace Hardware recommended him and I've used him a lot."

Savannah opened the door to Nicole's locker. It was completely packed to the gills with various bags and sacks shoved into the small space. "This needs to be sorted out for Elizabeth anyway, right?"

Edward was staring into the locker and nodded. "Yeah, right, for Elizabeth." He turned away. "I'll get a box. We can fill it up as we sort through things." He returned with a large box that had held the day's delivery of cauliflower. He pulled out a stray leaf and threw it into the garbage. "This should hold everything."

Savannah gently tugged on the scrapbook at the top while holding everything else in place. She set it aside. "Why would she keep all of this here?"

"Looks like she didn't want to trek back home

to get this stuff. It seems a bit weird since the pub is close to the graffiti action. Or maybe she wanted this stuff kept a secret from Elizabeth. I'm absolutely guessing."

Savannah picked up a bundle of dark clothing which turned out to be a black hoodie wrapped around a black canvas bag. She handed the hoodie to Edward and opened the bag. It was filled with a dozen spray paint cans of black and bubble-gum pink along with stencils, brushes, markers, latex gloves, a sketchbook, and several small pots of neon paint. There was also an opened package of face masks with two remaining.

They looked at each other.

Edward spoke first. "She was a graffiti artist. Well, you can knock me over with a feather."

"Let's look at the album." Savannah flipped it open. The first group of pages contained photographs of last year's mural festival. There was a gap of blank pages, and then there were images of true graffiti on abandoned buildings, railroad cars, and billboards in dodgy locations around town. "She took these at night, probably after closing up the pub." Savannah peered closely at the bright pink-colored images. "The signatures on this page are all the same."

"Would that be the SNARK guy?"

"No, his signature is unique and world renowned. This set of initials must be Nicole's. See the stylized letter N intertwined with a letter B inside a small triangle. That must be her mark."

On the last page of the scrapbook was a stapled five-page printout of an article about fake Vermeer paintings. It outlined the inclination for forgers to prefer anonymity and therefore were rarely remembered.

Savannah skimmed the pages. "This features a painter who became famous for his Vermeer forgeries."

Edward leaned over her shoulder and read, "Han van Meegeren (1889-1947). After World War II, he was arrested and charged with collaborating with the enemy and imprisoned.'" He pointed to a paragraph. "Look! He sold a fake Vermeer to Nazi political leader Hermann Goering. So that was the collaboration charge?"

"Weird," said Savannah. "His defense—wildly original, by the way—was that the Goering painting was created by his own hand. He painted it alone and in absolute secret. There was no collaboration."

Edward frowned. "Painting alone meant no collaboration?"

"He still died in prison."

"But why would Nicole keep this in an album of SNARK's images?"

Edward shrugged his shoulders. "I don't know, but this indicates that Nicole was obsessed with SNARK."

"Enough to start up graffiti as a hobby. That connects with her interest in SNARK. But what does the article about the forger mean?"

They looked at one another.

"Why would Nicole keep information about a particular kind of forgery?"

"It's not clear right now, but this must have

meant something to her. Why hide it from Elizabeth?"

"So, we just give all this to Elizabeth?" asked Edward.

"We don't have a clear reason for keeping it." Savannah raised her eyebrows. "Maybe Elizabeth will know what this all means."

"First, I want to make copies and then . . . Wait, there's something else back here." Savannah reached into the back of the locker. Crushed against the back stood a bundle of black envelopes tied with a red ribbon. The envelopes were addressed to "Darling Nicky."

They stared at the packet for a long moment, then Edward grabbed them and shut the locker door. "No one we know would ever call Nicole anything but Nicole."

"We obviously don't know this person."

Savannah slipped one of them out of the bundle. Edward reached over and grabbed her hand. "Wait. You can't do that. They're private."

"We're going to give them to Elizabeth, right?"

"Yes, but—"

"We need to make sure they have nothing to do with Nicole's death." Savannah opened the black envelope. "We need a chance at every lead that we can find. Let's start with the first one."

> *Dearest Nicky,*
> *I know you are married, but I can't help but observe how conflicted you seem.*
> *It shows up in the violent passion of your street art. What is causing you such pain?*

This truly breaks my heart. You deserve more.
You deserve to be the center of someone's universe.
I would like to do that for you.
SNARK

Just as Savannah started to open the next letter, she heard Elizabeth's voice.

"Hey, what's going on? I thought you would wait." Elizabeth was pale, with two pink spots on her cheekbones. She stood just outside the utility room with her hands on her hips. "Where did you get that?" She snatched the letter from Savannah's hand. "You have no right to read that. That belonged to Nicole. It's private."

Savannah recovered first. "Elizabeth, exactly as I texted, we were cleaning out Nicole's locker. As her employer, Edward has every right to examine everything on his property."

Elizabeth stepped back. "But—"

Savannah spoke up in a rush. "We also hoped it would help us figure out if anyone might have had issues with her. I'm uncomfortable about how callously she was run down in the street. That's not what a normal person would do. You want to know, don't you?"

"No. It was a terrible accident." Elizabeth looked down at the large cauliflower box. "Her death was not deliberate."

Savannah looked over to Edward and shrugged her shoulders. "I'm sorry, Elizabeth. I certainly didn't mean to offend. Although the case is classified as a suspicious death because of the behavior of the driver, I think it's more serious. Officer

Williams supports my working on Nicole's case, but I'm trying to find a stronger justification for helping in their investigation. I'm sorry that this is upsetting, but I'll be giving Officer Williams the contents of Nicole's locker."

Elizabeth covered her eyes with her hand. "Officer Williams has been trying to reach me. I ignored her messages because I needed some time to myself to deal with this nightmare. I didn't think things could get worse." She lowered her hand and pointed to the cauliflower box on the floor of the utility room. "Is that what was in her locker?"

Edward lifted the box and moved it over to one of the worktables. "We also found supplies and materials for painting graffiti. Did you have any idea that Nicole was doing that? I certainly had no clue."

Elizabeth carefully refolded the note and slipped it back into the black envelope. "She had a restless side to her personality. She would get intensely interested in something, a person, a craft, a type of music. Then she would feverishly collect or pursue the subject for a few months, then drop it like a hot rock. Her younger brother is very much the same."

"She has another brother?" asked Edward. "She never said."

"Well, if Nicole was the family's black sheep, Alan is the family's gray sheep. He supported Nicole against her parents' wishes, so they have that in common. Her parents will occasionally talk to him, so through him she had some idea about what's happening in the family. Nicole had a trust fund. He knew that I was the principle beneficiary upon her death and that the family was freaked out about that."

Savannah pulled a pen out of her pocket and looked for something to write on. Edward grabbed a napkin from the bar. "So, his name is Alan Borawski? Do you know where he lives?"

"I think he's involved in a farm-animal rescue organization. I can't remember the name, but its north of New Port Richey. We don't hear from him very often."

"Elizabeth, when we were in the hospital you— and you may not remember this—you said that Nicole had been courting trouble. Do you remember?"

Elizabeth huffed out an exasperated breath. "No, I simply don't. I only remember the terrible shock."

"Of course." Savannah rubbed the back of her neck. She didn't want to upset Elizabeth, but she also wanted to understand what Elizabeth had meant by her remark about Nicole courting trouble. "Could it be her new obsession with graffiti?"

"I probably reacted to her updating the will and how it would probably upset her family even more."

Savannah noted that. "What about you, Elizabeth? Do you have a will?"

"Nicole's family lawyer drafted one after we got married and he updated it to account for all the stuff in the trust fund. The one thing he told me I need is my own financial adviser right away. Nicole was pretty good with money, she had it growing up. I'm terrible. Can you recommend someone?"

"Sure, I'm using my dad's adviser. He's helping me grow the business while not losing my shirt. His name is Burkart. His office is just down the street on Central." As Savannah looked through her phone contacts, Edward handed her another napkin. She looked up Burkart's address and phone number, wrote them on it, then gave it to Elizabeth.

Elizabeth took it, then stared at the box. "Nicole was a very complicated person. I don't think we'll ever know everything about her."

Chapter 16

Savannah left Queen's Head Pub with a low-down feeling in her belly. Elizabeth's reaction to SNARK's letter seemed exaggerated emotionally. Could it be that she already knew about SNARK's infatuation with Nicole? SNARK needed to be found—but not right now. It was almost time for the flameworking class. She opened the back door to Webb's Glass Shop and found Amanda sitting at the oak roll top desk.

"Back early? How's your mother?"

"They needed to give her a bath and adjust her medications, so it's better if I'm not there. Then she feels free to ask her nurse questions that she doesn't want me to hear. Then she takes a long nap afterwards."

Savannah stood behind her and rubbed the tension out of Amanda's stress-tightened shoulders. "I'm sorry, Amanda. This is going to be a difficult time."

"Thank goodness for my morning class. It gives me a point of focus." She leaned back into Savannah's deep massage. "Wow, that feels good. So, where are you in the investigation of Nicole's death?"

"What?"

Amanda turned around and pointed to the small chair beside the desk. "You are investigating, aren't you?"

Savannah sat. "Yes, Officer Williams reactivated my consultancy contract. I told her what you said about SNARK. She's says it sounds a bit sketchy— mainly because it is."

"But this character is world famous." Amanda leaned back in the oak swivel chair until it creaked in protest. She sat forward. "Can I do some research?"

"I don't really think—"

"Please." Amanda mimicked a puppy-dog look. "I need something to occupy my mind. I have a new high-powered tablet PC that's incredible. The wireless internet at hospice is a high-speed demon. Please? Pretty please?"

Savannah nodded. "On one condition."

"Sure thing."

"You need to hear it first." Savannah reached over to hold Amanda's hand. "You have to text me a status every fifteen minutes while you're researching. Your mother's condition is serious, and you could get sucked into your research world and miss something important with your mother. So, let me know when you start and then when you finish."

"But that seems overly cautious." Amanda frowned and patted her soft, wavy hair.

"Maybe so, but it's the only way I'll let you get involved with Nicole's investigation. Agreed?"

"Agreed."

Savannah heard the doorbell jangle, followed by a familiar chatter at the front door. She smiled again at Amanda and walked toward the front of the shop.

Rachel and Faith Rosenberg were the first to arrive, almost immediately followed by Herbert. The remaining students trickled in so that at the stroke of one o'clock everyone was sitting at their stations.

Savannah stepped over to a small table that held six sets of hand-blown wine goblets with a matching stem placed inside the bowl. She held up a set and separated the stem from the globe. "What's missing here?"

Faith raised her hand. "The stem?"

"Yes," said Savannah. "That's what we're going to make today. I've already made the globe and the foot. All you need to do is make the stems."

"But—" interrupted Rachel.

Savannah looked over to Rachel. "No buts. You already have the skills to make a beautiful stem for these wineglasses. The technique we'll use for our first stem is called latticinio. It's a decorative type of twisted glass cane most commonly created from clear and white glass. After you have your stem thick enough and long enough, I will come around and attach the globes and feet for you."

"That's a relief," said Patricia. "I was going to leave before I embarrassed myself."

"I would never let you work outside your comfort level. That said, I have a few techniques to show you that will make your stem more interesting. First, I'll show you how to merge two colors, then twist and pull them into a cane." She lifted a shoebox full of glass rods. "I have our box of scrap rods for you to use as practice. Pick out two and punty them up on a clear rod. We're going to make several twisted canes."

She handed the box around and everyone practiced successfully. Of course, the twins needed special handling, but they were so delighted with the results, it was impossible to be annoyed.

Myla Kay appeared distracted and Savannah had to repeat an explanation of the process to her separately. It still didn't seem to sink in, but once Myla Kay got a good look at what the twins were doing, she picked up the technique right away and produced a beautiful stem. Again, she used strong contrasting colors that combined in unexpected beauty.

"Now I'm going to show you how to make a simple seahorse to use as the stem of your wineglass. I'm first going to mix two shades of blue to give the form some texture, then I'll make a rough shape and show you how to pinch out fins and the tail with a special tool."

The time flew by as Savannah helped each student fashion a seahorse. The twins used coral and yellow for their stems, and everyone was delighted with their final product. She took a group picture of the students holding their still warm wineglasses.

The purpose was to not only post the images for social media promotion, but as a practical way to identify who belonged to each individual goblet when she unloaded the kiln the next day.

"What a great class, everyone. See you tomorrow when we make our first bead."

Again, she asked Herbert to stay behind. "I am so impressed with your seahorse. You wield the tools well and your color choices are wonderful. Have you given any thought to my suggestion to join the teaching staff?"

He nodded. "I have. I talked it over with my wife." He looked up at Savannah with a wry little grin. "Apparently, she's been very concerned about my retirement. So far, she says I have spent more time watching TV each day than I did in a month when I was working. She would be delighted if I started teaching part time." He paused. "I would love to."

"That's wonderful. I'll refund your class fees and apply a deep discount to your materials. We'll need to teach one class together, and then you'll be on your own for scheduling future workshops."

He nodded. "I'm in."

After Herbert left, she cleared up the classroom and started preparing rods for the next day's bead-making class. The beads would be formed on mandrels—small rods that looked like barbecue skewers. The bead-release coating that she was painting on each mandrel needed to dry overnight. She coated her entire inventory of twenty-four mandrels and placed them upright in a rack to dry.

Her cell phone rang. "Hey, Frances. How's Jacob doing?"

There was a sharp edge to the judge's voice.
"I'm conflicted." Frances paused for a second.
"You know perfectly well Jacob loathes using tech-
nology, even though I kept telling him it would be
the perfect way for him to communicate. He's
been coping since he stopped speaking. He only
gets agitated when asked a question or told what to
do. Anyway, he's managed to text me five times
today about when he can come back to work. Five
times. All the texts were clear, no typos, very adult.
I want to hear what you think about it."

"He has gotten more comfortable with a phone
since the accident. How do you feel about him
coming back to work?" asked Savannah.

"Before this, he's never shown much interest in
using a phone. He's barely agreed to my insistence
that he carry his cell on his person at all times, just
in case he has an anxiety or asthma attack."

"Texting is the perfect way for him to communicate—I didn't think he would ever get comfortable with it." Savannah paused. "Why are you
conflicted?"

"This horrible event has had a strangely matur-
ing impact on Jacob. He's taking responsibility for
helping to find a cure for his mutism. He explained to me, using text messages, that he be-
lieves that the sooner he returns to his normal
routine, the quicker both his speech and memory
will return."

"Wow, that's a change. It's a good change isn't it?"

"It is. That's going from being compliant with
me and the specialists who advise us, straight to
being responsible for managing his own health
and welfare needs."

"Given that he's communicating so well, I'm fine for him to come back to Webb's Studio. Tomorrow, if he wants."

"I'll tell him. He'll be delighted. Am I the only one who is a bit upset at his behaving like a grown-up?"

"Isn't that what we all want?"

"It is, intellectually, what I have always dreamed Jacob would do."

"Then why are you conflicted?"

Frances sniffed. "My baby is growing up."

Chapter 17

Wednesday afternoon,
police headquarters

Officer Williams returned to the common squad
room and discovered it was completely empty.
Only the rumpled, worn, and carelessly torn carpet
remained. A memo was taped to one of the walls
announcing that the office was operational in the
new building.

She checked Detective Parker's office. There
was another note taped to the wall of the empty office.

> *To Whom It May Concern:*
> *My old office is as you see it, and my new office*
> *will not be ready until Friday. I appear to have*
> *been lost in the move to the extent that I'm*
> *unknown to the St. Petersburg Police Department.*
> *Getting my identity back, either physically or digi-*

tally, from the damaged data servers will probably take a few days. The friendly folks at Ferg's Sports Bar have given me the use of a booth, and I will be working from there until sanity has returned.

  Regards,
  Detective Parker

Officer Williams twisted her lips to one side and bit at the corner. She had a decision to make. Should she find him at Ferg's Sports Bar and risk his well-deserved wrath at the injustice of his situa- tion? Or should she could make her way into the new building and call him on her cell phone to make her report?

What would he do?

Decision made, she went out and crossed the street. Ferg's Sports Bar was owned by Mark Fergu- son, a native of St. Petersburg, graduate of Florida State University, and former teacher in the Pinel- las County school system.

In 1992, he had an idea to open a sports bar in a run-down area of downtown St. Pete, known as the Gas Plant District. With the help of family and friends, Mark purchased the Sunoco gas station that became the first Ferg's building.

He built the sports bar with reclaimed wood from torn-down houses and repurposed materials from All Children's Hospital and the Derby Lane Greyhound Track. It was now the most unique restaurant, bar, and event venue on the west coast of Florida. Mark was a mainstay of his creation, and Joy had met him several times. It was com- pletely in character for him to offer Detective Parker a temporary work space.

Officer Williams wandered through the rooms until she was at the back, farthest from the street noise. She found Detective Parker at a booth with a notepad, several manila folders, a white mug of coffee, his cell phone, and two pencils precisely arranged on the surface of the wooden table. His posture was ramrod straight, and he was staring at this cell phone like it was a live rattlesnake.

"Sir?"

Only his eyes moved to glare at Officer Williams. "Welcome to my office."

"What on earth is going on?" She scooted onto the bench across from him.

"There's been a mistake with the layout of the new offices. A big mistake. I don't have a new office."

"What? How did that happen?" She swallowed quickly. "I saw the final layout last week. Your office was clearly marked. It was one of the larger spaces. It had a window."

"Apparently the powers that be can't count. They were short by one office."

"Who's going to get yours?"

"I don't know, and I don't really care." He glanced back at his cell phone. "I had a pointed chat with the head of facilities. He's going to do a shuffle of some sort and call back when they get it straightened out." He performed an exaggerated eyeroll. "I merely need to be patient."

To keep from grinning, Joy pressed her lips together so tightly she could feel them tingle.

Detective Parker broke into a big smile. "Yes, I know I'm acting like a petulant nine-year-old, but a work space is important to me. I feel adrift without an office." He waved a hand to one of the servers passing by. "Coffee with cream for this officer, please."

The pent-up giggle exploded into a full belly laugh, and Joy couldn't speak for a few seconds. "I'm really sorry. I hope it gets fixed soon." She wiped the tears from her eyes, then planted her work face on. "However, I'm grateful for the opportunity to take the lead in this hit-and-run." She opened her notepad. "I've started our investigation with Nicole's family. There apparently was a split when she announced her marriage to Elizabeth. She has both parents and three brothers for immediate family, and an uncle as well. They all live nearby."

"How did they split over her engagement?"

"I don't know. I haven't been able to contact anyone yet. Everyone is out. I'll get more information from Edward Morris and Savannah. If I know Savannah, she'll have ferreted out all of Nicole's personal details."

"What has Savannah uncovered so far?"

Referring to her notes, Officer Williams reported, "I'm meeting her for coffee in a few minutes to get an update and the contents of Nicole's work locker."

"That should have been done by Forensics."

"Unfortunately, it was missed at the time of the hit-and-run, and apparently Nicole's wife, Elizabeth, was ready to take off with the contents. If Savannah hadn't been there, we wouldn't have anything to analyze at all."

Detective Parker folded his arms. "Fair point. Go on."

"Nicole seemed to be more than just an acquaintance with the graffiti artist SNARK. It appears that Nicole was beginning to paint graffiti herself in the late hours, after she closed up Queen's Head Pub. Savannah has also made an appointment with the SHINE Mural Festival organizer. The main office is near her glass shop, so I think I'll go with her."

Detective Parker furrowed his brow. "The graffiti interest seems completely out of character. I met Nicole a few times over this last year. I would never have guessed that she was interested in deliberately defacing property with self-aggrandizing variations of a secret name. I simply don't get it."

"Frankly, me neither. But it goes to prove we really don't know what secrets our friends are carrying around, do we?"

"Well said." Detective Parker's cell phone rang and vibrated on the surface of the scarred wooden table. He answered the call. "Detective Parker." He sat listening and then a smile slowly spread across his face. "That's very good. I'll be right over."

Officer Williams raised her eyebrows as a question.

"They've sorted out an office for me at last." Detective Parker began gathering up his possessions. "Stop by after your meeting with Savannah. Let's just hope those failed servers have been restored and we can get back to normal.".

"Normal, sir? We don't have normal—we investigate murders."

Chapter 18

Savannah walked through the front door of the nearly empty pub and spied Officer Williams seated at what was becoming her posse's favorite table, right in front of the women's restroom. "Hi, Joy. Have you ordered?"

"Yes. I'm trying something new, a green tea *maccha*-thingy. Edward recommended it."

Savannah raised her eyebrows. "It may not be drinkable. He has been experimenting with everything." She held out her hand and waggled it. "Some are fabulous, some are . . . less good."

"We'll see. He's bringing one for you as well." Officer Williams smirked. "We'll suffer together."

"I heard that!" Edward brought a tray with two glass cups of a green creamy liquid topped with an inch of white-frothed cream. He also set down a large plate of ginger-pecan scones.

Savannah clenched her jaw, then opened her mouth to protest. "Another new scone recipe?"

Edward tilted his head. "I'll get Nicole's locker contents." He left before Savannah could voice her concern over so much experimentation.

"We're still going to talk to the SHINE organizer?"

"Right after we down this horrible green concoction." Savannah lifted the glass cup to her lips and took a tentative sip. She turned down her lips, squinted her eyes and shivered. "Oh no. This is absolutely horrible." She eyed Officer Williams. "Your turn."

Officer Williams inhaled a bracing breath and took a sip. Her lips pursed, and she choked down a swallow. "This is awful. Where can we dump it?"

Savannah grabbed both cups and went into the ladies'. She quickly dumped the contents into the sink, returned to the table, and set the empty cups in front of them.

Edward returned from the back of the pub with the fauliflower box, securely taped.

Officer Williams took the box. "Thanks, Edward. I'll go through this and see what it adds to our investigation." She eyed Savannah. "We've got to go. Thanks for the tea." Officer Williams headed for the front door.

"You haven't touched the scones, and what did you think of the tea?"

"Hmmm. I'm not a real fan of green tea." Savannah gave him a tender kiss. "Stop with the experimentation for now. Focus on winning the Best Burger in the Burg competition. We're going to find Nicole's killer. I promise."

Officer Williams was waiting for her outside the pub. "How far is it to the SHINE headquarters? Can we walk?"

"Absolutely. Their office is across the street from Haslam's Book Store. I'm sure the SHINE organizers would appreciate it if we walked instead of leaving a patrol car parked in front for everyone to see. There would be questions." She raised her eyebrows.

"Funny how that makes people nervous," said Officer Williams. She adjusted her utility belt and waved an arm toward the street. "After you."

They walked into the small storefront that had a poster announcing the upcoming SHINE festival. The door was locked, but there was a small doorbell with a note taped over it to ring for access.

Officer Williams pressed the button and they heard the door lock click. A middle-aged man with a full head of shoulder-length white hair tied at the neck opened the door. "Hey, Officer. Has another mural been vandalized?"

"No, sir. Not that I've heard, anyway," said Officer Williams. "Can we come in and talk to you about one of the mural artists?"

"Sure, come on in."

The man stepped aside, and Officer Williams and Savannah entered a small room about forty feet deep that contained a large square worktable with stacks of mural drawings and two office desks at the back.

He stuck out his hand. "My name is Vince Currier. I'm the Director of the SHINE Festival this year."

Officer Williams smiled and shook his hand. "I'm Officer Williams and this my consultant, Savannah Webb. She's—"

Vince interrupted. "Aren't you the new owner of Webb's Glass Shop?"

Savannah shook his hand with an equally firm grip. "Yes, since the beginning of the year."

Vince waved a hand to a circled hodgepodge collection of chairs in front of the two desks. "Have a seat. If you don't have mural defacement to report, how can I help?"

Officer Williams cleared her throat and pulled out her notebook and pen. "We're investigating the hit-and-run accident that occurred on Monday afternoon. It appears that the young lady who was killed was involved in trying to identify a graffiti artist named SNARK. Are you familiar with that name?"

"You're talking about Nicole, aren't you?"

Savannah said, "Yes, she was struck right in front of my shop. She died in the hospital. We found all the materials that she would need for graffiti in her work locker. So she was obviously not public about her interest. Did you know she was an amateur graffiti artist?"

Vince lowered his head for a second, then looked at them each in turn. "I knew she was interested in the identity of SNARK. She was one of his regular commenters on his daily Facebook posts. She pestered me for more information about him for weeks before our latest SHINE Festival. I thought it was unhealthy, but I meet all sorts in this job. Artists are inherently strange and strangely obsessed."

Savannah pulled out her phone. "Hang on. SNARK has a Facebook page?"

"He does. It's simple—just SNARK."

Savannah opened the app and found SNARK's page. The first post was a graffiti image obviously taken in the dark, just after it was completed. She scrolled down in the comments and saw a comment from Nosy Barkeep.

"That's got to be Nicole's street name. It's her initials." She searched the comments on several earlier posts and each had one or more comments from Nosy Barkeep.

Closing the app, Savannah glanced at Officer Williams. "She was seriously obsessed. Also, the images are mostly in the area right around our section of Central Avenue. He must live nearby."

Vince agreed. "She kept asking me for more information about him—really made herself a pest."

"What did you tell her?" asked Officer Williams.

"Everything I knew," said Vince.

"Which was . . ." said Savannah.

"The same as everyone else. Absolutely nothing."

Chapter 19

Savannah shuttled out the last students from Webb's Glass Shop with no time to spare. Her meeting with Officer Williams was important, but she had been forced to invite Joy to meet with her at the shop instead of the new café, Bandit Coffee Company. Amanda had gone to hospice and there wasn't anyone else to keep the store open. She couldn't keep closing up and expect to keep her business open.

Joy walked in with two takeaway espressos and a six-pack of the little shop's signature specialty—pumpkin coffee muffins.

Savannah hurried over to give Joy a brief hug and took one of the espresso cups. "Sorry to deprive you of the atmosphere of the Bandit. News has gotten around that it's a great coffeehouse, so it might be around for a while. I'll be as quick as I can with an update. Mm, that muffin looks good." She and Joy went to the back office, where Savannah sat in the old oak office chair and Joy plopped down in the side chair.

"How's the move to the new building?" Savannah asked.

"My new digs are great. I'll unpack my single box this afternoon, but Detective Parker is still livid over the mix-up with the offices." She took a huge bite of her muffin, then mumbled, "But it's all right now, and he's moving in as we speak."

Savannah sank her teeth into one of the muffins and a silent reverence took hold. They both smiled, in pumpkin heaven.

"Do you have news?" asked Officer Williams after a quick swish of coffee.

"Yes, Vince called a few minutes ago. He forgot to tell us that Nicole was excited about engaging on-line with SNARK. This was right before her accident."

"How does he know?"

"Apparently, SNARK paints or bombs, as they call it, every Saturday. He has a huge social media following that are obsessed with being among the first to spot his newest work."

"How do you mean?"

"I looked at his website. Every Sunday morning, he posts an image of the night's work. Then he challenges his followers to find the newest one. There's usually a response within the hour with a picture of the new image."

"Does the winner get a prize?"

Savannah shook her head. "Nope, just the honor of being first. It's crazy."

"This is smart. But this also means, if he's working every Saturday night, he must scout out a location beforehand and then do the actual work. He must be operating in one general location somewhere close by, otherwise the travel time would make this impossible. It's an interesting subculture. Anything else?"

"I've got another approach to get in touch with SNARK. Amanda suggested that I pose as a potential client with the idea that I want him to paint a mural on the side of Webb's Glass Shop. I'm offering a fee large enough to attract his attention."

"If his identity is secret, how does that work? Someone must pay him. If he's expecting to make money, then everything associated with that must be in place. Well, you know about that part. Tax numbers, checking accounts, 1099 forms and the whole deal."

"Somehow he manages to do business in cash. I haven't asked my accountant yet about how I would expense it, but with a SNARK image on my building, the property's value will skyrocket. The least I can do is give it a try."

Officer Williams polished off the last few crumbs of her muffin. "That might work. You could get a jump on us. We're stuck with merely a description of a white car. Pretty much anything else would advance the case. Meanwhile, I need to get back and make sure no one jumps my claim in the new building." She sipped the last of her coffee and got up. "It's like the wild west up there."

Savannah rose as well. "Could you check for anything in your system about SNARK?"

"Sure, but since that's an alias, the probability of a decent result is dim. Plus, we are still in no-man's-land with restoring the servers, but I can tap into some of the global databases that aren't affected. Also, do you have time to go with me to interview Nicole's uncle? I know you're pressed for time, but he lives nearby, and I could use another pair of ears."

"Mmmgph," Savannah mumbled around her muffin. "I can go only if it's within the next hour. I'll leave a note on the door. Again."

"Terrific."

Savannah pulled a page out of the black backpack she took everywhere. "Edward and I are going to look for this." She placed it in front of Officer Williams. "According to the time stamp on the back, it's one of the last images that Nicole snapped. We want to see if it offers any clues or hidden messages."

"Thanks for getting an artist's view of this." She picked up the picture and frowned.

"What's wrong?" asked Savannah.

"I recognize that area. There was a house nearby that I considered buying. That's a pretty rough section of town."

"It's not that bad."

"Regardless, I'll alert the local patrol that you'll be in the area. They'll make a few extra circuits while you're looking around. I'll also have them connect with you, so look for them to make contact."

"Sure."

"Only if they don't get pulled away for something urgent, of course."

"Of course. Remember, we'll have the very large, very excited, very protective Rooney with us."

"Hah! You'll be fine then."

Chapter 20

Wednesday afternoon,
Nicole's uncle's house

Savannah rushed through the closing routine for Webb's Glass Shop, then hopped into the squad car with Officer Williams.

"This won't take long," said Officer Williams. "I've called ahead, so he's expecting us."

"Where does he live?"

"In the penthouse of the newest condominium tower downtown, ONE St. Petersburg."

The new development was a game changer in St. Petersburg. The forty-one stories contained only luxury condominiums that started at nearly a million dollars each. The influx of so many affluent residents affected the entire community in positive cash-flow ways. The St. Petersburg downtown ambiance would never be called sleepy again.

"Wow, he is the rich uncle. That's super exclusive and the tallest of the new buildings."

"So far, I hear there are plans for another one, even taller but farther west."

"I heard that too, but I think it's in either permit difficulties or financial trouble."

They pulled into the parking garage and Officer Williams found the guest parking the concierge had described. The concierge met them in the lobby. His uniform was the perfect replication of a New York doorman: a tailored double-breasted jacket with brass buttons and a silk top hat.

"Good afternoon, Officer Williams and Miss Webb. Mr. Borawski is expecting you." He led them to an elevator marked private. "Mr. Borawski has been rather fragile of late and he's naturally upset over the death of his favorite niece. I advise you to be as gentle as you can under the circumstances. Mr. Borawski's caregiver will meet you."

They zipped up to the penthouse in a flash. The elevator doors opened, and they stepped out to find a butler was waiting to greet them. He was in his late sixties, silver-haired, wearing a black silk crew neck with slim black trousers. "Good afternoon, ladies. I've been expecting you. My name is Arnold Banyon, Mr. Borawski's manservant. This way, please."

He led them into the entry that opened out into a great room that presented a magnificent view of Tampa Bay. Mr. Borawski was sitting in a lounge chair on the terrace, dressed in purple silk pajamas, a deeper purple silk robe, and covered with a cozy powder-blue woolen blanket. He gave them a wan smile and motioned for them to sit in the two chairs pulled up close beside him.

"Bert, this is Officer Williams and Miss Savannah Webb," said Arnold. Then he disappeared like a spooked cat.

"Please sit here." His voice sounded like an overplayed record that skipped its tracks. "My voice isn't strong, and I don't hear as well as I used to. I understand you have some questions about my niece, Nicky."

"Yes, sir. We're so sorry for your loss. It's especially tragic for such a young woman." Officer Williams took out her notepad and pen. "I have just a few questions about the circumstances between Nicole and her parents. Can you explain why they're estranged?"

A small table stood beside Uncle Bert that held a box of tissues, a tall glass of ice water, and a crystal dish that held a variety of pills, capsules, and lozenges. He pulled out a tissue, dabbed his eyes, and threw it into a small waste can next to the table. The can already held a number of discarded tissues.

"When Nicole announced that she was going to marry Elizabeth, it was an enormous shock to her parents. They had no idea she was gay."

"She kept that secret?" asked Officer Williams.

Uncle Bert raised his index finger, then took one of the tablets. After replacing the glass on the table, he said, "I knew from the time she was a toddler, that she would prefer girls to boys, but her parents were oblivious and are still extremely homophobic. Even now, they have no idea that Arnold has been my lover for more than two decades."

Savannah glanced sideways at Joy, who signaled her to go ahead. "Can you tell us about the trust fund?"

"I knew that Nicole's parents would be very angry when she finally came out of the closet with her engagement to Elizabeth. As I expected, they cut her off completely. She was attending the Massachusetts College of Art and Design and she had to withdraw from classes."

He paused for a moment. "I wish she had asked me for help at that point, but Nicole thought she could persuade her parents to accept the marriage. Then they canceled the lease on her car, so she bought an old junk car. That depleted her small savings. She had nowhere to live after she left the dorm, so she moved in with her brother and then quickly found a job as a waitress."

"You mean her brother Alan?" asked Officer Williams.

Uncle Bert took a sip of the ice water. When his hand began to tremble, Savannah jumped up and placed the glass back on the small table.

"Thank you. I have Parkinson's and sometimes my medications disagree with each other. It's unpleasant."

Officer Williams shook her head. "No problem. Take your time."

He smiled weakly, then continued. "Once I surmised that my idiot brother and his wife were determined to destroy Nicole's future, I set up a trust fund for both her and Alan. It pays out a decent annuity until my death, or when they reach age thirty. Then they will take over full control."

"What are the provisions for Nicole's death?" asked Savannah.

"Well, that's a little unique. I had it set up to transfer the annuity over to Nicole's wife and the remaining trust fund to her brother Alan." He raised his hands palms upward. "I have everything I'll ever want, and Arnold is set as well."

"How much is the trust fund worth?" asked Savannah.

"Five million dollars." He dropped his head back and closed his eyes.

Arnold instantly appeared at Savannah's side, pushing a wheelchair. "I'm afraid that the interview is over. He's exhausted himself."

Officer Williams immediately stowed her notepad and pencil while she rose from her chair. "Thank you for your time, sir." She looked over to Savannah then spoke to Arnold. "We can find our way out."

Arnold smiled his thanks and he began what sounded like a familiar argument in coaxing Uncle Bert into the wheelchair.

Uncle Bert took a long shuddering breath and looked up. "I'm so tired, Arnold. Very, very tired."

Savannah and Joy found their way back to guest parking and Joy unlocked the cruiser. They buckled up and drove down Central Avenue.

"Why do you think the trust fund is so tricky?" asked Savannah.

"I believe there are more secrets lurking within this family," answered Officer Williams.

Chapter 21

Wednesday evening,
on a street south of Central Avenue

Savannah and Edward left the house in her Mini with Rooney snuggled in his crate in the cargo area. "You know we're going to have to get a bigger crate, don't you?" Savannah said as she glanced in her rearview mirror.

"He's large for a puppy." Edward looked back as well.

"The bigger issue is that the current crate is the largest that will fit in the Mini. We're going to need a doggy car seat."

Edward pulled out his phone. "There are car seats for dogs?" He googled and turned his head to look at the back seat. "Brilliant! I'm putting one on order." He punched in the information. Then his phone pinged. "Great! It will be here on Friday. He's growing so fast this has got to be the last time we put him in a crate." He turned around again. "Right, Rooney?"

Rooney looked at Edward, whined for a moment, then tucked his head down between his huge paws. Even so he somehow managed to keep those betrayed puppy eyes on Edward.

"So why are we doing this at night?" asked Edward. "It would be a thousand times easier in the daytime."

Savannah expelled a deep, frustrated sigh. "I know it would. But with running both the shop and the studio, Amanda at hospice and Jacob not well enough to run either place, I'm out of options. If we don't do it now, I'll have to wait until Sunday. That's too long to wait." She patted Edward on his thigh. "You're my buddy on this adventure."

"It's lucky that Wednesday night is a bit slow. Samuel has been coming up to speed quickly, but I need to get back so I can teach him how to do the closing. I think I'm going to offer him a permanent job. He's a good sous chef and I'm sure it would simplify his life to have one full-time job with benefits rather than three part-time ones."

They pulled into an alley that the SHINE organizer told Savannah was the entry-level wall for beginning graffiti artists. Although technically the images could be considered defacing public property, the arts council had encouraged the SPPD to turn a blind eye. It was a chaotic jumble of images dimly lit by a street light.

They parked, got Rooney out on his leash, and Edward held him in close control. Savannah used a flashlight to illuminate the images. She scanned them carefully, looking for Nicole's signature bubble-gum pink with black paint in a triangle.

"Look!" Savannah pointed her flashlight to a lower section of the wall. "The color palette is right." She held the light steady on the image.

LOVE
IS
LOVE

The letters were a typical bubble-gum-balloon font with a thick black outline. Next to the last E was a little triangle with the stylized initials NB inside.

Savannah took a picture with her phone. "That's it, all right. It matches the little triangle image we found in her locker."

Rooney stiffened, then produced a low, rumbling growl. A small hooded figure dressed from head to toe in black was standing next to the wall. She pulled back the hood to reveal a shock of purple crew-cut hair.

"This wall is almost full. All the good spots are gone, but since I'm short, I take the low stuff anyway." The voice was soft but raspy, as if recovering from a screaming match.

Rooney stopped growling as soon as the artist began to speak.

"Do you mind if we watch?" asked Savannah.

There was a hesitation. "That would actually be helpful. I'm not very good yet, but I'm hoping to apply for one of the SHINE murals next year, and part of the event is to watch the paint-slingers work their magic. I need to get used to people watching me. So far, no one has been interested."

"Thanks. My name is Savannah." She waved a hand. "This is my fiancé, Edward." She bent to ruffle Rooney behind the ears. "And this amazing puppy is Rooney."

Rooney yipped and tentatively moved toward the artist.

"I'm Morgan. Who is this big hulk of adorableness?" Morgan slid the backpack to the ground and bent to give Rooney an experienced scratching behind his floppy ears. Rooney replied by licking a great wet path all down Morgan's face.

"Say hello to Rooney, the one-hundred-twenty-pound face-washing machine." Savannah hooked a finger under Rooney's collar. "Let the artist be." Rooney sat.

"Do you have a plan, or do you just wing it?" Edward stepped closer to the backpack.

"Normally, I just paint whatever comes to mind. But tonight, I'm trying out a new image, so I'm painting with a plan." Morgan unzipped the backpack and pulled out an index card and handed it to Edward.

"Wow. That's good." Edward showed the card to Savannah, who lit it with her flashlight. It was a colored pencil sketch of a realistic flamingo in flight.

"Thanks, but I may have bitten off more than I can chew." Morgan took the card back and began setting up her materials to paint the image. Then out came a small portable lamp and Morgan set it up to shine on a small blank space near the bottom of the wall.

Next came a wide range of spray-paint cans and a packet of stencils cut in meaningless shapes. Some had never been used. Some were covered in multiple colors. After laying out all the cans and stencils as if it were a personal ritual, Morgan put on latex gloves and slipped on a mask.

"This is the fun part for me. I love the process of getting ready to paint. It's my yoga."

She first sprayed the wall with a white base. Then Morgan worked efficiently and quickly using the stencils and shaping cards to build the flamingo, layer upon layer, starting from the broadest shapes and finishing up with details that brought the image to life. Stepping back to see the effect, Morgan stopped and added a few touch-ups.

"That's it. Now for the final step." In a few little sprays, Morgan left a signature in the right-hand corner of the image at the very bottom of the wall.

"That's gorgeous," said Savannah. "I thought you said you were a beginner. This looks very practiced to me."

Morgan shrugged and began gathering up her tools and materials and returning them to the backpack. "The more times you work with an image, the better it gets. This isn't my first time with the flamingo."

"I'm a little surprised. It's a bit cliché, isn't it?" Savannah raised her eyebrows. "Florida. Pink flamingoes can be viewed as kitschy."

"That's my signature image. I make sure they look like an Audubon image, not a cartoon."

"You've done that, all right. It looks like it will start preening any second. Thanks for letting us watch. Before you go, I was wondering if you ever met the artist who painted that?" Savannah pointed to Nicole's graffiti.

"Oh, sure. She was a rank beginner, but I was able to give her a few pointers. She picked up a lot of stuff from the locals. She had a job somewhere near here as a bartender."

"Yes, I was her boss," said Edward. "She worked for me at the Queen's Head Pub."

Edward thought those words sounded hollow. How could it be true that she would never come to the pub again? Nicole had been such a large part of the pub's quirky sense of fun and comradery. How would they be able to recreate the magic her big personality inspired?

"Apparently this was her main outside interest. In fact, her only interest outside the pub. Is there anything that you could tell us about her graffiti work?"

"Not much, she was just starting." Morgan turned away and then looked at them. "Wait a minute. She was obsessed with SNARK. Somehow, she almost always showed up when he was creating a new piece. I don't know how she did that. Maybe he told her. I only ever ran into him by accident."

"Do you know where we can find SNARK?" asked Savannah. "We'd like to talk to him."

"You and about a million fans and reporters. According to social media posts, he isn't in the area right now, but he is expected to return tomorrow. Rumor has it that he's painting his statement piece tomorrow night before he hops onto a train to the next mural festival in Montreal."

"Where does he stay?"

Morgan reached into the backpack for a thermos. "It varies. If it's a new town to him, he roughs it in the local homeless camps. But he's well-known around here, so I'll bet he is staying with some friends who have an actual house."

Savannah softened her voice. "Morgan, did you hear that Nicole was killed in a hit-and-run on Monday?"

Morgan's mouth flew open, but nothing escaped. "Killed?" The backpack dropped to the ground out of Morgan's limp, trembling hands.

Savannah stepped forward and grabbed Morgan by the arm. "Are you all right? Do you feel faint?"

Morgan jerked away from Savannah and stuttered, "N-n-n-no. I can't b-b-believe it. I don't have a television and I rarely hear the news." Morgan bent down and picked up the fallen backpack.

"It wasn't an accident," said Savannah. "We're trying to find out from her friends who might have wanted to harm Nicole. Was she involved in something dangerous? Do you have any information that might help us track down her killer?"

"I didn't know her all that well, but she was a regular in the late-night crowd."

Savannah pulled out a business card. "Could you give me a call if something occurs to you or one of your graffiti crowd?"

Morgan took the card and fingered the raised lettering. "Nicole was a kind and caring person. I'll find out what I can and give you a call."

In the next moment, Morgan was gone, leaving Savannah, Edward, and Rooney to stare at the delicate image of the flying flamingo.

Chapter 22

Savannah unlocked the shop and logged into the retail PC up front. When that was up and operating, she pulled out the wineglasses from the kiln and placed them at each student's workstation.

Her phone pinged. Jacob texted her that he was at Webb's Studio and would be working on the large stained-glass restoration project.

HOW DO YOU FEEL?
He answered: **FINE**

I've got to get over there and check on him. "FINE" means absolutely nothing.

Amanda came into the shop through the back door. She stowed her velvet patchwork hobo handbag under the sales counter. "Mom had a very good day yesterday." Her eyes shone, and she inhaled a quivering breath. "I was so happy. She was talking and laughing with the nurses. It was a wonderful afternoon. I stayed with her for supper. She didn't eat, but she was in such good spirits. So much like her normal self."

"That's wonderful."

"Hey, did you see the paper this morning?"

"No, Edward takes it into work with him. I don't even pick it up from the sidewalk in front of the house anymore." She frowned. "Why?"

"It appears that Nicole's will and testament was revealed by her lawyer to her heirs yesterday. It names Elizabeth as the sole beneficiary of her trust fund."

"That's what I would expect," said Savannah. "She is the surviving spouse."

"Here's the surprise. The value of the fund is five million dollars. Five. Million. Dollars. Can you believe that?"

"Yes. I knew that. Sorry that I didn't fill you in. I didn't want to disturb you at hospice."

"Oh, that's all right, but anyway, the reporter could have been given the value of her estate by someone in the family."

"Or close to the family."

"What about the lawyer?" asked Amanda.

"Not likely. This is all purely speculation, but if the lawyer did this, he's not a very ethical lawyer. The lawyer represents the family, so if there is discord about a will he drew up, he is not serving the family by publicizing it." Savannah folded her arms.

"Also, not a good recommendation for the quality of his services if he is caught violating the confidentiality a will."

"Agreed. No one had any idea that Nicole had a fairy-tale rich uncle. He stepped in after her family disowned her when she announced her intention to marry Elizabeth."

"Oh yuk. Poor Nicole."

"That puts a new perspective on Elizabeth's motives, wouldn't you say?"

"Oh yes, the paper said that she appeared shocked," said Amanda.

"That could be false. We already know about Nicole's brother. Do you think he was mad that he gets no share of the trust?"

"No, he's been rescued by the same rich uncle, so you would have to assume that he knew about the trust from the start." Amanda tilted her head and smiled. "What are you going to do about it?"

Savannah shrugged her shoulders and thought for a few moments. "I think we need to know even more about Nicole's family. Uncle Bert appears to be a true savior to both Nicole and Alan. Maybe we can find out if there's more to the story."

"Easier said than done," said Savannah. "Elizabeth wasn't very cooperative the last time Edward and I talked to her. We have no real reason to talk to her about anything. She's not connected with the SHINE Festival or anything else associated with the art community."

"That leaves us with no opening," said Amanda.

Savannah ran a hand through her tight curls. "Maybe not, but if she's not involved in Nicole's murder, she might be very happy to help us prove that she's not the killer. Right?"

Amanda nodded.

Savannah picked up her cell. "Let's find out. I'm calling her."

When Elizabeth answered, Savannah put the phone down on the sales counter and set it to speaker. "Hi, Elizabeth. This is Savannah Webb and I've got Amanda Blake here with me. I've been hired by the St. Petersburg Police Department to help with the investigation into Nicole's hit-and-run. Do you have time for a few questions?"

"Isn't that unusual? I mean, you are a civilian, right? I don't have to answer your questions."

"Yes, but I've been helpful to the police in the past and they sometimes need expert advice in cases involving special topics—like graffiti artists."

"Oh, you mean Nicole's obsession with SNARK."

"Do you have any idea why Nicole was interested in him?"

"I have a suspicion, but no real evidence—just an opinion."

Savannah looked over to Amanda and winked. "I'll gladly listen to your opinion."

Elizabeth's voice dropped into a monotone that gave the impression of boredom but was more likely to protect herself from becoming emotional. "Nicole bought a painting for her uncle, which looked exceptionally well done. She wouldn't tell anyone where she got it, even under pressure. She thought Uncle Bert would appreciate the quality of the aspiring artist."

"That doesn't sound suspicious."

"Well, Uncle Bert became very suspicious. He recognized it as the image of an obscure canvas by the famous Dutch artist, Johannes Vermeer. Uncle Bert thought the painting was a copy of the famous forger, Han van Meegeren, a famous character during the World War II criminal trials. The canvas might be of value in itself for a blatant con of forging a forgery. The painting is especially fine in its own right, but even more interesting for its checkered history. He appreciated the skill of the artist and wanted Nicole to contact the artist for him."

"How does that involve SNARK?"

"Nicole looked closely at the painting and saw some correlation between the painting and some of SNARK's graffiti. She was embarrassed that she had been taken in, and by giving that painting to her uncle—she was doubly embarrassed. I knew she was trying to find SNARK, but I didn't know how far she was willing to take it. If she believed SNARK was a forger, what would she do?"

"Could you possibly bring me the painting in question? I would like to follow the trail of Nicole's reasoning for thinking that SNARK was the forger. Painting styles can be deceptive. I want a much closer look."

"Sure. I'm deep into estate paperwork, but I can have Phillip drop it by sometime this afternoon. I'm sure Uncle would be happy to lend it to you if it will help find Nicole's killer. Oh, by the way. Nicole's final wishes were for her body to be harvested for organ transplant and to science. She wanted it that way. But there's also a celebration of her life scheduled for the middle of next month. I hope you can be there. You guys meant a lot to her."

"Thanks, Elizabeth." Savannah ended the call. She looked over to Amanda. "I'm not sure why she was so chatty. But at least we have a more substantial justification that SNARK could be the hit-and-run driver."

Amanda folded her arms in front of her generous chest. "It's still weak, but so far—he's all we have."

Savannah blew out an exasperated puff of breath. "You're right, but I'm very anxious to look at the painting."

"You know who an even better expert might be?"

"Who?"

"Why, Jacob, of course. He looks at everything from such a different point of view. It might also be a bit of useful therapy or at worst a distraction for him to study it closely."

"You're right. I'll round up some pictures of SNARK's graffiti for Jacob to compare to when we get the painting. He can write down his analysis for me."

"Another way he could help would be to investigate the background of Nicole's family."

"Great idea, if he's up for it. Remember that friend of his? She's a reference librarian with a keen interest in historical St. Petersburg. Okay, I'll leave you to get your class underway while I find this rescue farm that Alan runs."

Chapter 23

Thursday morning,
rescue farm

Savannah pulled up to a mailbox at the end of a dirt road that her GPS barely recognized. It seemed remote, although she was only a few miles from US Route 19, the main north/south thoroughfare. The carved wooden sign on the rickety gate across an even sketchier dirt and sand road read, WELCOME TO THREE PINES ANIMAL RESCUE. A plastic-coated index card was tacked to the sign. VISITORS PLEASE ENSURE THE GATE IS FASTENED BEHIND YOU.

Following those instructions, she drove down the sandy road to a cluster of outbuildings that surrounded an old cracker-style farmhouse. In the center of the circular drive stood three tall Ponderosa pines that had shed enough pine needles over the years to ensure nothing grew underneath them.

She parked beside the main building. At least, it was most likely the main building, although not a single structure had a lick of paint anywhere to be seen. She got out of her Mini and a scruffy sandal-clad young man in a holey T-shirt and even more ragged denim shorts barged through the screen door, letting it slam behind him.

"Welcome to Three Pines. I'm Alan Borawski." He stretched out a callused hand with fingernails black with imbedded dirt.

Savannah shook his hand. "I'm Savannah Webb. I own Webb's Glass Shop and I was a friend of your sister, Nicole. I'm so sorry for your loss."

"Loss?" Alan put his hands on his hips. "That's choice. She screwed up our whole family. I never forgave her for that. She was Mom and Dad's favorite. They've never been the same since she outed herself with that money-grubber, Elizabeth."

Savannah stepped back. "I'm sorry that you feel that way. Nicole was the manager of my fiancé's restaurant, Queen's Head Pub. I've had nothing but wonderful times with her. You know that her accident is under investigation, don't you?"

Alan dropped his hands, dropped his head, and his mouth dropped open. He stood absolutely silent for a few long moments. "I did not know that."

"You haven't heard from Officer Williams of the St. Petersburg Police Department?"

He shook his head, then looked straight at Savannah. "I let the machine answer the phone in the mornings. I've got animals to feed and water, and pens to muck out. I'm just finishing my chores for the morning or I wouldn't have heard you drive up."

"Would you mind if I ask you some questions about Nicole? I'm investigating her relationship with a graffiti artist named SNARK."

Alan crossed his arms. "I've still got to fill up the water tub for the horses and donkeys, feed the sheep, and check on the sick animals. If you can wait ten minutes, I'll tell you what I know. Otherwise, you'll have to come back some other time."

"No need. I can stay."

"Come on in. You may as well wait in comfort." He held the screen door for Savannah and she stepped into the dark, low-ceilinged kitchen. "There's coffee but no cream and no sugar. I'll get along now."

The kitchen was basic to the point of austere. Cups and plates were stacked on open shelving. Underneath were narrow, hand-crafted cupboards that closed with a bit of wood that swiveled on a nail. There was a 1950s chrome dining set with original red plastic–covered chairs so well used that much of the red was worn pink. Savannah grabbed a sturdy white mug and poured her coffee from the vintage Mr. Coffee machine.

On a shelf over the dining table was a row of books on every kind of farm animal she had ever heard about. Dairy cows, steers, pigs, horses, mules, donkeys, chickens, and dozens more. There were also vintage veterinary textbooks mixed in with *Farmers' Almanacs* dating back to 2002. *Someone does his research.* She had nearly finished her coffee when Alan burst into the kitchen, again letting the screen door slam.

Alan nodded a greeting, then went directly to the white porcelain farm sink and washed his hands thoroughly up to his elbows with a bar of soap. He dried them on a thin towel and hung it back on a bare nail.

He filled a mug with coffee and sat at the table. "What do you need to know?"

Savannah noticed the word *need* rather than *want.*

"Were you here when Nicole was hit?"

He stood up and pointed to the door. "You can leave right now if you're going to talk like that. She was my sister no matter what I felt about her personal choices. I had nothing to do with her death."

"That may be true, but you must expect that the police will be interested in the family first. In most cases, the victim of a homicide knows her killer."

"Is this why the police have been calling me? They think I killed Nicky?"

"Calm down, Alan. You're going to have to give your answers to Officer Williams anyway. You might as well tell me now, because I can always ask her after she interviews you. By the way, you would be wise to return those calls. You don't want to be uncooperative. Call her back. She's a good police officer."

He sat and expelled a breath. "I'd better get a volunteer lined up for tonight's chores. I'm careful not to exhaust my trusted supporters. Nicole was always creating drama. Now she's continuing that." He sniffed and looked into the distance, his eyes unfocused. Then he spoke in a near whisper. "But this time, she can't make it better. She's dead."

"Nicole appeared to be investigating the origins of a forged painting that she gave to your Uncle Bert as a birthday present."

"I've seen it. She was intrigued about the techniques the artist used. Our uncle was curious as well. Don't see the value in it myself."

"Do you know anything else about the situation?"

Alan brought the mug to his lips and looked over the rim at her while he drank. "The problem is that it upset Uncle Bert that she had been conned into buying a forgery—even worse, a forgery of a forgery."

"But it was a gift. Surely he wouldn't be angry with her for thinking of him on his birthday?"

Cupping his hands around the mug of coffee, he leaned forward. "But that's the thing. He was questioning her judgment on whether she was shrewd enough to handle the money in her trust fund. He still had the power to dissolve it and take back the money. She was desperate to change his mind."

"I know it's a lot of money, but why would that really matter? She had a job, a house, a wife, basically real happiness."

"Right, but those things come at a price far higher than a bartender makes. She needed that monthly income from the trust to keep Elizabeth happy. Elizabeth is an expensive wife."

"In what way? I don't get the impression that she spends a lot. Except that she does visit her family in Laguna Beach. She's a freelance writer."

"She's been trying to get a movie script accepted by one of the major studios. That's an expensive process. Fruitless, if you ask me. Unless you're Steven Spielberg, you need to live in Los Angeles if you want to write for Hollywood."

Alan took another sip of coffee and grimaced. "This has been on the warming plate for too long. I'm going to make another pot. Do you want another?"

"No, thanks. What's this about Elizabeth spending a lot of money?"

"Well, in her case, she needed money to crew these fabulous yacht-racing events in expensive parts of the world. Because she was a gifted sailor and crewed nearly for free, she was in demand."

Savannah furrowed her brow. "Really? That doesn't sound all that expensive."

"Well, she was also learning how to write screenplays."

"Okay, I didn't see that one coming. How could that be expensive?"

"Attending workshops, getting feedback from script doctors, and attending pitch sessions with producers in Hollywood. All of that is very expensive. It appears that she was quite good. She had several scripts get to the development stage, but then the productions fell apart before they could be filmed."

Alan dumped the coffee grounds into a blue plastic bin, refilled the coffeepot with tap water, poured the water in the reservoir, and placed the pot back in the Mr. Coffee. He spooned more grounds into a fresh filter, then pressed the brew switch.

He stood in silence for a few moments. "That was the big problem with what she was trying to do. She had a script she was pitching to the big studios. She had an agent and the whole ball of wax."

"That sounds serious. How close was she to selling the script?"

"How long is a piece of string?" Alan shrugged his shoulders.

Savannah looked at her watch. She was cutting it close for getting back to the shop on time. She got up. "So as far as you know, the only questionable part of Nicole's life was the problem of the forged forgery?"

"As far as I know."

Savannah looked around the room at the sparse furnishings, the sagging screens in the open windows, the bare floors that needed a good sanding and finishing polish. "Was she helping you out with the farm?"

"Sometimes she gave me some working cash, you know, to help with the expenses around here." He sighed deeply. "But not lately. Especially after she married Elizabeth." He looked sad. "In fact, not at all after she married Elizabeth."

Chapter 24

Savannah grabbed a Taco Bell drive-through burrito, then made the long drive back to St. Petersburg and walked into Webb's Glass Shop at a quarter to one.

"Hey, I was beginning to get worried." Amanda looked up from the desk back in the office. "It's been quiet since my class left. How did you get on with the brother?"

Savannah plopped down in the guest chair. "Not what I was expecting. He seems to have been ignored by everyone in his family and is struggling along by himself. The rescue farm must take enormous resources to keep running. He's certainly not spending money on anything not pertaining to the animals."

"What do you mean?"

"Well, the old farmhouse hasn't been painted in at least a decade. No air-conditioning, only a fireplace for heating, no real creature comforts at all. Apparently, Nicole was working with him prior to her marriage to Elizabeth, but not so much since."

"Well, that's natural. I mean, they had a fantastical wedding, a honeymoon in Greece, and they just bought that little house in Gulfport."

"He also complained that Elizabeth was spending tons of money on editors and conferences trying to get a script produced out in Hollywood."

"I didn't know that. I thought she was a ghostwriter for some of those celebrity books that keep coming out."

"Yeah, she made some scraps of money that way, but it seems she wanted her own name on the big screen, so she stopped taking on new projects. She's still working over in Tampa writing tech manuals, but she hates that job." Savannah noticed the time. "Hey, you've got to go see your mother, and my class is about to start. Let's meet up tonight at Queen's Head Pub and share what we know."

The hanging doorbell jangled. It was time for class.

Savannah enjoyed the delight each student expressed with their completed wineglasses.

"I think we need at least four more," said Rachel. She compared her two wineglasses to Faith's.

"Oh, I agree." Faith turned to Savannah. "Is it true that Herbert here is going to be an instructor for flameworking?"

Herbert raised his eyebrows. "Where did you hear that?"

"We know everything," the twins said at the same time.

Savannah pointed both her index fingers at the two. "That's true, but things are not yet settled. There'll be a trial class in a few weeks. Don't go jinxing this for Herbert. More importantly, don't jinx it for me. I need the help."

"We won't mess it up. We want to sign up for his first class," said Rachel.

"Can we make martini glasses?" asked Faith. "That would suit us better. We serve lots of martinis."

Savannah felt her lips spread into the biggest smile of the day. "Yes, your parties are legendary. I'll make sure you're signed up as soon as things firm up." She held up a small single-color glass bead. "This is what we're going to make today. You already have most of the skills you need, but in any case, I'll pass this around so you can see what we're trying to make."

She handed it to Myla Kay, who seemed to be operating at half speed. She dreamily held the bead up to the light and looked through the hole in the center. She stared at the glass bead so fiercely, Savannah thought she was trying to bore another hole in it.

"Is something wrong?" Savannah asked.

Myla Kay slowly turned to look at Savannah. Wordlessly, she finally passed it on.

After the last student quickly examined the bead, Savannah asked, "Any questions?"

Patricia raised her hand. "My sister has one of those fancy charm bracelets. You know the kind. They're in malls and airports everywhere."

"You mean a Pandora charm bracelet. Right?" said Lonnie. "I would like to make one for my mother for Christmas. Are we going to do that today?"

"Not in this class, but I'm considering setting up a one-day workshop just for that purpose. They require a larger diameter mandrel—which I have on order, but I won't receive them until next week. This class would be a prerequisite for the workshop, anyway. How many of you would be interested?"

All but the twins raised their hands.

Savannah tilted her head. "I thought you two would jump at the chance. Why not?"

"Oh, we'll be there all right," said Rachel.

"But we don't wear bracelets," said Faith. "Especially charm bracelets that make noise." She shivered. "Too distracting."

"But we have friends with charm bracelets who need birthday gifts, so that makes it unanimous—we'll all attend." Rachel smiled at a smiling Faith.

"I'll set that up then. Now back to this lesson. It's the oldest of the glassmaking techniques, glass beadmaking. The resulting beads can be worn on a charm bracelet, on a necklace, or on a keychain. You're going to find making them takes a good bit of practice, but it's well worth the effort. Watch closely."

She lit the small torch and picked up one of the mandrels she had coated in bead-release liquid last night. "The mandrel is the support rod for making your glass bead."

She looked squarely at Rachel and Faith in turn. "Do not attempt to make a bead anywhere else on the mandrel except this gray section. Let me re-

peat that. Do NOT attempt to make a bead anywhere else on the mandrel. If you do, it will fuse
there and become a permanent part of the mandrel. I'll have to throw it away. There's no recovery."

Next, she held up a thick cobalt-blue glass rod.
"Notice that I'm holding it with my left hand like a
pencil. I'm turning the mandrel in my right hand
slowly toward myself." She looked up. All the students were spellbound. "You may need to experiment. Try it this way first and then if it doesn't feel
comfortable, switch hands and try again. If that
doesn't work, let me know. I've seen some creative
approaches that I can show you."

"Heat both the mandrel and the glass rod." She
put both into the sweet spot of the flame. "You are
also heating the bead glass so that it will form easily around the mandrel. It's a Goldilocks thing.
Too cool and it won't form onto the mandrel. Too
hot and it will be unstable, and your bead will be
uneven."

She held the blue rod close to the mandrel and
began pressing the glass onto it while rolling the
mandrel. She applied the color for several turns.

"Now that I have enough material around the
mandrel, I can finish off shaping it by using a small
marver." She heated the bead and pressed it gently
onto the flat surface of the marver paddle. She re-
peated those steps until she had a cobalt-blue bead
about the size of a dime.

She walked down the row of workstations, letting everyone see the finished bead. "You can
make the bead slimmer or wider, but the impor-

tant part is to keep the glass on the coated part of the mandrel. When you're happy with the shape, you put it in the oven. After about thirty minutes, we'll take them out and the bead should release. We'll use a toothpick to clean out the center and then it will look like this one I passed around a few minutes ago. Now, it's your turn."

The students began the delicate process.

As an exception to their normal classroom attempts, Rachel and Faith were reasonably competent at making a bead.

Herbert concentrated on keeping the pressure of the colored rod even so that the bead was uniformly round. Savannah stood beside him while he used the marver to even out the bead.

"That's great, Herbert. Now, for your advanced assignment, make a bead three times as wide out of three colors."

Herbert grinned like a child.

By this fourth day of class, Savannah usually knew which students needed extra instruction—like the twins—and which students were practically independent, like Herbert. Myla Kay confounded her. It appeared to Savannah that Myla Kay's skills fluctuated up and down every day, and she was sometimes both brilliant and dull during a single classroom session.

Today was a needy day for Myla Kay and Savannah practically took over making each bead that Myla Kay attempted. Savannah wondered if she had a drug problem that would cause frequent concentration lapses.

* * *

Just as Savannah was cleaning up the flame-working workstations and making sure she had enough supplies for tomorrow's session, a couple entered the shop. The man opened the door for the woman to walk through. They were dressed in jeans, rubber sandals, and oversized fishing shirts with a bright red logo over the chest pocket. The logo was the silhouette of a fishing boat and the writing said BORAWSKI FISHING GUIDES.

"Are you Savannah?" asked the woman.

"Yes, ma'am." Savannah walked toward the couple with her hand extended. "I'm "Savannah Webb. How can I help you?"

"You can get your nose out of our business. That's how you can help!"

Savannah took a step back, then straightened herself to her full height so that she towered over the couple. "I'm sorry? I don't understand."

"Sorry isn't going to cut it with me, missy." The woman shook a pointed finger in Savannah's face. "You have no right to meddle in our business."

The man sidled in front. "You stay away from our son Alan. He's got health issues and we had to take him to the emergency room after your visit."

The woman stepped in front and placed her hands on her hips. "If you dare show up at Alan's farm or at our fishing business, we'll call the police on you for harassment."

Savannah put her hands up in front of her. "Look, you've got this all wrong. I'm working with the police as a consultant. They know what I'm doing."

Well, maybe not.

Mrs. Borawski took her husband's arm. "I don't care if you're working for the police or anyone else for that matter. You don't have the authority to interfere with our private lives."

"But, Mrs. Borawski, don't you want to know who killed your daughter? You could have left me a message on my phone. Why did you come all the way down here?"

Mrs. Borawski stiffened. "I wanted to see you in person. You're turning my family inside out. I want this business to be done with. Your interfering is keeping everyone upset."

Savannah relaxed her posture. "But surely you understand that until the real culprit is found, your whole family will live under a cloud of suspicion. Trust me, I know what that feels like. There's no shortcut here. The more cooperative you are with me and the police, the quicker everyone can get back to the business of normal daily life."

"There is no normal in our family. Not since Nicole married that—that—that person."

Mrs. Borawski grabbed her husband's arm. "Come on, Thomas. I don't want to be here."

"Don't pull on me, Deloris. I can't stand when you pull on me."

She dropped her arm and left in such a temper that the bell clanged for a full minute after they were gone.

Why are they so upset?

Alan is accepting money from both sides of this divided family. That could cause quite a bit of tension if either side found out. I don't know for sure if anyone had. Alan also hadn't told Nicole that the family had forgiven him. Motive?

Savannah's phone sounded the text message ping. It was from Jacob.

He texted: **NEED GREEN CATHEDRAL GLASS**
She answered: **NO PROBLEM. ORDERED LAST WEEK. ARRIVED TODAY.**
He responded: **BRING TO STUDIO**
She replied: **ABSOLUTELY**
He continued with: **NEED NOW**
She responded: **WILL BE RIGHT OVER**
He finished with: **C U**

I'll bet anything he's avoiding the sidewalk in front of the shop, where he witnessed the hit-and-run. But I still need to see how he's doing.

She wrangled the lightweight but awkward package of glass into the back of her Mini Cooper and drove over to Webb's Studio. A few moments after she pulled into the gravel parking lot, Jacob appeared at her elbow as she was opening the hatch door.

Savannah took note that Suzy was on leash beside him, looking alert but calm.

Hmm, that's a good sign.

Jacob reached into the trunk and carried the box into the studio. Savannah followed him as he put the box on an empty worktable in his sectioned-off area of the studio.

"Wow, you've made great progress," she said, leaning over the large medallion-shaped stained glass panel. "Does the new glass match?"

Jacob lifted his eyebrows and turned to open the box with a box cutter. He removed the packaging material carefully and placed the half sheet of cathedral glass next to the medallion. He reached up and turned on an additional work lamp above the table and leaned over to compare the new glass with the existing portions of the stained-glass medallion. His eyes beamed, and he grinned wide. Then he pulled his phone out of his back pocket.

PERFECT

Chapter 25

Thursday evening,
Queen's Head Pub

Savannah locked up Webb's Glass Shop and scurried next door to Queen's Head Pub. Officer Williams and Amanda were sitting beside each other, huddled together at the far table. It was the most remote table in the restaurant, always the last one to be filled, in front of the women's restroom. They looked up when she got close.

"What are you two conspiring about?" Savannah asked.

Amanda lifted her head in mock horror. "We're not conspiring."

"Just wondering," added Officer Williams.

"Just wondering what?" Savannah pressed.

Amanda looked at Officer Williams again, shrugged her shoulders, and looked back to Savannah. "We may as well confess, or she'll start interrogating us." A tilted grin briefly swept over Officer Williams's face.

"We were wondering if you had set a date for the wedding."

Savannah tilted her head back and lifted her fists at the ceiling. "Grr. Not you two as well? I'm having enough trouble keeping Edward and his mum at bay. Why is it so important to know the exact date?"

Officer Williams patted the surface of the table in front of an empty chair. "Sit."

Savannah eased into the chair.

"Look." Officer Williams spoke softly. "I know I'm not much older than you, but frankly, for a person your age, you've seen a fair amount of tragedy."

Amanda piped in. "We think you should be getting on with those wedding plans."

Savannah covered her face with her hands for a few moments, then looked at her friends. "It seems ridiculously self-centered to be planning for a wedding before we've even had Nicole's funeral."

Joy propped her head in her hands with both elbows on the table. "That's a tender view and it shows that you were raised properly, having such a kind heart. But . . ." Joy paused.

"I knew there was a *but* coming." Savannah closed her eyes. "Say it."

"Okay, here's the *but*. You must put yourself first for a change. I really can't see why you haven't come to that conclusion yourself." Joy sat back in the chair and folded her arms. "You're a clever woman. Set. The. Date."

"I will." Savannah raised her right hand. "I solemnly swear that a date will be carved in stone before the end of this weekend."

Edward walked up and stood at the end of the table. "What are you talking about?"

Amanda piped up. "We want Savannah to set the wedding date now, but she wants to wait until after Nicole's funeral."

"She's promised to set a final date before the end of the weekend," said Joy.

"You honestly think Nicole's murder will be resolved by then?" Edward rolled his eyes. "I think you're underestimating the complexity of the case. If it were a simple hit-and-run, it would have been resolved by now."

"Yes, I know that," said Savannah. Her eyes commanded silence from Joy and Amanda. Then she looked up at Edward. "Can you take a little break for a powwow?"

"Sure, I'll be back in a second. I've got something new for you to try."

"But Edward," Savannah said to his receding back. "You don't have to do that."

"Is it my imagination or has Edward been spending a lot of time in the kitchen?" Joy looked at Amanda, who raised her eyebrows in agreement.

"He creates new dishes when he's upset." Savannah pressed her lips together. "This is at least the fourth new recipe in the last two days."

Edward appeared with a tray containing four copper mugs of chilled cider and a heaping plate of pumpkin spice scones. "Try these. I'm thinking of having an afternoon tea. We're not busy in the late afternoon and there isn't anyone nearby who's offering a proper British high tea. We would have fixed seating and strictly reservation only, so we could prepare properly and take advantage of how limited the seats would be. I think it's a niche market that we could fill. I mean, the kitchen is already open."

"Edward, please sit." Savannah waved her hand at the empty seat next to her. "You're making me crazy with all this energy. We need to focus on getting those energies working in the right direction. You have two big things to worry about right now. One is getting more staff and the other is winning the Best Burger in the Burg competition."

He sat. "I'm sorry, I know I'm at the babbling stage. I promise to concentrate."

"Before we get started," Savannah began, "Jacob is avoiding coming over onto Central Avenue to pick up supplies. I think he doesn't want to look at the spot where Nicole was hit."

"Interesting," said Amanda. "Maybe that's the key to getting his memory back. Could we somehow reenact the accident?"

"Whoa, that's a big leap into the black pit of the unknown," said Savannah. "But I'll bring it up with Jacob's mother. Since he's been taking an active interest in his recovery, maybe she will approach Jacob directly to see if he wants to take that leap."

"Would she permit it?"

"Hard to say. I know she's at her wit's end with his therapist. The therapist wants to administer drugs, but Frances knows that the side effects can often be worse than the condition they're trying to treat. Judge Underwood is leaning more toward some physical action or situation to encourage the

return of his speech. I'll bet she would be willing
to help us if we set it up."

"I don't think that's a good idea." Officer
Williams frowned. "There's so much that's unknown about teenagers on the autism spectrum.
They don't make good study participants. His situation is complicated by mutism and memory loss.
Jacob is the Underwoods' only child and they've
proven that they're willing to move heaven and
earth to help him. My guess is that she'll wait."

"I agree. I'm chuffed that he's texting," said Edward. "He's never done that before. As usual, what
we think might be comfortable for him could be
the exact opposite." He stared pointedly at Savannah. "Leave him to work this out by himself. He
knows what's good for him—none of us understand
how his condition affects his thought processes.
He's the best one to oversee his recovery. We only
know that he thinks very differently."

"Okay, okay." Savannah grabbed a scone. "You're
right. None of us are trained to handle this situation. I'll leave it alone for a little while longer, but as
soon as the painting shows up, I'm going to take it
over for him to do his magic, if his mother thinks
he's up to it. I trust her instincts over any therapist.
I hope he can tell us something useful about the
forger by comparing SNARK's graffiti to the painting."

"Okay, guys, catch me up on what's happening."
Officer Williams pulled out her notebook and
pen. "I want to resolve this case as quickly as possible. I think the disastrous move from the old police
building to the new one has exhausted Detective
Parker's last vestige of mortal patience. However, it

has given me the chance to take on the role of principal investigator in an informal way."

"Informal?"

"That means I get to do all the work without the pressure of being"—she finger quoted—"officially in charge." She lowered her hands to the table and folded them in front of her. "I'm actually good with that. I personally think he's on edge because there's a promotion afoot. Everyone thinks he's too young for the position, but closure rates are more important than age to the chief of police."

Savannah sipped her hot cider, "If he is promoted, how will that affect your work situation? Do you get promoted as well? You've been working together pretty consistently over the past few months."

Officer Williams put her hands flat on the table. "I can't believe I'm saying this because you guys are usually pretty helpful, but could we get back to the case? At the end of the day, I want justice for Nicole. No matter what happens to any of us."

"Agreed. This is for Nicole," said Savannah. "I know your time is limited. Let's get back on track. So, where are we?"

Officer Williams flipped back to a page in her notebook. She turned to Savannah. "Let me see. What have you found out about the connection between Nicole and SNARK?"

Savannah took a deep breath. "The connection was strong between them, but it wasn't simply a case of Nicole wanting to learn how to paint murals. I think she was trying to figure out if he was the artist that painted a forged picture that she had given her rich uncle."

Officer Williams squinted. "SNARK is a forger?"

Savannah nodded. "It's possible. Nicole's brother Phillip is bringing over the painting so that Jacob and I can compare it to his mural paintings. There should be some stylistic evidence if he is the forger."

"Fine," Officer Williams said. "Let me know what you come up with. What else?"

Amanda lifted her hand. "I've been researching the backgrounds of the organizers of the SHINE Festival and trying to determine who might have helped Nicole with finding SNARK. She must have asked them for help at some point. It's where I thought of, first thing."

"Did you find out anything?" asked Officer Williams.

"Not yet, but I've barely scratched the surface." Amanda widened her eyes. "The SHINE Festival took off like a rocket and no one was prepared for its overwhelming success. I'm trying to track down some of the early volunteers to find out how SNARK approached them. It is completely possible that there are no records."

Officer Williams made a note. "I can pull their paperwork from when they first applied for permits. There might be some names of the original organizers on them for you."

"Thanks," said Amanda.

"Meantime, I found an investigation thread regarding the trust fund." Officer Williams scanned the room and ensured no one was near the table. She leaned forward. "Nicole's brother Phillip may gain control if Elizabeth dies or is found incompetent. Apparently, this came about because even the uncle had concerns about the stability of Nicole's marriage.

"Really?" Savannah sounded disappointed.

"Yes. Her uncle has been recently more focused on the details of the trust. He'd just been admitted into a rehabilitation home due to a bad interaction with the medications that he's taking. So, he's had more time to think about it. That's the official reason. Personally, I think the mobility impairments go along with the progression of his Parkinson's disease. He usually recovers—well, enough to go home in a few weeks."

From the corner of her eye, Savannah noticed that Samuel hovered near their table, staring at Officer Williams in her uniform. Savannah tapped Edward on the arm and tilted her head toward the obviously eavesdropping cook. When Edward turned to look at him, Samuel scurried back into the kitchen. They immediately heard a great clatter of broken glassware followed by loud cursing. Edward shot out of his chair and ran into the kitchen. Savannah heard him gasp and knew this wasn't just a matter of smashed stock. She bolted for the kitchen.

The floor was covered in broken pieces of white plates. The signature square plates had been specially ordered when Edward opened Queen's Head Pub a little more than a year ago.

Edward stood at the back door, and Savannah rushed to join him just in time to watch the taillights of a car as it turned the corner onto the one-way street of First Avenue North. The driver was certainly familiar with the city. It was the best way to leave the area fast.

"What was that all about?" asked Savannah. "Could that have been Samuel?"

"Possibly. He's been acting strange since he took over more of the kitchen work."

"Which he started to do after Nicole was killed." Savannah folded her arms over her chest. "We need to tell Officer Williams that, so she can add him to her list of suspects."

They returned to sit at the table. "Samuel left." Edward shook his head. "I hope he isn't quitting. That would be the last straw. It would just about kill my chances in the Best Burger in the Burg contest. He's been doing a lot of the preparation work. Because the contest ends on Saturday, everyone who comes in is ordering our burger."

Savannah patted Edward on the shoulder. "It will be fine in the end."

Edward turned to Officer Williams. "Samuel has been behaving strangely. It might be the stress of the additional hours I've been giving him. Of course, it could be that he's terrified of police."

"Has he quit his other jobs?"

Edward ducked his head and squinted. "I don't know—I'm finding out that Nicole really ran almost everything. I'd better get myself sorted out, or this pub is going to suffer a serious problem."

Officer Williams made another note. "I haven't gotten around to adding his name to the list of background investigations. Argh! I hate getting behind in an investigation. What's his full name?"

"Samuel Joven," said Edward. "I'll get you his address."

"Actually," said Officer Williams, "while you're at it, could you get me a list of all your employees?"

He slipped out into the kitchen area and returned with a photocopy of handwritten index cards. He read off Samuel's address to Officer Williams. "It's one of those transient places not too far from here. I didn't know he had a car. It must be borrowed."

The posse disbursed, with Officer Williams leaving in the squad car, and Amanda driving her mother's pink Cadillac to the hospice facility. Edward and Savannah stood looking at each other. Savannah reached over and took his hand.

"I'm concerned about our ability to manage two businesses within one relationship. Maybe I shouldn't have taken on the consulting job."

Edward shook his head and folded Savannah into his arms. "That was never going to happen. We need to know what happened and this is the way to find out."

Savannah leaned into his body and nuzzled into his neck. "Maybe we should see a relationship therapist. I don't want to end up in trouble over this."

"Let's not panic yet. I don't think we need outside help to solve our very minor problems. We're not crazy. Well, at least not in that way. We're just overwhelmed, and I don't need outsiders poking their noses into my business."

"One way to help is have Amanda limber up her IT superpowers and do a bit more social media investigation. Her mother seems to be making another miraculous recovery."

"That's incredible. That lady is tough."

"Another way I can help is to contact a staffing agency to help with the rush in the pub. But you need to stop experimenting in the kitchen. I know it's keeping you calm but not really helping anything else."

"You're right. No more new recipes until this investigation is done."

Savannah backed out of his embrace. "Thanks, honey. Now we need to figure out what frightened Samuel. I'm going to check out his place and talk to the building manager."

"Hang on, I need to go with you. I'm his boss and I could legitimately be checking up on an absent employee."

"True, but you need to stay here and run Queen's Head Pub until we get you some replacement staff. Outside of classroom hours, I can simply close my shop and customers will come back for their supplies later. You simply can't leave. It's still daylight—I'll be fine."

Edward rubbed the back of his neck, "I don't like this."

"Fair enough. I'll be fine."

Chapter 26

Officer Williams took the single box of her personal property from the trunk of the patrol car. She had been carrying it around with her for several days. She usually got the same patrol car when she needed one, but since there was no way to count on that—she simply carried the box around with her. It didn't weigh much.

She walked into the new lobby. The smell of drywall, paint, and floor cleaner grabbed her by the throat. She coughed, sputtered, and nearly fell in front of the new revolving door. The entrance hall wasn't even close to being finished.

One of the antiquated badge scanners had been salvaged from the old building and put into service. She placed her ID on the scanning screen, but it didn't register. The security officer, also from the old building, grinned and his crinkly eyes lit up when he saw her.

"Hey, Joy. I'm back to work! This newfangled scanner needs a reboot followed by a restart every five minutes. So, I'm going back to the old-fashioned way to sign people into the department. All I need is coffee."

"Coffee is my favorite payment system."

She signed his chipped and worn clipboard with the pen attached by a scruffy bit of string. Both had seen better days.

Joy handed it back.

"Old-school always works." He touched two fingers to the brim of his hat. "Go forth and save the day."

The farther she made her way into the new building, the more chaos infested the hallways. There were scissor lifts for the electricians wiring the fluorescent light fixtures. There were crumpled drop cloths beneath the white-spattered boots of the painters. There were several colors of fiber optic cable being unwound from enormous spools in the ceilings.

She finally found the open-plan area where she was assigned. Her desk was near the back with a brand-new ergonomic office chair in front of a new desk that had her name scribbled on a piece of plain copy paper taped to the surface. She was the only one there. She placed her box on the desk. The first thing she took out was her coffee cup, followed by a simple name plate in a small stand.

The name plate traveled with her wherever she was assigned. Her father had given it to her when she graduated from the police academy. The next personal item was her diploma, but there was nowhere to hang it in this open bullpen, so she put it in the bottom drawer of the desk. The box also held a good supply of notebooks, a pottery cup to hold her pencils and pens, and a colorful stock of Post-it notes. The last two items had belonged to her mother—a gray Swingline stapler and its matching tape dispenser.

She flattened the box, stored it in the bottom drawer of the desk, and then considered herself moved in.

Now to find Detective Parker.

She phoned him rather than run around the building.

"Officer Williams," said Detective Parker, "I certainly hope you have some progress to report. I could use some good news."

"Sir, where's your office? This place is a total mess down here."

"It's not much better up here, but I'm on the fourth floor overlooking Second Avenue. It's left as you get off the elevator. Then follow your nose for the strongest odor of noxious paint, and that will be my office."

Officer Williams followed his instructions precisely and was rewarded with a back view of Detective Parker looking out over the street. His office had been freshly painted and was incredibly small with barely room for a desk, an office chair, and a side chair. However, the window was a floor-to-ceiling treasure of light.

She knocked on the doorjamb. "Sir, your new office is very small."

"Good detecting, Officer Williams, but I'm lucky to have a window view." He turned and motioned for her to sit in the side chair while he sat in his new ergonomic office chair. "How are your digs?"

"The new bull pen is huge. There are no sound dampeners like carpet or individual partitions. It's going to be a noisy nightmare and I won't be able to have a cogent thought. Luckily, I don't spend a lot of time at my desk. I'm sure I'll find somewhere quiet as soon as the construction is finished." Officer Williams stood, stepped into the doorway, and looked up and down the hall. "Are we anywhere near the conference rooms?"

"I'll show you where they're going to be." He hopped up and marched down to the end of the hallway and turned left. "I'm told there will be four of them here, but so far—definitely not ready." He opened a door and let her look inside. The room wasn't there yet. All the studs were in place and the electrical conduits weaved in and out of the upright two-by-fours like a clothesline. The sub-floor was still the fiberboard panels. The ceiling was completely exposed, with the air-conditioning ductwork snaking through the framework that would hold the squares of acoustic tiling. No walls, no floor, no ceiling, no work space.

Officer Williams whistled. "This is going to take some time. What can we use?"

"I've gotten hold of the maintenance fellow from the old building and he's gotten us two standalone whiteboards and an old-fashioned corkboard. He says he can deliver them tomorrow morning."

"But where will we put them? Your office isn't big enough to change your mind."

"No problem. We're going to use your open-plan office." He finger-quoted the words *open plan*.

She shook her head and wondered why everyone had regressed into finger quoting. She grinned. "Unconventional, but I'm guessing that that is your point."

Chapter 27

Savannah went home, changed her clothes, and took Rooney for a nice long run. It was a way to let her subconscious think. Frequently, simple answers to complicated questions appeared to her while her mind floated during the run.

Instead of their normal path, she headed south and crossed Central Avenue into the area that she now knew displayed the paint-slinging of the graffiti artists in training. Her eye was tuned to catch out any new images as well as spot the artists.

The graffiti artists were easy for her to spot with their unofficial uniforms of black hoodies and bulky black backpacks. They were a contrast to the business casual wearing day workers walking unknowingly past the new breed of night workers. It was a new mix highlighting the changing demographics in her hometown. No longer a retiree's winter respite, it was an urban cultural village.

In her dad's time, St. Petersburg had been a haven for middle-class Northerners wishing for a few warm weeks in the middle of the harsh winters. The town's famous green benches used to be filled with the leisured elderly. Now, the predominant group was around her age and the art culture had boomed along with it.

When she returned home she called the office of a local temp agency and left a detailed message. Edward had a history with the agency and they would call him tomorrow for times and types of staff he needed.

Savannah sat in her Mini and rang Samuel's cell phone. There was no answer and a message informed her that the customer had elected to decline voicemail. She frowned.

I didn't know you could even buy phones without that feature. Of course, I would never get a phone without it.

She drove to the three-story run-down apartment building and parked in the one visitors' spot off the alley. She entered the main hallway, found Samuel's apartment on the top floor, and knocked.

There was no answer. She knocked much harder and she heard the chain rattle on the door behind her. "He's not here anymore." A single eye peeked out of the crack in the door. "Stop making a ruckus."

Savannah turned in time for the door to slam shut. She headed downstairs and knocked on the door labeled RESIDENT MANAGER.

"Coming," was followed by a horrific bubbly cough that made Savannah's lungs hurt in sympathy. The door opened and a gentleman in his late seventies stood in sandals, cargo shorts, and a plaid shirt that was worn so thin that his white undershirt was plainly visible.

"Good evening, I'm looking for Samuel Joven. This is the address he gave to his workplace."

"He cleared out a little while ago. You just missed him."

"Cleared out?"

"Yep, he slipped an envelope under the door with a note and the key. Before I could get up he was gone."

"Did it say why?"

"Nope. With no notice, I get to keep his security deposit." The manager started to close the door.

"Wait." Savannah put her foot in the door. "Did he say where he was going?"

The manager looked down at Savannah's foot. He kept staring at it until she moved it out of the way. Then he looked up at her.

"The note didn't say. That young man has worn a worried look since the first time I saw him. He still had it."

"Thanks. If he comes back or if you hear from another resident that someone else sees him, tell him to come back to Queen's Head Pub. He's not in trouble. The owner wants him to come back as a full-time cook. He's good."

"Don't hold your breath." The manager quickly closed the door.

Darkness had fallen—she had taken too long. Before stepping out onto the broad porch that ran the length of the building, Savannah got her keys out of the side pocket of her backpack and held her car key tightly in her fist like a small wine screw.

Although this section of town wasn't far from her house and Webb's Glass Shop, it had a sketchy reputation—not a particularly good place to be alone after dark. She skipped down the front steps and hustled around the corner into the alley toward her parked Mini Cooper. She clicked the car door open and was reaching for the handle when she heard a roaring engine behind her.

Using all the strength in her well-trained muscles, she leaped onto the hood of her Mini and scrambled up to the roof on hands and knees. She felt the whoosh of a white car speeding along the side of her Mini and a spray of gravel hit her cheek.

She looked at the retreating car and tried to pick out the license plate, but it had been obscured by what looked like reflective duct tape. She pulled out her phone, fumbled with trembling fingers for the phone app, and managed to take a picture of the car before it careened onto the next street. It was a long shot, but maybe the forensics experts could enhance the image. Phone cameras were amazing nowadays. She had to try.

Even with her heart pounding and blood rushing in her ears, all Savannah could think was that Edward was going to fuss—and he had every right.

Chapter 28

Thursday evening,
Savannah's home

After she pulled into her carport, Savannah sat in the car for a few minutes taking deep breaths and trying to calm herself. She didn't want to worry Edward with her act of bad judgment, but she had chosen to ignore his advice and the attack had happened. He deserved to know about it.

"Where did you get those cuts?" Edward asked her as soon as she walked into the living room. "What happened?"

Savannah lifted a hand to feel her cheek, and her hand came away spotted with blood. "It must have been the gravel."

"What gravel? Tell me how, luv." Edward motioned for her to follow him down the hallway to the single bathroom. He opened the mirrored medicine cabinet and took out the small first aid kit. "I thought you were only going to talk to some of the local business owners."

"That's exactly right. But just as I was leaving, it occurred to me to see if Samuel was hiding out in his rented room. His situation sounds a little Dickensian to me."

"Good plan, then what?" He pulled out a small tube of cream and a packet of cotton balls and put them on the counter. He grabbed a clean washcloth, wet it in the sink, and lathered up with antibacterial soap.

"Ugh! You know I hate that stuff."

"You might, but I'm going to clean up this little mess. When was your last tetanus shot?"

"Sometime last year after one of my more serious glassblowing burns."

"Okay, that's recent enough." He gently washed her cheek and used her hairdryer to blow her face dry. "Go on. Tell me the rest of the story." He opened the tube of antiseptic cream.

"Ouch!" Savannah yelped. "That stings!"

"Oh, don't be a baby. You're tougher than this. Get on with it."

"I crossed the sidewalk into the adjacent alley and our famous white car came barreling down the street and turned into the little alleyway. The only way to save myself was to scramble onto the hood of the Mini Cooper. That's where I got the peppering of gravel. I scrambled up on the roof as quick as I could."

"As soon as I finish here, you have to call Officer Williams and report this as a threat on your life."

"But . . ."

"No buts. She needs to know what happened.

It's not right to keep information from her that could help the investigation."

"I know, I know!" Savannah could hear herself yelling. She swallowed and dropped her head. "I'm sorry. I'm just embarrassed. After all that blustering that I can manage a simple interview, I blew it big-time."

Edward kissed the top of her head. "It's a wise investigator who learns from her mistakes."

"If I hadn't been keeping up with my tai chi classes, I don't think I would have made the leap so quickly. Those classes saved me."

Even though it was late, and she wanted nothing more than Edward's best comforting embrace, Savannah called in the incident to Officer Williams.

Chapter 29

Savannah sat at the oak desk in the back office, catching up on tax paperwork. She loathed this task, but if she didn't keep her reports up-to-date, the consequences were severe. She could lose her license if she failed to file her taxes on time each month. Luckily, her accountant's operations manager, Stefanie Brinkley, was relentless with timely reminders.

Amanda bustled through the back door. She was wearing a lime-green cold-shoulder blouse paired with white jeans and lime Converse sneakers, although her hair was still a plain color. Savannah was glad to see her cheerful wardrobe choices.

"Guess what?" Amanda announced. "My mom is one hundred percent better. I think she's having one of her miraculous recoveries. She was awesome last night. I haven't seen her act this chatty and engaged in a long time. She still needs to be in hospice, of course, but it was a fantastic evening."

"That is remarkable. I'll be able to come over for a little while tonight and read to her if she's awake."

"Well, she did fall rather deeply asleep just before I left." She fluttered her hands like bird wings. "But here's the good news on the investigation front. Officer Williams has shared her information about Nicole's phone, and I was able to discover her password. Anyone could have figured it out easily anyway, since it uses a variation of Nicole's birthday. I downloaded the folder where she stored the photos she had taken of SNARK's graffiti as well as her own."

"Wonderful." Savannah got out of the office chair. "Use your best judgment to print out the ones that you think show the most diversity in painting techniques. As soon as Phillip arrives with the forged painting, I'm going to have Jacob do a comparison. He has the best chance of spotting telltale patterns that would indicate that SNARK created the painting."

Amanda fired up the color printer with eight examples of SNARK's graffiti. She placed them in a folder and handed them to Savannah.

They heard knocking at the front door. "Oops, sorry, I haven't opened up." Amanda sprinted for the front of Webb's Glass Shop and unlocked the door.

Phillip Borawski stood on the sidewalk with a deep furrow in his brow. "I thought you wanted this painting as soon as possible." He stepped through the doorway. "I thought you open at nine." He looked at the large schoolhouse clock on the wall. "It's nearly half past."

"I'm sorry. I completely forgot to unlock the door. We were working in the back and I lost track of time." Amanda blushed.

Savannah looked at the brown-paper-wrapped package. "Is that the painting?"

"Duh!" Phillip placed it on the checkout counter. "How long do you think you'll need it? I took it off the wall in my uncle's home. We're not sure when he's coming back from the rehabilitation facility, but he gets anxious if he thinks anything has changed while he's gone." Phillip shrugged his shoulders. "It's possible that this time he won't ever return, but so far he's made an unbelievable rebound from each health crisis. He's pretty resilient."

"You told him you were taking the painting?" Amanda frowned. "Is there any chance that it might worry your uncle when he's ill? Some of the oddest things can affect the recovery time of a patient that is under stress. I've had lots of experience lately. My mother is in hospice with lots of ups and downs in the state of her health."

Phillip looked stunned. "That's where things are with Uncle Bert. I never thought of what might affect his health. He's always ill. But I guess I could have kept it from him." He turned pale. "You don't think this would make him worse, do you?"

"I don't know your uncle, but my mother in hospice gets all sorts of weird notions."

He nodded. "I'll be more careful in the future."

"We'll need the painting for at least all of today

and possibly tomorrow. If we discover something, I'll have to turn it over as evidence to Officer Williams."

"That seems a very long time. What gives?"

"I'm not sure how long Jacob will need to analyze the painting to his satisfaction. He won't know either." She tucked the painting under her arm. "But I'll take this over to Jacob right away so that he can get started."

"Fine, give me a call when he's done."

Phillip left, leaving behind a sense of relief.

"What on earth is he so annoyed about?" asked Amanda. "We're only trying to help solve Nicole's murder."

Savannah shrugged her shoulders and went out toward the back. "He might just be impatient. We don't know him." She placed the painting and the folder of graffiti in the back of the Mini. She got in and stared into the rearview mirror at the scratches that her leap the previous night had caused. It reminded her to be careful more effectively than Edward's warnings. It took only a few minutes to drive to Webb's Studio.

She placed the wrapped painting on the small end of the long wooden table in the conference room at the studio. She positioned the folder of graffiti images beside the painting.

Jacob appeared at her elbow and he adjusted the folder to align perfectly square next to the painting. Service beagle Suzy stood at attention beside Jacob. She was on full alert to any change in his emotional state.

"Jacob, I want you to study this painting and compare it to the pictures in the folders. The images are from Nicole's cloud storage and might give us some ideas to go further in our search for her murderer. That said, you have all the time you need to perform a thorough comparison. I'm not going to tell you what I suspect because I want your objective assessment. When you're finished, write down your conclusions then send me a text. I'll come over and get them."

He turned to look straight into her eyes and made a tiny nod to acknowledge that he understood.

A shiver rolled down Savannah's spine. Jacob had never, ever, ever made direct eye contact before he witnessed Nicole's hit-and-run. He had always looked at a spot near the center of her forehead.

In the end, Nicole's accident had already affected Jacob. When his speech and memory returned, Savannah considered that some changes might be permanent. She hoped those changes would be for the better, but there was an equal chance that he would have more trouble interacting with others. She shook that thought out of her mind.

"I've got one more task for you, if you feel up to it."

Jacob tilted his head to the side.

"I need to know how Nicole's family established themselves as pioneers here in Pinellas County. Hopefully, you can visit your friend at the main library and have her scour the records for information on those early days."

His eyes narrowed, and he continued to look her in the eye.

"Okay, Jacob." She bent and started to give Suzy a little scratch on the top of her head, but quickly withdrew. It was a no-no while a service animal was on duty. "Sorry. Anyway, I've got to get back and teach the flameworking class. Remember, text me before you go home—even if you haven't finished your analysis."

By the time Savannah ate her packed peanut butter sandwich, followed by one of Edward's cranberry scones, she had completed the required tax forms for this month. She confirmed that the calendar reminder was on the right day for next month and started toward the flameworking classroom.

She heard the bell ring. "Hi, ladies."

The Rosenberg twins entered wearing a combination of teal and hot pink that shouldn't have worked on the octogenarians, but they absolutely rocked it. Savannah felt her eyebrows try to park in her hairline. "Can you help me for a few minutes? I'm running behind. Can you empty the kiln and put each student's beads at their workstation?"

"Not a chance," said Rachel.

"We're not staff," said Faith.

They hooked their arms together and stood like a two-person protest march.

Savannah gasped. *Have I been so rude that these gentle women have taken offense?*

"I'm so sorry." She placed a hand over her heart. "I didn't mean to—"

Rachel and Faith leaned back and roared peals of laughter. "Gotcha," they said in perfect unison.

Savannah sighed heavily in joyous frustration. The twins were more support to her than they could ever imagine. With their advanced age came an instinct for lightening the emotional load for the friends around them.

I'm lucky to have such friends. And Edward. And Amanda. And Jacob with Suzy. And Joy. And Rooney. And Snowy. What a wonderful family.

She finished her setup chores while Rachel and Faith distributed the beads from the kiln. By that time, the remaining students were present, and Savannah started the class.

She held up a bead that combined two colors side by side. "This is the first bead we're going to make today." She handed the bead to Myla Kay, who again examined it in slow motion before she passed it down the row.

"After we master that one, we'll tackle another one that is a little more complicated." She held up a lime-green bead with purple stripes and orange protruding nodules. She handed it to Herbert. "I'll expect you to make at least three of these."

Herbert inhaled a deep breath and then studied the bead carefully. Savannah thought she could see his mental wheels spinning—already planning on how to make it.

When the beads had been returned to her, she held up a bead that had a wide, bright red base, two narrow strips of white, and a ring of small black dots that protruded from the surface like tiny octopus tentacles. "This is our master bead. Once you've made a bead like this, it indicates that you have mastered all the skills necessary for flameworking beads."

Myla Kay raised her hand. "What if I can't manage to make that last bead? Will I get a failing grade?"

Savannah chuckled and shook her head. "No one fails this class. The whole purpose of this workshop is for you to determine if this is something you want to pursue. It's an introduction to the various techniques, not a master class. It takes a lot of hours in front of this frightening flame here to get good at making beads. By the end of today, for each of you, that decision will be clear."

Herbert laughed. "I love this."

Savannah pointed to the box of glass rods. "Okay, everyone. Pick out enough colors for your beads, then punty them up for the first bead."

It was a cheerful class with everyone caught up in bead colors, spinning the mandrels so that the beads lay even, and making dots and stripes for at least three beads each. Herbert made about a dozen, more than enough for a small necklace.

At the end of the session, Savannah took a picture of the entire class holding their beads on mandrels. She made sure each student understood that they could pick up their beads tomorrow, any time after one in the afternoon. She explained that by using the slow cooldown, their beads would have less chance of cracking.

Savannah plastered her customer smile on her face until each student left. She was exhausted. This class was a reminder that she frequently took on more than she could manage. Six students required too much hands-on assistance for one instructor. She knew she needed an assistant instructor, but she envisioned continuing as principle instructor.

The new teaching structure would pay out if she expanded the class to eight or even ten students. Still, not a huge profit, but if each workshop introduced flameworking to a new hobbyist, that would be wonderful. A new hobbyist who would purchase their materials from Webb's Glass Shop.

After performing all the tasks for clearing out the classroom and closing the shop, Savannah nearly collapsed into the oak chair in the office. The chair squeaked at a screaming pitch.

"Sorry," said Savannah. She paused for a second, then sighed. "Great—I'm so tired, I'm apologizing to a chair."

Her phone pinged. It was a text from Jacob.

FINISHED ANALYSIS
She replied: **DID YOU FIND ANYTHING?**
He replied **YES**
I'LL BE RIGHT OVER.

Now fully awake, Savannah plowed through her remaining tasks and closed up the shop. She hopped into her Mini and in five minutes walked into the conference room at Webb's Studio.

Jacob sat in his usual chair at the far end of the conference table with Suzy in his lap. A slight smile played on his lips. The graffiti pictures had been spread out on the conference table in an exact grid. On the other side of the painting was a ruled tablet with pages and pages of writing.

"What did you find?"

Jacob pointed to the tablet. He picked up his phone and showed it to her, then started typing away.

Her phone pinged for each message.

MULTIPLE ARTIFACTS

"Point them out to me," said Savannah. Jacob pointed to a small flower in the upper right-hand corner of the painting. Then he pointed to a bright red bird in the lower left-hand corner.

ALSO IN GRAFFITI

Jacob pointed to an identical flower and an identical bird in one of SNARK's larger mural paintings.

USED MANY TIMES.

Jacob flipped through a stack of SNARK's graffiti images and pointed out many variations of both flowers and birds.

SAME ARTIST DID BOTH.

Savannah picked up the ruled tablet and began to read the detailed analysis. If Jacob hadn't discovered his talent for glass, he would have made the best art investigator ever. His eye was incredible. After she scanned the analysis, she gave a thumbs-up to Jacob.

Next to the ruled tablet was a stack of books that did not have binder labels to indicate that they were from the library. Each book had more than half a dozen bookmarks in it.

"Jacob, how did you get these?"

He reached for his phone.

LIBRARIAN HAS PRIVATE COLLECTION

Savannah raised her eyebrows. "She gave these to you from her personal library?"

ON LOAN UNTIL TOMORROW

"Thanks. I'll have them back, no problem." She gathered them up, along with the ruled tablet. "I'll see what comes from your research. Thank you, Jacob. I have no clue how this might be connected to Nicole's murder. In fact, it could be totally unrelated, but we need all the information we can get." She smiled brightly. "Let's close up shop here and I'll drive you home."

He deliberately looked her in the eyes and grinned from ear to ear.

Chapter 30

Detective Parker and Officer Williams stood before the whiteboard in their temporary staging room for the murder room. A single whiteboard had been delivered to Detective Parker. He rolled it into an empty cubicle near Officer Williams's open-plan office. He had researched the personnel records to determine who was on vacation and appropriated use of that office.

"I thought you had found another whiteboard and had your eye on a corkboard," said Officer Williams.

"I did. It appears that other clever officers have cottoned on to this trick. This was the only one I could get."

A picture of Nicole's smiling face was at the center top of the first whiteboard. Beneath Nicole's image was a printed copy of the trust fund that their uncle had written up to protect Nicole's share of his fortune. In the same row on the far left was a picture of her parents, her brother Phillip, and next to him her brother Alan. To the far right was a picture of her wife, Elizabeth, and next to her was a social media picture of the graffiti artist SNARK, the face shrouded by a black hoodie.

Officer Williams shuffled the second row of pictures over to the right to add a picture of Samuel Joven.

"Who's that?" asked Detective Parker.

"He's a server who works part time at Queen's Head Pub. I ran a background check, but he has no priors. While I was getting an update from Savannah, Edward, and Amanda, this guy dropped a tray of glasses and ran out the back door. He was driving a white car."

"That's not particularly suspicious. There are masses of white cars."

"According to Savannah, he's skipped town. She went to his apartment to follow up on why he fled the restaurant. It appears that he left without collecting his security deposit, not to mention his wages."

"Still not overly suspicious. Honestly, he could be undocumented and nervous around police—not a thing to do with Nicole."

"Savannah called me last night and said that a white car tried to run her down while she was leaving Samuel's apartment building."

"Now, that might be something. Did you add that to the case file?"

"I tried. I got half done and the server kicked

me off and wouldn't accept my password. I've applied for a new password through the IT department, but I rather think they're a little busy."

"I would hope so."

Standing back from the whiteboard, Detective Parker folded his arms across his chest. He stared at the board. "The two most promising leads are still with Nicole's wife and possibly her brother Alan. Alan has that rescue farm that is failing. Have you confirmed an alibi?"

"Not for Alan, but I've verified that Phillip was at home in Zephyrhills. His phone recorded his location when he received the call from Elizabeth about the accident. Also, Savannah says that he's been helping her obtain a forged painting from Nicole's uncle that may be relevant to the case."

"How is a forgery pertinent?"

Officer Williams paused a moment. "I'm not quite sure, but Savannah insists that it is a significant lead."

Detective Parker removed Phillip's picture. "Trust Savannah to stretch her authority as a consultant into the thinnest thread possible."

"But she's proved herself useful in the past."

Detective Parker turned to Officer Williams. "I'm concerned about the hit-and-run. Her curiosity and knowledge may be causing the killer to feel threatened. Warn her to keep her nose out of the investigation side of the business."

Officer Williams rolled her eyes. "I'll repeat my memorized warning to Savannah the next time I see her."

"What's new on this SNARK character?"

"Savannah has tracked down a correlation between a little-known forged masterpiece that Nicole gave to her uncle, and some contemporary murals. The murals are by SNARK. She's letting Jacob take a closer look at both the murals and the painting. She says he has several pages of notes that indicate that SNARK is the forger."

"That's promising. Any progress on identifying SNARK?"

"None. It seems unbelievable that he could remain unidentified. It not like he's an international spy—or double agent. He could be keeping his identity a secret out of habit, or to generate an air of mystery. There are precedents, however, of famous graffiti artists who just plain don't want to be known."

Chapter 31

Friday evening,
Queen's Head Pub

After feeding Rooney and Snowy, Savannah skipped her evening run and returned to the pub to help Edward with the last Friday night of the Best Burger in the Burg competition. It was one of the busiest nights. Traditionally, the very busiest night was always the last day of the contest, which would be tomorrow. But tonight's crowd threatened to break all prior records.

Savannah wore a Queen's Head Pub polo shirt and a long black apron over her jeans. She was helping to cut down the time required to serve the burger orders by staging the cheese, bacon, raspberry sauce, lettuce, tomato, and fried eggs. Edward was working the grill. The regular chef was preparing the remaining standard menu dishes.

Now Savannah remembered why she had avoided

food service jobs while she was in high school. She hated the repetitive preparation tasks that were absolutely mandatory if one expected a signature dish to taste exactly the same every day. It was different for a dish on the daily special menu. That one could end up however the chef felt like doing it, using whatever ingredients were handy. It was vital that the burger recipe be prepared the same way every time. She could see how some felt the mind-numbing drudgery to be soothing—an antidote for the constant demands of a stressful life—but not for her. For her, it was torture.

Out of the corner of her eye, she saw Samuel walk in the back door, go straight to his locker, and put his backpack away. He put on an apron and headed to the prep table and started chopping the red onions that were obviously running low.

"Samuel!" Savannah turned to face him. "What are you doing?"

He frowned and gave her a *what gives* look. "I'm chopping onions."

Edward came in from the dining room. "Samuel! What are you doing?"

Samuel gave Edward the same *what gives* look. "I'm chopping onions. What's the big deal?"

Edward puffed out his cheeks and threw his hands up in the air. "You did what every bar owner despises! You left in the middle of service last night without a word."

Edward was within a foot of Samuel when Savannah stepped between them and Edward crashed into her, knocking both her and Samuel into the stainless-steel prep table. The containers of condiments and chopped salad vegetables tottered like little drunks, then spilled onto the floor. That little distraction allowed Edward to regain his composure.

"Calm down, both of you," whisper-shouted Savannah. "You're going to scare away the customers."

That worked instantly with Edward. "Right, sorry." He pointed a finger at Samuel's chest. "Where have you been? You know this is our biggest week of the year. Why did you leave your station and then your apartment?"

Samuel held both hands palms-out in front of his chest. "I know. I know. Let me explain."

"Hurry!" said Edward. "There's a ravenous crowd out there."

"Fine," said Samuel. "I got a call from a friend at my apartment house that my landlord was furious with me. My rent check bounced. He threatened to confiscate what little I own out of my room. Then he threatened that he was going to call the police."

"For a bounced check?" Savannah's eyebrows raised.

Samuel studied the floor. "It wasn't the first time, and I knew my deposit would cover everything, but I couldn't afford to lose my stuff. I left here, packed up my stuff, and left the suitcase with my friend."

Edward put his hands on his hips. "Everything you own fits in a suitcase?"

"Yes."

But you could have told me what was going on. It was leaving without saying anything that stings."

"I'm sorry. That's why I came back. I know you need the help and I thought you might forgive me. Besides, I didn't know if you would find out that Nicole had given me a warning."

"She threatened to fire you?"

"Yes, but she didn't. I thought she might after she caught me panhandling for rent money near here. It's a last resort when I haven't made enough money at my part-time jobs. I hate it. But it works."

"But she didn't say anything to me," said Edward.

"I didn't know that. As far as I knew, she was going to tell you after the burger contest was over. She kept looking at me and pressing her finger to her lips. It was a threat to be quiet."

"She wouldn't have fired you," said Savannah. "She liked to help people with their problems. She's sent more than one of the staff here to rehab centers. If they weren't insured, she would pay."

Edward's mouth dropped. "I didn't know she was doing that."

"That was her thing. Earlier this year, I found her out behind the dumpster talking to one of the homeless guys. I overheard her telling him where to meet up with a social worker that she knew. He ended up in rehab and went back to his family. I kept her secret." Savannah stared at her feet. "She was complicated."

"No kidding?" said Samuel. "She was trying to help me—not turn me in?"

"Yes," said Edward. "That was perfectly Nicole."

"Okay." Samuel looked from Edward to Savannah and back. "She was helping Myla Kay somehow."

Savannah tilted her head. "My student?"

"Yes, she told her she needed to sign up for the class."

Savannah and Edward looked at each other in disbelief.

"Why would she do that?" Savannah frowned.

Edward frowned in the exact same way. "It makes no sense. There's got to be something more to this. Anything else?"

"Just one more thing." Samuel's voice dropped to a whisper. "That's who Nicole was meeting out in the street when she was killed."

"Why didn't you tell anyone?" asked Savannah.

"Because I didn't want to call attention to myself. Just because I'm here legally doesn't mean that I'm free of harassment. I work hard to stay out of the notice of the authorities." He looked from Savannah to Edward then back to Savannah. "What now?"

Edward and Savannah both shrugged their shoulders.

Edward turned to Samuel. "We're going to do what Nicole would have done. You've got a full-time job with us on the condition that you stay out of trouble. I want you to apply for US citizenship. I will sponsor your application. That will help."

Samuel looked at his shoes for a long moment. "That's a hard one for me."

"I know. That's why I'm asking for that as an employment condition. It's important that you start the process before things change."

Samuel whispered, "Yes."

"Yes, what?" asked Savannah.

Samuel nodded. "Yes, I'll apply for citizenship." He looked up. "Thanks." He fetched the broom and dustpan and cleaned up the condiment debris. In a few deft moves, he had resupplied and the prep station was ready to go.

Just then, Savannah's phone rang. She quickly wiped her hands on her apron and pulled the phone out of her back pocket. It was Amanda. Savannah slipped out the back door so she could hear.

"Hi, Amanda. What's up?"

"Oh, Savannah. I need you. Mom is much worse. It looks like she'll pass away tonight."

"What? But you said she had a terrific day yesterday. She was as bright and cheerful as ever. What happened?"

"The hospice counselor said that it happens this way quite often. She said that there is usually a big rally right before the end. They use all their strength to have a final perfect day. I need you. I can't do this by myself."

"You're not alone. I'm so sorry. I'll be right there."

She went back inside. "Edward, I just got a call from Amanda. It looks like her mother is in her last few hours. I—"

"You need to be there with Amanda," he said.

"But what about all this?" She waved a hand to the frenzy in the kitchen.

Edward grabbed her by the shoulders. "This is just burgers. It's only a meal. Besides, Samuel's back. He might be a mess, and his judgment appears questionable, but he's great in the kitchen. Go to Amanda. That's where you need to be right now."

Savannah pulled her apron over her head and

threw it in the kitchen's laundry basket, then drove over to the hospice center. She made her way to Mrs. Blake's room and entered the dimly lit interior. Soft music played in the background and Savannah found Amanda holding her mother's hand in both of hers. Amanda looked up through red-rimmed eyes. "She's slipping away."

"I'm so sorry, Amanda." Savannah went around the bed and pulled Amanda up into her arms. As soon as Savannah folded her into a warm hug, Amanda sobbed like a child. "I can't let her go. She's all I have."

"I know. I know." Savannah released Amanda and pulled a chair right beside Amanda's. "This is hard, but you have so many good friends."

Amanda took a tissue from the box sitting on the bedside table. The only other item on the table was a picture of Amanda laughing, in full rainbow mohawk. It was her mother's favorite. After a hearty blow and wipe, Amanda stood and tossed the used tissue into the practically full wastebasket. Then she straightened her mother's pillow, which had a hand-crocheted lace trim, and tucked in the soft pink quilt in a stunning wedding-ring pattern.

"She had me bring these from home yesterday. Honestly, you wouldn't believe how energetic she was. She made sure I understood which dress she wanted to be buried in and where all her important papers were filed. She even told me to take the afternoon to catch up on my chores." Amanda looked at her mother's placid face. "It's like she wanted to go without me in the room."

"That's certainly a possibility." Savannah kept her voice low and measured.

There was a soft tap on the door and a hospice nurse slipped into the room. "Hello, Amanda. Is this the friend you called?"

"Yes." Amanda stood without releasing her mother's hand. "This is Savannah Webb. She owns the glass shop where I work. She's been good enough to let me off most afternoons since Mom came here."

The nurse looked at Savannah. "I'm so happy you're here to be with Amanda and her dear mother." She leaned over Mrs. Blake and checked her pulse, holding her wrist while looking at her plain silver wristwatch. She nodded slowly. "Indications are that these are Mrs. Blake's last hours, if not minutes. Now that your friend has arrived, I expect that it won't be long."

Amanda sat and put her mother's hand to her lips. "What do you mean?"

The nurse put her hands behind her back and leaned against the wall as if she had all the time in the world to spend with Mrs. Blake. "That is one of several scenarios that we've seen with parents who are leaving their unmarried children. One scenario is that they'll slip away while their child is out of the building."

"That's why she sent me to do my chores yesterday." Amanda got another tissue.

The nurse stroked her chin. "Yes, I think that could have been the reason. Another scenario we see is that they'll wait until someone comes to support their loved one. At that point, they'll leave. I have a feeling Mrs. Blake was waiting for your friend to arrive."

Amanda grabbed a tissue and blotted her eyes. "Can you tell if she's in pain?"

"She's resting easy and completely pain-free. It would be helpful if you told her how much you love her and what a good job she's done raising such a confident young woman." She waved a hand to Savannah. "You, too. Tell her that you will look out for her daughter."

The nurse left the room without making a sound.

Amanda turned her tear-filled eyes to Savannah. "I'm not ready."

Savannah inhaled a deep breath. "This is where you need to be brave for your mom. She is ready. You must tell her that she can go. You must thank her for loving you. You must tell her that you will be fine."

Amanda took another tissue, wiped her eyes and blew her nose. She stood and gathered up her mother's frail and mottled hand. "Mom, I want to thank you for giving me a strong sense of right and wrong. I want to thank you for instilling a moral compass so strong that I'll never get lost. I want to thank you for teaching me by example the importance"—her voice broke and she swallowed quickly—"of being true to my spirit."

Amanda stopped and kissed her mother on the cheek. "Thank you for being my mom. I will love you forever."

Savannah stood by Amanda and put one arm around her shoulders. They stood as Mrs. Blake's breaths came softer and slower and softer and slower. Finally, no more breaths came, and the soft pink of her skin drained away to a chalky dust.

Chapter 32

Saturday morning,
Webb's Glass Shop

Drained, Savannah barely managed to stumble through her morning routine to open Webb's Glass Shop for her students to pick up their glass beads. As usual, the first to arrive were the Rosenberg twins. They were wearing a soothing palette of dove gray, from their oversized silk shirts down to ballet slippers. It was the perfect note for a somber morning.

"We heard about Amanda's mother," said Rachel.

"We sent a substantial donation in Mrs. Blake's name to Suncoast Hospice," said Faith.

"I know Amanda will appreciate that." Savannah placed their beads in separate jewelry presentation boxes. "I hope you can come to our house next Saturday for her Celebration of Life ceremony.

Amanda is attending her mother's cremation this morning."

"Alone?" said Rachel.

"All by herself?" said Faith.

"That's the way she and her mother planned it."

The twins looked at each other. "Of course, we plan to be there on Sunday," said Rachel.

"We'll send flowers to your house. We already know your colors," said Faith.

"You don't have to do that." Savannah frowned. "Edward and I can manage. Budgets are always tight with small business, but we're doing fine."

"Agreed, sweetie," said Rachel. "We're not doing it for that—"

"—reason," said Faith. "We know how busy you are. We love picking out flower arrangements. We'll have our caterer friend drop by a few dishes for nibbling as well. You two don't have the time."

Rachel patted Savannah on the arm. "It's our way of honoring a properly old-fashioned lady. Don't resist. Mrs. Blake would agree with our wishes."

Savannah could see that they would not bend, and it would be a great help to her and Edward for them to organize the memorial.

"It would be wonderful. I accept."

Several hours later, Herbert walked in. "Hi, I'm here to pick up my finished beads. Are they ready?"

"Sure, everything's ready." She placed the beautiful beads in his hands. "Have you decided to accept my offer to work here?"

Herbert shrugged his shoulders. "I'm still thinking. Although the thought of more students isn't what I would have predicted after so many years, I'm surprised at how much I miss the excitement."

"No pressure, Herbert. I'm doing fine, but you seem like a natural."

"I also miss the reward." He reached into his back pocket and handed her his employment application. "I'm in."

Savannah felt tension melt away that she didn't realize she was holding. The next class would be so much easier with an assistant. Not only that, she would be able to spend more time with Edward. They needed more time together.

After Lonnie and Patricia had picked up their beads, Savannah turned to the painting and the notes that Jacob had written comparing it to Nicole's phone images of SNARK's graffiti and murals.

Sorting through the printed pages, she saw that he had written that the strongest link appeared to be a stylistic treatment of the eyes. In the painting, the glint painted in each eye was asymmetrical. This effect added to the realism of the portrayal but was not a common technique of the original forger.

The doorbell jangled and Myla Kay walked up and leaned over the table. "What's this?"

Savannah shrugged. "It's a special project I've given to Jacob. He's working through some health issues and he's a particularly sharp analyst." Savannah turned his notes facedown on the workbench. "I hoped this would be a great distraction."

Myla Kay rubbed her hands together. "Are my beads ready? I want to string them up today. They're a present I'm giving to me."

In no time the beads, a length of rawhide, and a clasp were wrapped up for Myla Kay to take with her.

Savannah returned to the graffiti images and confirmed that Jacob's assessment was correct. The glint in the portrait's eyes mimicked the exaggerated images in SNARK's murals and graffiti. He also mentioned a tendency to include small elements of bright high-contrast color pairs.

She flipped through the notes again. There was a doodle in the margin. Jacob had drawn a small car.

He saw the car that hit Nicole!

That drawing might be the resolution to the case. She called Jacob's mother.

"Frances, Jacob sketched a car on one of his analysis notes. Some part of him must remember the car that hit Nicole. Do you think the reason he doesn't want to come over to Webb's Glass Shop is because it's where he saw the accident?"

There was a moment of silence.

"So, it's possible he saw the license plate," Frances replied in a low, pensive voice. "I've talked to his therapist about a reenactment to unblock Jacob's speech, but as a therapist, he's incredibly conservative and he's unwilling to agree. But he also thinks it might work—irritating man."

"What do you want to do?"

"Jacob is much stronger than he appears. Let me just ask him." The phone went silent for a few seconds. Savannah could hear Frances talking to Jacob, but the words were muffled. She was probably holding the phone against her chest. "As I thought, Jacob is impatient with these additional disabilities. He is so frustrated that he has agreed to go forward with this. I'm going to bring him over. Let's hope this will remove the uncertainty."

"Park in the alley. There's a reserved parking spot back there."

Savannah was as nervous as a newly adopted kitten. She wanted to help Jacob recover his voice and memory but didn't want to be the cause of something worse. She admired Frances for all the times she had to be strong for Jacob's welfare.

In a matter of minutes, there was a knock on the back door. Savannah opened it and Frances entered, followed by Jacob holding Suzy in his arms.

Frances headed for the front of the shop. "Let's do this quickly." She spoke over her shoulder. "It will either work or fail and there's no reason to procrastinate. Follow me, Jacob." She opened the front door and motioned for Jacob to come through.

Jacob's jaw tightened, and he adjusted his hold on Suzy. He trudged through the shop as if he were being dragged to jail. He stood on the exact spot where he had witnessed Nicole's hit-and-run. He stood rock still in absolute silence.

Savannah slipped out the door and stood next to Frances. They glanced at each other. They waited.

Jacob looked at a spot in the road just a few yards in front of him. He adjusted Suzy once more. Savannah felt like her insides were quivering. Would he regress even further? Maybe physical paralysis? His face was pale, and his jaw was clenched rigid, with his lips pressed into a thin line.

Jacob continued to stand in deathly silence. Then he turned to Savannah. "I remember," he said.

Frances grabbed Savannah's arm with the grip

of a power lifter. Savannah heard Frances gasp, then she swallowed and said in a low, calm voice, "What do you remember, Jacob?"

"I saw a white car. It was going too fast. Nicole was crossing the street. It crashed into her." Jacob put Suzy down on the sidewalk next to him. Suzy looked at him intently—her eyes alert. Jacob pointed down the street. "That's where the car turned. It turned right at the very end of this block. It was still going too fast."

Frances released her iron grip on Savannah's arm and made a single step toward Jacob, then stopped. "Did you see the driver?"

"The driver was wearing dark clothes."

Savannah hung her head down. She was over-come with relief that Jacob had regained his speech and memory, but his description brought them no closer to identifying the killer.

Jacob picked up Suzy and stood next to his mother. "The driver sat tall behind the steering wheel. You can't hide your height with a hoodie." He looked at his mother. "I feel much better now. I remember everything."

Frances covered her eyes with both hands and quickly scrubbed away her tears. Her voice was thick with suppressed emotion. "That's very good news, Jacob." She scratched the top of Suzy's head. "Suzy can get some rest now. You've been giving her a worrisome time."

"The license plate was BDR 529."

Savannah speed-dialed Officer Williams.

Chapter 33

"What are you doing here?" Detective Parker stood in front of Officer Williams's spartan desk.

"I know, I know. I adore my lazy mornings at home, but I wanted to trace this license plate that Savannah phoned in. What are *you* doing here to catch me?" She grinned up at Detective Parker. She seldom got a chance to pull his chain, but never let an opportunity go by.

"My office is finally finished."

Officer Williams replied, "Uh-huh," while she typed the number into the Florida Department of Highway Safety and Motor Vehicles database. "The servers seemed to have recovered from the move." She filled in the remaining data and clicked the search button.

"What's the hurry with a license plate?"

"Jacob's memory and speech returned this morning. He saw the hit-and-run and got a glimpse of the car's driver."

Detective Parker folded his arms. "That's huge."

"Yes. He remembers the license number and that the driver wore a dark hoodie."

Detective Parker moved to stand behind Officer Williams and they both stared at the screen as it searched through the Florida database. After a few moments of watching the search wheel spin, the application displayed the details.

Officer Williams leaned back in her chair and looked up at Detective Parker. "That's not what I expected."

Detective Parker bent down and squinted into the screen. "It's an expired plate issued to Nicole Borawski." He stood up straight. "That's a puzzle. Decidedly unhelpful."

"Nicole drove a new red BMW SUV. I've seen it. The hit-and-run car was white. We need to get Jacob to give us more details—which I'm sure he can. Maybe I can reach them."

She phoned Savannah. "Hey, Savannah. Is Jacob still there?"

"Hi, Joy. Yes, he's picking up supplies for the project he's working on. Why?"

"We've checked the plate Jacob remembered and it's issued to Nicole, but it expired about eighteen months ago."

"Really? That's about the same time that Nicole broke the news of her engagement and her family disowned her. That's got to be the junk car her uncle told us that she bought with the last of her savings."

"Is Jacob ready for an interview?"

There was a pause on the line.

"It just happened a few minutes ago. I think tomorrow at the earliest."

Savannah said, "Jacob's mother says not today—perhaps tomorrow."

"Fantastic. Do we know who has the car?"

"Nope, no one mentioned anything about her getting rid of it."

"Okay," said Officer Williams. "One more thing. Does Jacob remember any details that could help—the make or model of the white car?"

"Hang on. I'll ask. He still hates talking on the phone."

Officer Williams could hear that there was a discussion between Savannah and Jacob, but she couldn't make out enough words. She chuckled. It sounded like the adult-speak in the Charlie Brown movies she had seen as a child. She modified her expression, suddenly aware that Detective Parker was looking down at her with a frown. "Patience, sir. Savannah needs to wait for Jacob to reply. Sometimes it can be minutes."

Savannah returned to the phone. "He says that it was an older Toyota Corolla with a baseball-sized rusty dent on the left-hand side of the rear bumper."

"Thanks, that matches the records. Tell Jacob's mother that we'll arrange to interview Jacob at home." They ended their call.

Officer Williams turned back to her computer console and typed into another database query page. "Let's see what happened to that car."

In a few seconds, the screen displayed the information on the car. "Sir, she's still the registered owner. It looks like she kept the car after her uncle set up the trust fund. It could be one of those situations where she feels like she needed a safety net."

Officer Williams's cell phone rang. "It's Savannah." She listened for a few seconds. "Thanks." Officer Williams turned to Detective Parker. "Jacob remembered something peculiar about the driver's hoodie."

"What?"

"Jacob noticed a graffiti-type logo on the sleeve of the hoodie and . . ."

"And?" prompted Detective Parker.

". . . and he saw it as the car turned the corner. The logo said SNARK."

"That's it. SNARK drove the car that killed Nicole," finished Detective Parker. "But, who is SNARK?"

Chapter 34

"What are the police going to do?" asked Edward after Savannah told him about Jacob's recovery.

Savannah sat at the bar. It was too early to open the pub for business, but yesterday had been so busy that Edward hadn't turned in his merchants' orders. Although most vendors would automatically send him the same quantity that he had ordered last week, some vendors would skip him this week and give their stock to other restaurants. Another vital task that Nicole had managed for him.

"Would you make me a cappuccino? I just can't seem to wake up." She propped her chin on her hands over steepled elbows. "The prosecution is going to have a terrible time making a case to find SNARK guilty."

"They haven't identified him yet," Edward said. "Let alone arrested him."

"I think the big problem is that Jacob could be considered an unreliable witness. That's not the reality, of course, but it will take some significant groundwork to educate the jurors about his abilities, not just his disabilities."

She was stopped by the loud whistling of the espresso machine, followed by the steaming of the milk. Edward placed the white porcelain mug in front of her. "Sadly, I agree. Now that we know SNARK ran Nicole down, the problem with Jacob as the only witness really starts to pile up."

After slurping down half her cappuccino, Savannah leaned back and massaged the back of her neck. "Jacob will not testify well. He won't look at anyone. He'll mumble. There will be long pauses while he holds Suzy."

"That will give the prosecutor fits."

"Right. I can hear the prosecutor saying, 'Your star witness goes mute with amnesia whenever he gets upset.' " Savannah stood and downed the rest of her coffee. "This is assuming that the police are able to find SNARK. According to his social media feeds, he has fans who can help him out of town or maybe out of the country."

"They would be happy to help a murderer?"

"How would they know that? He must be an expert at posing as a persecuted graffiti artist."

"There's got to be a way to draw him out into the open. What set of circumstances would entice him to come out of hiding?" Edward took Savannah's cup and automatically started making her another cappuccino.

"SNARK doesn't know that Jacob has identified him as the forger. He's still worried about my investigation activities. How could we take advantage of that?"

Edward placed the cup in front of Savannah. "What about exposing him to the SHINE organization as a forger?"

"That has possibilities. I could take the painting over to their headquarters and make a big show of comparing the markers that Jacob found. I could insist that he be stricken from the competition."

"That wouldn't be out in public," said Edward.

"But if we also got the organization to remove his mural, that scandal would sweep through the graffiti underground like lightning. If we made it known that I would be present, maybe that would draw him out."

"There's a lot of ifs and a fair bit of risk."

"Not if I suggest that Officer Williams needs to be ready to apprehend SNARK."

"Do you think he'll be drawn out?"

"Well, he's already tried to run me over. If I weren't fit, I wouldn't have been able to hop out of his way."

"I'm not happy about the whole drawing-him-out scenario. There are so many things that can go wrong."

"I agree," said Savannah, "but I can't think of anything else that will ensure that Jacob is not the only witness. Even with his mother coaching him, this will be a traumatic experience. What if he turns mute again? We can't risk Jacob."

"Too right," said Edward. "But how?"

Savannah stood and put her hands on her hips. "If he finds out about it, SNARK is going to go after Jacob, no matter what. I would prefer that we control the situation rather than have SNARK stalk Jacob's house. All he would have to do is wait for him to take Suzy for a walk."

Edward inhaled. "That's not good."

"Then there's the fact that Jacob is relatively alone at the studio all day. A perfect target."

"Right. I say we try to get your mural-removal scheme in place as soon as possible. How soon can you make that happen?"

"I can call the organizer later today and let her in on the forgery suspicions and suggest that they act quickly in order to salvage their reputation. All she has to do really is spread the word that the paint-over is scheduled for tomorrow."

"Thanks for that. Today is the last day of the Best Burger in the Burg competition. We're going to be jammed to the gills. In fact, I'm going to ask you for a giant favor."

"Ask away."

"Can you work in the kitchen? Although my temp agency is sending over food service laborers, they don't have enough experienced staff. I'm still going to need everyone I know to pitch in for today. In fact, Amanda called to offer to help, as well as Arthur."

"Of course, I'll help. Will that be enough?"

"I think so. I'm not expecting to win. I only want to survive the onslaught with our service reputation in reasonable shape. Otherwise, I'll be in real trouble with bad reviews. With the loss of the best day-to-day person I'll probably ever have, a lot must change. I don't mind losing the Best Burger in the Burg competition, but I don't want to lose the high ratings that Queen's Head Pub holds as well."

Chapter 35

Saturday,
new police headquarters

"**I**f he's the one who tried to run over Savannah, then he's probably still in town." Officer Williams stood in front of the whiteboard in the borrowed office.

Detective Parker rubbed his palms together. "I'm going to get the chief to boost the priority of our BOLO. Since SNARK is using Nicole's ordinary-looking white car, finding him will be difficult."

"But not impossible."

"I'm going to increase the number of patrol vehicles around the Grand Central District. Since Jacob is the only credible witness to the hit-and-run, we should keep an eye on him when he's out in public."

"What about the eyewitness at the Mustard Seed Inn? He saw the hit-and-run. Should we include looking out for him in our patrol checks?" asked Officer Williams.

"Yes, but nothing he saw can tie anyone to the car. Jacob saw the license plate and the sleeve logo. Without Jacob and the car, there is no case."

Detective Parker left and Officer Williams returned to her desk.

Her cell phone rang. Officer Williams listened carefully while Savannah explained the plan to paint over the mural.

Then Officer Williams yelled into the phone, "Are you crazy? Why am I asking that? Of course, you're crazy."

Savannah interrupted. "Joy, listen for a moment here. We can't let this situation go on. Jacob won't be safe once word gets out that he's an eyewitness. He won't be safe. SNARK has already proved that he's willing to kill. It's unreasonable to ask Jacob to hide until some random event may or may not cause an officer to find the white car."

Joy puffed a breath out her nose. "It's annoying when you're right. In fact, starting now, I'll make sure there's plenty of unmarked cars in the area. The Best Burger in the Burg contest was already on our schedule for increased coverage. I'll make sure that we expand on that with more officers on foot as well."

"What about painting over the mural?"

"I'll bring that up with Detective Parker. I think he's going to object."

"Think about Jacob and Suzy."

"Good point. I'll call Frances to warn her about the new risks. Then, I'll make a strong case for more protection. I promise."

Chapter 36

"We need another burger for table fifteen!" Amanda yelled back into the kitchen.

Savannah turned from the preparation table to Samuel at the grill. "How many does that make so far?"

"More than a hundred," said Samuel.

"And it's only seven o'clock." Savannah grumbled as she started forming more patties. She and Samuel had worked out an efficient workflow to keep up with the busiest day of the Best Burger in the Burg competition. Samuel grilled the buns and patties while Savannah formed the patties, restocked the condiments, and managed the fries.

Samuel looked up from the grill. "Only three more hours. The dinner menu officially closes at ten."

"That seems like years away." Savannah grabbed another handful of ground meat and placed it on the scale for an exact six ounces.

Every table in the pub was filled, as were all the seats at the bar. Edward was behind the bar wishing he had four hands to keep up with the drink orders. As hostess, Amanda was managing to seat new customers. The large patio out front had been converted from casual seating to even more dining space by adding folding tables covered with tablecloths.

Amanda was surprised to see Jacob and his mother approaching the pub from the sidewalk. Suzy was on leash without her service harness, and her tail wagged like a windshield wiper.

Jacob walked up to Amanda. He looked at her left ear, then smiled. "I am here to buy my mother your entry in the Best Burger in the Burg contest. If we like the burger, we will vote."

Amanda looked at his mother.

Francis looked tired, "Jacob insisted and it is easier to go along than risk a relapse. I know there are extra patrols for our safety." She shrugged her shoulders.

"It's so nice to hear your voice, Jacob," said Amanda. "It's a mad house inside that I don't think Suzy would like. Is it all right to sit at a small table here on the patio."

"That will be perfect." Frances patted Amanda tenderly on the arm. "May I offer you my sincere condolences?"

Amanda blinked her eyes and dipped her head a fraction. "Thank you very much."

"I hope you're taking care of yourself. Are you

sure you should be here? This is a large crowd. It's well-known that in the days immediately following the death of a family member, you are especially vulnerable to illness. The shock affects your immune system."

"Thank you, Mrs. Underwood. Helping Edward and Savannah is the only thing that makes me feel human right now. They've been so generous—it's a pleasure to be able to help them when they need a hand."

Amanda blinked hard again and led them to a small temporary table next to the sidewalk. Suzy tucked herself underneath Jacob's chair. "I'll send one of the servers out right away. It may be a few minutes—they're super busy."

Officer Williams drove north on Sixteenth Street. She was only a few blocks from home when the police radio announced that a citizen had seen a white car bearing license plate BDR 529. It had been spotted heading west at the intersection of Eighteenth Street and Central Avenue. Officer Williams called dispatch that she was nearby and on her way to the area.

He's near Haslam's Book Store. That's only a few blocks from Queen's Head Pub. She made a U-turn, then headed for Central Avenue with her lights flashing and blaring a few taps of the siren.

Officer Williams spotted the white car and moved close enough to verify the license plate number. She called for backup and reported the driver to be wearing a black hoodie pulled over his head. She signaled with her siren and lights for the white car to pull over. Officer Williams reported that it looked like the driver would comply but was having difficulty finding somewhere to pull out of traffic.

The driver motioned with one hand out the window, indicating a turn into the parking lot of Haslam's Book Store.

Instead, after idling a few seconds, the driver sped down the alley behind the bookstore and nearly ran down one of the owners, who was feeding the birds behind the store. Officer Williams followed as quickly as the rutted alleyway permitted. The driver turned left at the end of the block to get back onto Central Avenue.

Officer Williams groaned when she cleared the alley. The driver had run the last few seconds of the light and by the time she reached the intersection she screeched to a halt to avoid crashing into a group of pedestrians.

Officer Williams tooted on her siren and the pedestrians stiffened up to look at her, then hurried out of the street. She was now only a few blocks away from Queen's Head Pub. She turned off both her siren and lights and searched the street for the white car.

Amanda sent a server out to the patio and yelled back to Savannah in the kitchen. "Hey, guess what? Jacob is treating his mother to one of our burgers. Make sure it's a good one."

"Jacob? Jacob never eats burgers. What has gotten into him?"

"He's changed since he recovered his voice."

Amanda shrugged her shoulders and returned to the line of customers wanting a table.

Savannah nodded and noticed which server was taking their order. "Samuel. Let me know when you've got their order ready to deliver. I want to take it out myself."

"No problem, the next two are almost ready." Samuel gently flipped over two perfectly charred patties. As soon as they were equally charred on the bottom, he plated the order and yelled over to Savannah. "Jacob's order is ready."

Savannah took the platters and approached Jacob's table. "These are indeed the best burgers in town." She set them down. "Hi, Frances, wonderful that you could stop by."

Frances waved her hand at the packed crowd. "I've never seen this place so busy! How's Edward doing in the competition?"

"Right now he would be delighted to come in in the top five. He hopes to not embarrass himself, but he certainly doesn't expect to win. But, just in case, make sure you vote."

She watched as Jacob stared at the burger intensely, then took his knife and cut it in half. He inhaled a deep breath and took a bite of the burger. He craned his head and widened his eyes. "This is excellent. Edward will win."

Savannah nodded. "I think so, but you'll never get that from Edward."

Edward walked out to their table. "Who, me? Cheers, Jacob. Good to see you." He heard the thumping of a tail underneath Jacob's chair. "And Suzy as well. I hear from the kitchen that you're treating your mom to one of my burgers. I see—"

Suzy barked sharply and poked her head out from under the chair. An instant later they heard the roar of an engine.

Then a siren shrieked to life in front of Queen's Head Pub. The patrol car was inches behind a white car hurtling toward Jacob's table.

Frances screamed, "Jacob! Watch out!"

Savannah screamed, "Move, Jacob!" Then she grabbed Jacob beneath his arms and hurled him away from the speeding car.

In the next slow-motion moment, Savannah felt Edward give her a powerful shove that drove her and Jacob down onto the concrete patio floor. She heard Amanda screaming, "It's Myla Kay! Grab her! Myla Kay is SNARK!"

Then she blacked out.

Chapter 37

The wee hours of Sunday morning,
hospital emergency room

Savannah kept falling asleep, and then waking up because she couldn't move. Each time, Edward's voice would break into her fuzzy thoughts.

"You have to stay awake, luv," he said. "If you get through the next few hours without showing signs of concussion, we can go home."

Savannah wrinkled her brow in concentration. "I'm not home?" She opened her eyes to the bright lights and energetic bustling of doctors, nurses, orderlies, and emergency personnel in the cramped emergency room. "Why can't I move?"

"You're wearing a neck brace. They don't want you to move your head until the results of the CAT scan come back."

"I've been awake before?"

"Yes, which is a good thing, because they won't talk to me. They will only let me sit with you because you have no relatives. I could at least prove that we're engaged and living together. Thanks for badgering me into getting the address changed on my driver's license."

Savannah looked around as much as she could with her limited head movement. "This is the same place where Nicole was brought, isn't it?"

"Yes, luv, but you're going to be fine. You need to stay awake for another couple of hours and they'll let us go."

"Us?"

Edward took her hand and cupped it between his. "You're not in here alone. Never alone."

Savannah exhaled a long *umm.* "You always know exactly how to make me feel wonderful."

"That's my job."

She scooched up a little higher in the bed. "What happened after—"

A nurse pulled the privacy curtain aside with a lively flourish. "Hello, hello! It's time for your vitals check. Let me check your wristband." She examined the printed hospital band on Savannah's left wrist. "Good. What's your name?"

Savannah frowned." Savannah Webb."

"What day is it?"

"Umm, by now, I think Sunday."

"Do you know where you are?"

"Bayside Hospital emergency room."

"Where do you live?"

"St. Petersburg, Florida."

The nurse let a tiny smile escape, then took Savannah's temperature, blood pressure, and pulse. She turned, twitched the privacy curtain back in place, and left the room.

Edward's eyebrows shot up like twin darts. "That was abrupt."

"Has she been asking me questions since I got here?"

"No, this is the first time I've seen her. Your original nurse must be busy elsewhere."

"How many times have they checked me out?"

"This is the third time."

Savannah frowned. "I don't remember the first two."

"Well, you did get quite a knock. They took you away for a CAT scan, but I don't know the results." He cupped her hand again. "I'm not a relative, so they won't tell me what the scan showed."

Savannah tentatively explored the back of her head and found a tender spot.

"Ouch." She smiled up at Edward. "That's going to be tender for a while. What happened to everyone?"

"Well, that's a good sign." He smiled and kissed her hand. "Curiosity has always been your greatest strength. Sadly, also your greatest weakness."

"Come on. Stop stalling." She gingerly lifted herself upright in bed. "Jacob! Is Jacob all right? I remember that I made a grab to pull him out of the path of the white car. Is he hurt? Is Suzy hurt?"

"Calm down. Everyone else is fine. You're the only one who made it here."

Savannah felt a wave of tension leave her shoulders.

Edward continued. "Jacob was the first to recover and he snatched up Suzy, who was howling up a storm just like she did when Nicole was hit. I was the next to get up from the pile and I helped Officer Williams secure SNARK. When I turned back to you, Frances was trying to wake you up. That's when Officer Williams called for the EMTs."

"I don't remember any of that."

"You just wouldn't fully wake up. You seemed to be mumbling in a dream. The EMTs put you in this neck brace and whisked you away to here. I followed them in your Mini."

"What happened to Myla Kay?"

"Also known as SNARK?" Edward tilted his head. "That was a big surprise. It was a miracle that she wasn't killed outright in her attempt to run down Jacob. It turns out she was full of drugs and couldn't even tell Officer Williams who she was."

"Where's Amanda? How is she holding up?"

"She's fine," Edward answered tersely. "You need to stop asking questions and rest. If you keep agitating yourself, we'll never get out of here."

"But what about the Best Burger in the Burg competition? You left the pub on the most popular voting night."

Edward opened his mouth to answer and was interrupted by the sound of the privacy curtain being drawn aside.

A thin, dark young man in blue medical scrubs entered with an electronic device in his hand and a stethoscope draped around his neck. "Savannah Webb?"

"Yes, that's me," said Savannah. "When can I go home?"

The young man smiled and looked even younger. "That's a healthy attitude." He looked at Edward. "Is it okay to share the results?" He then looked at Savannah. "Would you like some privacy?"

"No, Edward is my fiancé. I want him to know if there's a problem."

"Perfect. The news is good. Your CAT scan is clean. There are no fractures in your neck or spine."

Savannah grinned so wide her cheeks nearly cramped. "So, you can take off the neck brace?" She started to reach around to the back of the brace.

"Yes. Hang on." He placed his device on the side table. "Let me help you get that off. Sit up."

Savannah sat forward while the doctor pulled on the Velcro straps and removed the brace. She rolled her neck from side to side. "Oh, wow. That feels wonderful. How much longer do I have to stay?"

"Only two more hours. We need to make sure there's no delayed bleed at the impact site. Stay quiet. Stay in bed. Two more interviews by one of the floor nurses and I'll release you."

He picked up his device and turned to Edward. "Make sure you watch her closely for the next day or so. They'll tell you what to look for when they release her."

Edward stood to shake the doctor's hand and yelped when his left foot bore his full weight. He stumbled into the doctor's midsection and they both tumbled onto the cold tile floor.

The doctor recovered quickly and helped Edward hop back into the chair without using his left leg. "So, when were you going to let somebody know that you injured yourself?"

"It didn't seem to be so bad. Until now."

"Right. Let's get you checked in and examine that foot. It may be broken."

Chapter 38

The scent of flowers reached the guests before they even stepped on the porch. The Rosenberg twins had run amok at the florists and huge bouquets covered every flat surface inside and outside the bungalow.

Beside the propped-open screen door was a small book stand with an album for guests to jot down a few words on how they knew Amanda's mother. There was a line awaiting their turn to sign the guest book, but no one was the least bit impatient.

When the guests moved into Savannah's living room, they met Amanda dressed in all white with a flowing skirt topped with white tulle. Savannah hadn't known that Amanda owned a skirt before today. The gauzy confection set the joyous mood.

Amanda had bleached her hair white and had placed a stripe of mourning black across her forehead. The Rosenberg twins stood on each side of her in support and had chosen to wear soft lavender. There was a reunion of sorts, with people calling out to friends that they hadn't seen in months or years.

The atmosphere was joyous, with laughter and smiles along with the occasional emotional memory that produced a flurry of tissues. Savannah was grateful that Amanda had agreed to postpone the memorial for a week. Edward's injured leg had turned all their plans upside down, but Samuel had saved the day by convincing two friends from his previous part-time jobs to fill in the gaps. With him stepping in to manage Queen's Head Pub, everything had fallen back into a comfortable rhythm.

As guests moved into the kitchen, they were greeted with an assortment of finger foods. There were sliders made with various meats, cubes of cheese, a huge assortment of crackers, flatbread mini pizzas, a giant bowl of fresh berries, and potato chips with dipping sauces. The dessert tray held bite-sized portions of pecan pie, eclairs, tarts, and custard pudding. Everyone was wandering around with plates of food accompanied by Bloody Mary, mimosa, and screwdriver cocktails, espresso, or sparkling, mineral, or plain water. There must have been over a hundred guests.

Edward was resting comfortably in his recliner with his booted and braced leg propped on a bed pillow. Savannah had covered it with a childhood treasure—her purple Winnie the Pooh with Eeyore pillow slip. Edward had responded by asking Jacob to place purple Wolverine stickers all over his recovery boot. All perfectly aligned, of course.

Elizabeth and Phillip both dropped in to pay their respects. "Nicole's family have ended their feud with us," said Elizabeth. "They have opened their hearts to nontraditional families. I'm very happy because I'm pregnant." She rubbed her little baby bump.

Phillip smiled broadly. "It's going to be wonderful that I get to be an uncle."

"We had been trying to conceive for months, but my eggs weren't good enough." She rubbed her tummy again. "Nicole's worked the very first time."

Officer Williams stopped by to express her condolences to Amanda. "I'm so sorry I didn't get a chance to meet her. From knowing you, I can tell she was a magnificent woman. You really can't have too many strong women in your life." Joy looked over at Savannah and the Rosenberg twins. "Take advantage of them."

"Joy!" Savannah approached and gave her a big hug. "Thanks for coming. We're a little overwhelmed. Let me get you a chair next to Edward and we'll try to talk."

Savannah moved a chair beside Edward and motioned for Joy to take a seat. Savannah perched on the arm of Edward's lounger so that he was bookended by them.

He looked from one to the other. "Trapped, I see."

Savannah leaned over and kissed him on the cheek. "Loving it, I see."

"How's the leg?" asked Joy.

"It's going to be out of this boot by the end of next week. I still have to keep it elevated as much as I can, but the pain is better each day."

Savannah leaned forward. "What's the status of SNARK's case?"

"Well, she's in the county jail awaiting trial. She confessed outright to the hit-and-run. Apparently, she was under the influence of some powerful opioids and when she saw Nicole, she swerved into her. Nicole apparently was one of the few people who had discovered her true identity and it sent her into a fugue. She hadn't been thinking clearly for quite some time and her attachment to reality was paper thin. I think it was a tragic combination of deep anger and then a sudden opportunity."

"What's next? She tried to kill Jacob."

Officer Williams shrugged. "With only the single witness, it looks like she thought it could be contained. She'll be charged with both attacks. But she seems to have turned a moral corner. She's in a voluntary rehab program and apparently is expressing deep remorse."

"That doesn't help Nicole's family," said Edward.

"No, but while she's awaiting trial, she's started to teach a traditional drawing class for inmates who are also recovering from drug abuse. Her class is so popular that they've had to move it to the cafeteria to accommodate the number of students."

"I hope this isn't an act to win sympathy from the authorities," said Savannah.

"I don't really think it is," Officer Williams responded. "I know I haven't had that much experience with criminals and their prevarications, but she seems truly remorseful."

At sundown the memorial moved outside to the backyard, where the guests related their favorite memories of Mrs. Blake. The closing performance was Amanda reading her mother's favorite passage from Tim Dorsey's *The Pope of Palm Beach*. When she thanked everyone for helping her to celebrate her mother's wonderful life, there wasn't a dry eye in the place.

Within the next half hour, the only remaining guests consisted of Savannah's and Edward's closest friends: Amanda, Jacob, Rachel, Faith, Frances, and Joy.

Edward stood, with Savannah's help, and pointed to a tray of filled champagne flutes. "Please take a glass for a toast. We have an announcement."

There was a murmur of excitement while Amanda took the tray and made sure that Jacob got the glass of sparkling water.

Edward wrapped his arm around Savannah's waist. "We wanted you to be the first to know that we've decided how to celebrate our wedding with both our UK and US friends and family." He beamed at Savannah.

She beamed back. "We're having a formal wedding at Edward's ancestral church in the village of Saint Albans in England on Boxing Day, the day after Christmas. All of you are invited to the service, though of course we understand if you can't make it across the Atlantic."

"Then we're taking our honeymoon right here in downtown St. Petersburg at the historic Vinoy hotel," said Edward. "It appears that they still adore the plate chargers that Savannah made them for their formal events. Huge discount!"

Everyone oohed and aahed. Except Amanda. She flushed pink with concern. She bolted out of her seat. "What about a wedding dress? You can't have one made before the wedding—it takes six months to have one made."

Savannah tilted her head toward Edward. "I had a look in the attic among my mother's things." She paused. "I'm going to wear my mother's wedding dress. It's almost a flawless fit and the preservation process has kept the dress in wonderful condition."

"It will be perfect." Amanda beamed.

Savannah continued. "Then after we return, we're having a reception for friends, Webb's Glass Shop students, and loyal patrons of Queen's Head Pub. We're going to have a celebration tent in the parking lot between the two businesses. The date for the reception is the second Saturday of the New Year."

Edward nodded toward Jacob.

Jacob put Suzy down beside him, reached into his pocket and pulled out an index card. He cleared his throat and read.

"When Edward asked me to give the wedding announcement speech, at first I refused." He looked over the card directly at Edward. "But then I remembered—he has no friends! He's always in the kitchen."

For a moment everyone held their breath. Then Jacob cracked a smile, and a wave of laughter sped through the crowd.

Edward's and Savannah's eyes met. They shared a twinkling gaze—Jacob had successfully told his first joke.

"He has found his best friend, his true partner, his forever love in Savannah. Savannah has found her best friend, her true partner, her forever love in Edward. Raise your glasses with me to wish them a long and happy marriage."

CAST OF CHARACTERS

Savannah Webb	Protagonist. Owner of Webb's Glass Shop.
Edward Morris	Savannah's boyfriend. Owner of Queen's Head Pub.
Amanda Blake	Office manager of Webb's Glass Shop.
Jacob Underwood	Apprentice at Webb's Studio.
Judge Frances Underwood	Jacob's mother.
Suzy	Jacob's service dog.
Rooney	Savannah Webb's young dog.
Snowy	Edward's kitten.
Nicole Borawski	Manager of Queen's Head.
Elizabeth Hartford	Nicole's wife.
Phillip Borawski	Nicole's brother.
Alan Borawski	Nicole's brother.
Rachel Rosenberg	Glass student. Faith's twin.
Faith Rosenberg	Glass student. Rachel's twin.
Myla Katherine Nedra	Student #1.
Lonnie McCarthy	Student #2.
Patricia Karn	Student #3.
Herbert Klug	Student #4.
Viola Blake	Amanda's mother.
Charlotte Gray	Coroner.
Samuel Joven	Part-time prep cook.
Deloris Borawski	Nicole's mother.

Thomas Borawski	Nicole's father.
Uncle Bert	Nicole's uncle.
Arnold Banyon	Uncle Bert's manservant.
Vince Currier	Director of SHINE Festival.
Tim	Staff at Mustard Seed Inn.
Gregg	Witness to Nicole's hit-and-run.

Glossary of Terms for Flameworking Glass

Bead Separator (also known as Bead Release) is a thick liquid that is applied to a mandrel to keep the hot glass from sticking to the stainless steel. A simple bead mixture contains alumina and high-fire clay mixed with water.

Borosilicate Glass (also known as Hard Glass) is a glass composed of boron and silica. A well-known example would be Pyrex.

Cane is a thin rod of pulled or twisted glass.

Cold-working is mechanically altering the appearance of glass when it is cold, meaning room temperature. Grinding, etching, cutting, and faceting are examples of cold-working techniques.

Didymium Lenses are used by lampworkers for eye protection from infrared and ultraviolet radiation from hot glass. They also eliminate the yellow sodium flare to make it easier when glass is worked in the flame.

Fire Polish is a process used to create a glossy smooth finish on glass using heat.

Flame Annealing is a method of slowly cooling a bead in the outer edges in the flame of the torch.

Flameworking is the manipulation of glass, usually glass rods, by means of a torch.

Frit is crushed glass of varying sizes (usually sorted through a screen).

Fuming is the process of melting or burning a metal or metallic salt onto a glass surface. The metal, most often gold or silver, is heated within a flame until it vaporizes. The vapor is then deposited onto the surface of the glass. Metallic vapors can be toxic so safety precautions should be taken.

Fusing is the process of heat bonding two or more pieces of glass together. This can be done in a kiln or using a torch.

Gather is a glob of glass on the end of a punty or blowpipe. In flameworking, the gather is formed by melting the end of a rod and feeding more of the rod into the flame to increase the molten area of the glass.

Glass is a non-crystalline material with the mechanical rigidity of a solid and the atomic qualities of a liquid. Most glass is composed of silica, sodium oxide, along with a stabilizer such as calcium oxide.

Glass Enamels are powdered glass applied to and bonded by heat to a heat resistant surface such as glass, fine silver, copper, or pure gold.

Graphite Marver is a flat heat-proof surface. It provides an area for glass to be rolled into shape.

Hothead Torch has as big a flame as you can get with this style torch. The bigger the flame, the more BTUs and faster you can work the glass. Most commonly available brazing torches have a smaller sized flame which means less BTUs and less heat.

Lampworking is a term derived from the original method of working glass with an oil lamp or Bunsen burner. Today this technique is commonly referred to as Flameworking.

Latticinio is a decorative type of twisted glass cane. The Italian word literally translates into "little milk-white strands" and referred to canes made with only clear and opaque white glass. Today the term includes all color combinations of twisted cane.

Mandrel is a stainless-steel rod used in beadmaking. It gives the artist a handle and space to start making a bead.

Striker is used to light torches. You must quickly squeeze the handles together to cause a spark.

Tweezers have many uses for the flame worker. They are used to set in decorative chips, pull contamination out of the molten glass, hold and shape hot glass, etc.

Information about Glassblowing Instruction

Making gifts with glass is my favorite hobby. My husband, George, and I have a large kiln in the small studio behind our house, which we use to fuse glass. In addition, we have been creating a series of etched-glass books depicting the covers of each book in the Webb's Glass Shop Mystery Series. They are simply gorgeous, and I always have one with me when I have an event at a library or festival. To see the process we use in making these books, go to the website sponsored by Kensington Books, https://www.hobbyreads.com.

On occasion, we take classes to make blown-glass pieces. There are several hot shops in St. Petersburg, and we have enjoyed participating in the "date night" workshops. Our first session was at the Morean Art Center on 719 Central Avenue. The format is simple—each couple has a hands-on experience culminating in one piece of glass art. It is typically a solid sculpted paperweight, or a blown-glass ornament made by the two of you in collaboration with an instructor.

Webb's Glass Shop is inspired by the real-life Grand Central Stained Glass & Graphics business owned by our good friends Bradley and Eloyne Er-

ickson. Their website is http://www.grandcentral
stainedglass.com. Visit if you can.

You can find a class in your area by searching
the web for fused, etched, or stained-glass classes
in your city.

My husband and I have scaled back our glasswork. We've restricted our work to making gifts for
friends, family, and book promotion. My current
interest is in making glass beads in a technique
called flameworking. I'm taking classes at one of
the local glassblowing shops, Zen Glass Studio. It's
located near the imaginary Webb's Studio in the
Warehouse Arts District of St. Petersburg.

Working hot glass is a little intimidating, but I'm
getting more comfortable with the torch and how
the molten glass behaves. George says he'll set me
up a workstation in our studio behind the house.
Maybe.

Right now, I'm concentrating on writing the
next book in the Webb's Glass Shop Mystery series.
Since millefiori is the featured glass art in one of
my next books, I predict that I will need to find a
way to do both.

ALSO IN THE WEBB'S GLASS SHOP
MYSTERY SERIES

Shattered at Sea

**A Mediterranean cruise gives glass shop owner
Savannah Webb a chance to demonstrate her
expertise—and fire up her skills when it comes
to foul play . . .**

Enjoy the following excerpt from
Shattered at Sea . . .

Prologue

At sea, cruise ship Obscura,
security office

"There's no way he's dead," Savannah shouted at the security guard. "No one saw it. You haven't found a body."

"Miss, that's often the way it is for these cases," said the security guard. "We are proceeding with the investigation. You have no authority here. You're not even related to the passenger."

"But . . ."

"Leave it to us. We're the only authority out here in international waters."

Savannah turned away with her fists clenched and her eyes narrowed to small slits.

Leave it to you? There's no way.

Chapter 1

Friday morning,
Webb's Glass Shop

"It's a terrible time," said Savannah Webb. "I can't take a week off and leave everything to Amanda and Jacob. It feels wrong."

"It's the chance of a lifetime." Edward Morris folded his arms over his chest to reflect Savannah's stance. "The offer is a seven-day cruise in the Mediterranean that begins and ends in Barcelona, Spain. What's a little scheduling sacrifice compared to this opportunity?"

They stood eye-to-eye and toe-to-toe for a few moments. Savannah once again appreciated that Edward felt unthreatened by her six-foot height and unusual strength built by years of glassblowing large objects using heavy molten glass.

"What opportunity?" asked Amanda Blake, assis-

tant manager and part-time stained-glass instructor. Savannah and Edward broke apart quickly.

Amanda stood next to them at the checkout
counter of Webb's Glass Shop. "I'm always a little
suspect of the word *opportunity*." She finger-quoted.
"It can mean many things."

"In this case," said Savannah, "the opportunity
is to work as the substitute glassblower on a cruise
ship in the Mediterranean."

"That's awesome! When do you leave?" She adjusted the large statement necklace on her generous chest. It was made of saucer-sized glass
medallions that clinked when she moved. Amanda
was always moving. "How long will you be gone?"

"The problem is that the cruise is for a week,
and since it leaves out of Barcelona, Edward wants
to go a day early so I can meet his family in England. Then we'll fly out to board the ship on Sunday."

Amanda clapped her hands. "So, what's the
problem? I can handle Webb's Glass Shop and the
beginner's stained-glass class by myself. Jacob is
perfectly happy over at Webb's Studio. It's only a
few blocks away, so I'm not too far if he needs
something."

Jacob Underwood, Savannah's apprentice, had
recently moved to her expanded business site in
the Warehouse Arts District of town.

Edward spoke up. "He's been handling things
very well. Your student clients know about his Asperger's syndrome. He knows everyone who rents
a studio. If a new student wants to rent space, he can
send them over to Amanda to handle the paperwork and payments."

Savannah momentarily tried suppressing a giant grin, but it forced its way out into a hearty laugh.

"You're absolutely right." She gave Edward a big hug. "This opportunity will not come around again. There's a bazillion things to get organized, but I really want to go."

Savannah Webb checked her watch, then looked out the rental car window for the sixth time in thirty seconds. "Are you sure they open this early?" She looked over to Edward, who sat beside her on their way to the Miami Passport Office. They had taken the 7:30 A.M. flight from Tampa International Airport, which had meant a 4:30 A.M. wake-up call.

"Our appointment is at ten forty-five. It's only nine thirty. We're in good time." Edward looked back at Savannah. "I still can't believe you don't have a passport."

"Not as many Americans travel outside the US as you Brits; you guys are always looking for holiday trips abroad."

"If you spent one dreary winter in England, you would go mad. You take the sunshine for granted."

"True. Anyway, Dad did so much traveling when he was working for the government. He always said that there was so much to see in this country, why go to foreign parts while we still have so much to enjoy right here? You have wanderlust—not me."

Savannah enjoyed the occasional weekend trip, but most of the time she was perfectly content to kick back in her little Craftsman cottage with Edward and their dog and cat fur babies, Rooney and Snowy.

"It's not only about seeing more sights. It's about experiencing different cultures in a way you can't appreciate without walking around on their streets, eating their food, and facing their weather. You grew up in St. Petersburg, then spent a few years in Seattle at the Pilchuck Studio. Quite a narrow view."

Savannah tilted her head and turned toward Edward. "But I read a lot of books—more than any of the kids I grew up with. All the librarians knew me."

"Doesn't count. You can't smell the spice market in New Delhi without standing there."

Savannah reached over and held his hand. "Okay. I'll give you that point. But you must agree I'm certainly changing my outlook today. This is an incredible opportunity for me. Thanks for helping."

"I only helped with the passport—stuff I know. My travel agent did the rest. Jan is a miracle worker with travel challenges. You're the one who's done the impossible to get everything arranged so you can spend ten days away from the shop." He looked at her slip of paper. "Thirteen? Really?"

"Shush up," Savannah whispered as they sat. "It's my lucky number."

"Number thirteen," the receptionist announced to the waiting room in a strong voice that hinted she had a musical background.

Savannah jumped up so abruptly that she dropped the folder containing her documents all over the floor. She stooped to gather them up and bumped heads with Edward. "Ouch!" She plopped down on her behind and rubbed her forehead. "What are you doing?"

"Trying to help." Edward gathered the papers and slid them into Savannah's bright green folder, then pulled her up by the hand. "You seem flustered."

"Good guess." Savannah felt a flush rising in her cheeks. She looked over to the receptionist, who was frowning like a judge sentencing a convicted drug dealer. Savannah resisted the urge to step forward at once. She first straightened her papers. Then she put on her brightest smile and walked up to the receptionist's desk.

"Hi, I'm appointment number thirteen."

"If you're ready, step through the aisle over to cubicle number eight."

Number eight—hmmm. That's lucky in China and unlucky in India. I think I'll lean toward China's belief.

Savannah stepped into the tiny space that held a desk barely wide enough for a computer monitor and a mouse. There was enough room for a guest chair and the passport administrator—nothing else.

"Hi, my name is Margie Adams. Please have a seat, Miss Webb." Savannah smiled and sat. Margie must have been the oldest civil servant in the world. She looked to be nearing ninety, if not already there. However, she was meticulously groomed and had curly white hair, a smooth ivory complexion, and maroon eyeshadow that accented her piercing eyes. "Good, it looks like you have your documents. Hand them over and I'll fire up the application program. We'll get this passport process steaming along so you can go to"—she looked at Savannah's passport request form—"London, England."

"Yes, we have tickets to leave on this evening's eight-o'clock flight from Miami."

Miss Adams was flipping through Savannah's papers and her fingers were flying over the submission form entries. "Everything looks good, Savannah. I always appreciate an orderly mind." She paused. "Wait. Here's your driver's license, but where's your birth certificate?"

"It should be right there." Savannah reached out for the folder. "May I check?"

"Sure." Margie closed the folder and handed it over.

Savannah flipped through the documents and sure enough, the birth certificate wasn't where she had placed it. Her heart jumped two beats. Without that, there was no way she was getting a passport, flying to London, or boarding that cruise ship. She flipped through the papers one more time. It was gone.

"Excuse me," said Edward from the narrow hallway. "Are you looking for this?" He held up her birth certificate. "The receptionist said I could bring it down."

Savannah gave him cow eyes in relief, took the paper, and put it where it belonged.

Margie stretched out her hand for the folder. "Louise must like the looks of you. She would normally have let this explode into a massive issue, then play the martyr." She grinned at Edward, then turned back to her computer screen. "You can go back to the waiting room. It won't be long."

Edward left and Margie peered at the justification section. "It says that you're going to work on a cruise ship?" She scanned Savannah from top to bottom. "You don't seem like a cabin porter type. What are you going to do? Are you an entertainer?"

"More like an educator." Savannah smiled and leaned forward. "I'm taking the place of an injured glass artist on a cruise ship leaving out of Barcelona. I'll be doing glassblowing demonstrations on one of the larger ships for the seven-day Mediterranean cruise. The poor girl will be released from the hospital in a few days, so I'm only filling in until she returns."

"Glassblowing? On a cruise ship?" She lifted a single eyebrow. "You can't even have candles in your cabin on a cruise ship. How can they have glassblowing demonstrations?"

"It's a special setup. The hot shop was designed by Crystal Glass Works to run on electricity instead of gas fires. The techniques are a little different, but they heat the glass in electric furnaces—no fire at all. It will be tricky for me to learn how to work the glass without using a blowtorch, but what a wonderful opportunity to see the Mediterranean!"

All the while, Margie was tapping away into the application form template. It was disconcerting that she could hold a conversation and simultaneously type at lightning speed. Margie filled in the last field and pressed the enter key with a flourish. "There, now let me check one last time for accuracy." She sped through each field, delicately flicking the tab key. "Fantastic. Everything looks perfect. I'll submit this to the back-room clerks who will create your brand-new passport. All you have to do is come back here at two today and it will be ready."

"Thank you very much." Savannah grinned like a Cheshire cat. *It appears that thirteen and eight are my lucky numbers.*

She returned to the reception area. Edward stood and splayed both hands palms up. "So? You look happy."

"Yes, we can pick up my shiny new passport this afternoon. I'm hungry."

"Of course you are. When there are issues, you can't eat. As soon as the issues are resolved, you're starving. I've sussed out the pattern."

They arrived back in plenty of time. Margie nodded and waved to them. They only had to wait a few minutes until Savannah's passport was ready. Then they drove to the Miami International Airport to turn in the rental and check in for the flight to Heathrow Airport. They received special treatment because Edward's parents had upgraded their economy-class tickets to business class as soon as Edward told them they were coming to visit. Jan had used her insider contacts to make it happen.

"They must be anxious to make you welcome," said Edward.

"What do you mean?"

"The two of them travel business class across the pond each and every time, but when they send me a ticket? It's crunch class both ways," said Edward.

Squeezing in a family visit before the cruise ship

embarked was an opportunity Edward couldn't resist. Savannah was looking forward to seeing Edward's parents again.

The first special treat was the short line for business-class passengers at the check-in counter. The second treat was the pre-check TSA line through security, followed by the third treat, a pass to the airport lounge to await boarding time.

They enjoyed a local craft beer accompanied by small plates of finger food. Savannah pulled out the illustrated instruction manual she had received from Crystal Glass Works that detailed the procedures for glassblowing with the electric hot shop on board the cruise ship. She reviewed the handwritten notes she had made in the margins when she took the training class.

When their boarding time was called, Edward and Savannah walked into the business-class cabin and Savannah gaped at the size of her personal space. Their large, wide seats were in the center aisle so that they sat side by side yet each had unrestricted access to the aisle. She hefted her carry-on into the ample overhead compartment.

In her seat, the best available noise-canceling Bose headphones were sitting on top of a decent-sized pillow and a quilted duvet. A small amenity kit contained slip-on socks, a sleep mask, ear plugs, moisturizer, toothbrush, toothpaste, lip balm, and breath mints.

As soon as Savannah had settled into her seat, a flight attendant offered her a glass of champagne. "Welcome aboard, Miss Webb. I hope you enjoy your flight."

Savannah turned to Edward, who had also received his glass of champagne. They looked at each other and clicked glasses. Savannah toasted, "Good luck to us on the first of many international adventures. Cheers."